To Tempt a Scoundrel
The Brethren Series

For more information about the author:
www.christicaldwellauthor.com
christicaldwellauthor@gmail.com
Twitter: @ChristiCaldwell
Or on Facebook at: Christi Caldwell Author

For first glimpse at covers, excerpts, and free bonus material, be sure to sign up for my monthly newsletter!
Printed in the USA.

Cover Design and Interior Format
© KILLION
THE KILLION GROUP, INC.

To Tempt a Scoundrel

THE BRETHREN
THE SERIES

USA TODAY BESTSELLER

CHRISTI CALDWELL

DEDICATION

For Kimberly Rocha

On this journey I've been on as an author, I've been s
o very grateful to find you. Thank you for being
such an ardent supporter of not only me and my
works, but to the entire romance community.

And *most* importantly…thank you for
being a wonderful friend.

Alice and Rhys are for you!!

CHAPTER 1

London, England
Winter 1820

Wʜᴇɴ ᴛʜᴇ ɢʀᴇᴀᴛ ʟᴏᴠᴇ ᴏꜰ her nine and ten years broke their betrothal to wed his employer's daughter, Lady Alice Winterbourne had been rather certain life could not be any worse.

Particularly after one was jilted in a note, and then stormed the dastard's offices—pleadingly, no less.

Just as Alice had been wrong about her betrothed, the bookish barrister Henry Pratt's *affections*. So too had she been wrong about the state of her currently, and perpetually very sad affairs. The passing months after The Scandal, as Society had taken to referring to it, had proved how very wrong she'd been.

"Oh, Alice."

It was peculiar just how many different meanings could be infused into that phrase; "Oh, Alice" and by so very many different people.

In this particular moment, in that particular place, it was none other than her sister-in-law, Lady Daphne Winterbourne, the Countess of Montfort, whose "Oh, Alice" was infused with sadness.

Which was only marginally better than the self-blaming of Alice's brother.

Grin through it.

Grinning was easier.

Plastering on a smile that threatened to shatter her cheekbones, Alice glanced up from the small stack of books she'd been piling atop her mahogany tester bed. "Oh, come, Daphne! None of that! It will be good fun."

Tremendous fun. Heaps of it. Bountiful supplies—

Liar.

At the answering silence, she turned her lips up another smidgen, which strained every muscle of her face.

Who knew there were so very many muscles in a person's face? Grinning so, only highlighted that peculiar fact.

Alice neatly deposited her stack inside the valises on the floor.

Ice pinged against the windowpanes, while the fire crackled in the hearth, punctuating the silence of the room's occupants: Alice, Daphne...and the bustling maid hurrying about packing Alice's belongings.

Not quickly enough.

The quiet *thunk* of Daphne's cane striking the floor, and the shifting boards, indicated her sister-in-law had moved. Closer. She was coming closer. And the nearness of any person—particularly one as astute as Daphne—would reveal the strain at the corners of Alice's lips. The tightness about her eyes. The wretched dark circles that gave her the look of one of those deuced raccoons she'd read of in a book plucked from the Circulating Library.

Devoting all her energies to the mounds of books resting about, she put her hands on her hips and made a show of contemplating them. All the while, seeing not a single title or author's name... or topic.

But then, such had been the way since Henry Pratt and The Note and Alice's subsequent flight to his offices...and then worse still, to St. George's.

And then, of course, had come her blasted arrival at St. George's, the day of his wedding.

What a bloody, pathetic fool. Her throat worked painfully. For that pitiable display, she was deserving of Society's scorn.

Blasted Winterbourne passion. It was a curse inherent in their line. The wild displays of emotion: rage, love, desire coursed in their blood. They wore their emotions for all the world to see and Alice had once celebrated their unwillingness to dissemble.

She cringed. And how very poorly she'd worn it that fateful day in London when The Scandal had become THE SCANDAL, in all the papers. And in all the ballrooms and drawing rooms… and really anywhere and everywhere people were or had been.

After all, it was not every day a young woman interrupted the wedding services of her former betrothed.

"…*Therefore, if any man can show any just cause, why they may not lawfully be joined together, let him now speak or else hereafter forever hold his peace…*"

Daphne settled a hand on Alice's shoulder, interrupting those cursed memories.

Please do not offer an apology… do not…

"I hate that you'll be gone so long. Please consider returning at least for Christmas," Daphne said quietly, sadly.

Sad. They had all been so very sad… because of Alice. The servants; old loyal ones… and new, recently hired ones, her brother, his wife: the young, blissfully in love, recently themselves wedded couple should not have to hide their laughter or conceal their smiles.

But they did.

"I will, of course, miss you," Alice piped in, delivering the rote reply. It was not untrue. She desperately loved her family. "But it will be such good fun." *Smile.*

Alice flashed another overstretched grin.

Sadness deepened within her sister-in-law's always expressive gaze. "But this is a time of year to be with one's family." How was it possible for there to be such varying depths and degrees of sadness in a person's eyes? And yet, there it was in Daphne's. Her sister-in-law gave her a probing look, bringing her back from her meandering thoughts.

Dropping the books in her hand, she turned and hugged her arms about Daphne's shoulders. "Come. It is but for a fortnight." A blessed, welcome fourteen days… away from the pitying glances and sad-eyed stares from her well-meaning brother. "You will have Daniel and Alex." The couple's young babe.

I wanted a tiny babe, too. I imagined being a bucolic family and—

Her heart wrenched all over again.

"You belong with us."

Alice cringed.

They meant well. All of them. Alice's only recently devoted brother and Daphne, her former companion turned sister-in-law. But there was something so very humbling in going from cherished sister and friend... to pathetic aunt.

Alice's future flashed behind her mind's eye: she a spinster aunt, reading from her books while her nephews and nieces pondered over their unwed aunt and—

"I have to go," she finally managed. "I *want* to go," she swiftly corrected. And she did. For what was the alternative? To remain with her family and be constantly reminded of the mistakes she'd made?

Invited by Lady Lettice Brookfield, to join her family at their Somerset estate for a winter house party, she'd rather face the company of a friend who hadn't yet once uttered "Oh, Alice" and instead chatted and plotted with Alice the way she might any young lady—and not one like Alice who'd scandalized the *ton.*

Alas, her sister-in-law was too clever, and snagged on Alice's former words.

"But you do not *have* to go. You have to be with your family, the people who love—"

Alice recoiled.

"Alice," Daphne said, an apology heavy in those two syllables.

"It is fine." It hadn't been fine in so very long. "I know you love me," she acknowledged, taking Daphne's spare hand, her other gripping her cane, drained of blood from the hold she had upon it. "I know you and Daniel and Alex... all of you. I never doubted nor ever will..." Alice held her gaze, imploring Daphne with her eyes to understand. "But I need to go." It was all she offered. She could not share this aching need to escape the greatest mistake she'd ever made and the perpetual state of sadness in which she'd left her own family.

Daphne sighed. "There is nothing I can say?"

"Daniel?" she ventured.

The hint of a smile hovered on the other woman's lips. "He insisted I was not to leave your chambers unless I'd secured your pledge to remain with us for the holiday."

Alice's maid rushed over and scooped up the remaining gowns. The neatly folded garments held with the reverence one might show the queen's jewels; Lucy laid them in the trunk and then closed it. That faint click resounded with an air of finality and decisiveness.

Daphne caught the maid's stare.

Lucy promptly stopped arranging the trunks and dipped a curtsy. She hurried from the room, closing the door behind her. Shifting her weight over her cane, Daphne urged Alice to sit.

Oh, blast. She didn't want another lecture about family being with family during the approaching holiday season.

Alice just wanted to be away… from their stares, from the reminder of her folly… from all of it.

"Please," Daphne said quietly.

And it was that slight imploring when Daphne had only been like another sister that brought Alice reluctantly down onto the edge of her mattress.

Daphne lowered herself to the spot beside her. She fiddled with the ivory handle of her cane. "When I entered your brother's employ," she began slowly. "Your brother was so very adamant that…" *Say it. Just say his name because not saying it did not make any of this less real.* "Mr. Pratt was undeserving of you."

Henry Pratt.

A barrister who'd earned a living when most men were indolent lords, content to wager away their fortunes. He had helplessly captivated Alice.

Fool. You bloody twit.

Daphne cleared her throat. When she spoke, emotion clogged her tone, making her voice husky. "I insisted he was. I insisted that, despite Mr. Pratt's lack of funds and his commitment to his work, he cared for you and…" She grimaced, and gave her head a slight shake.

"Mm. Mm," Alice said adamantly, facing the other woman. "I'll not have you do that. I'll not have you take ownership of my folly in trusting my heart to… to Henry."

In the immediate aftermath of his treachery, even the mention of his name had gutted her. With time, it had faded, lessened. Now, there was nothing more than the sharp tug of resentment of him… and *herself* for that great mistake.

A proud smile curved Daphne's lips upward. "You are an amazing young woman, Alice."

Alice didn't want to be admired. She was undeserving of those sentiments. For inside, she was still the angry, hurt young woman who'd been jilted, and then gone on to humiliate herself. As such, she met that statement with silence.

Daphne's smile faded. "We have been worried about you since…"

"The Scandal?" Alice ventured. "Or… THE SCANDAL."

Daphne wrinkled her nose. "Both," she confided, and Alice loved her sister-in-law all the more for her honesty. This, she appreciated.

Not the tiptoeing about, or the averted sad-eyed stares, or hurriedly altered discussions. But this. Not talking about it and not acknowledging what had happened with Henry Pratt did not make that betrayal go away. It just highlighted it in a viciously stark way that deepened the pain of her naiveté.

"Your brother insists you remain here, with us, but I believe it will do you good to join your friend, Lady Lettice, and be away from this place. Sometimes, the change of place, or people is good for one's heart."

Good for one's heart.

Was such a thing possible when one's heart had been smashed by a man who, as her sister-in-law had so rightly claimed, had been undeserving of that organ?

Alice forced another one of those painful smiles. "Thank you, Daphne," she said gently, in a bid to mark the end of the discourse.

Her sister-in-law shoved herself upright. The minute she'd presented her back to Alice, she let her grin die. With slow, careful steps, Daphne limped to the door. She paused at the entranceway and glanced back.

Restoring her false grin, Alice stared expectantly back.

"I've wanted to say something to you…" Daphne said somberly. "I've searched for the perfect time or way but have not found it. Until now." Her sister-in-law brought her shoulders back to a determined little set. "I want you to know… that your heart is breaking," Nay, broken. It had already been smashed under the hands of Henry Pratt's ink-stained fingers. "And it will not matter what anyone says; about Mr. Pratt's worthlessness or your own strength… because those are just words. But in time, you yourself will come to find that there can, despite his treachery, be true love and…" Mayhap that it hadn't been that emotion with Henry after all.

That supposition hung silent, as loud as if it had been spoken, and insulting for what it implied about Alice's knowing of her own mind and heart.

Color suffused Daphne's cheeks. "I am merely speaking as a woman who once gave my... heart to a dastard, only to have him shatter it." And now she'd found love with Alice's brother.

"Thank you, Daphne," she repeated.

As soon as she'd gone, Alice stared at the closed door, waiting, waiting.

She hurled herself backwards, crashing down on the down mattress. Shooting a hand out, she dragged the pillow over her face.

She was not so destroyed by her pain and humiliation that she didn't see that true love did exist. Daphne and Daniel were proof enough of that.

What she did recognize, however, was that happening to find the precise gentleman deserving of one's love, and being the recipient of his devotion in return was as rare as catching a shooting star amidst a winter's storm. It was unlikely. And nigh impossible.

And given her rotted luck with Henry Pratt, the last things Alice believed in were shooting stars and the wishes they'd bring.

But mayhap her sister-in-law had been correct in another regard—it would do Alice good to be away from this place and the lingering presence of Henry Pratt's gloomy shadow.

CHAPTER 2

LORD RHYS BROOKFIELD, BROTHER TO the Marquess of Guilford, and bane of his proper mother's existence, had not balked at much in the course of his eight and twenty years.

He'd outraced, outdrank, and outwagered some of London's most wicked scoundrels.

Rhys had deservedly earned a reputation as a rogue, who'd never met a widow or scandalous lady he could not charm.

For all his moral failings, however, he did draw the proverbial line somewhere.

Leave it to his pinch-mouthed, propriety-loving mother to find it.

Standing in the doorway of his brother's parlor, he briefly contemplated the path to escape over his shoulder. Perhaps he'd heard her wrong?

"Don't you dare think of leaving this room, Rhys Winston Grayson Brookfield," his mother snapped from her spot in the upholstered King Louis XIV chair where she sat like the Queen of Sheba upon her throne.

Oh, he'd heard her, all right. Even as he wished he hadn't…. or that he'd misheard or mistaken her. Dragging his heels, he forced himself to enter the rooms.

"Absolutely not."

"I'm pleased that you'll join me and—"

"That is certainly not what I was 'absolutely-notting'. Rather, the first part," he said tightly, plopping down on the seat opposite hers. "The…" He tried to force the word out. "The…" He strangled on it. By God, he couldn't.

"Marriage, Rhys," his mother scolded. "The word is marriage."

And not just any marriage at that, but rather the talk of a possible and proposed match between Rhys… and a child. That was the line that he'd never even toe, let alone cross.

Not picking her head up from her embroidering, the Dowager Marchioness Guilford directed her reply to that small wood frame between her fingers, never missing a stride. "The Cunnings will be arriving tomorrow and the expectation is clear." She pierced the needle through with such ferocity, there could be no doubting Rhys had gotten under his mother's skin—as he'd always invariably managed to do. *And this time, I did not even have to try…* There was some solace in that. "You have responsibilities to this family, now." *Now.* "As such, I'm not begging, Rhys. Why, I am not even politely asking because, frankly, that is far beneath me. I am—"

"Oh, yes," he drawled, interrupting her. "Politely asking is the stuff of the masses and hardly the distinguished dowager marchioness."

She gave a pleased nod. "Precisely." God, was a person born this insolent? Or was it something learned? Fortunately, where the Brookfields were concerned, it was not a trait that traveled through their blood. "As such," she patted her greying chignon. "I am telling you."

"You are telling me?" he asked dryly. "How positively medieval of you." Ironically, with the marriage of his eldest brother, the Marquess of Guilford, to a young widow with two children, Rhys should have been absolved of further expectations where responsibility was concerned. Alas, that union had brought about an even more tenacious urgency on his mother's part.

"Medieval," she snapped, surging forward in a shocking break in her usual composure. "Is it medieval that two centuries worth of properties, history, and legacy have not been, as of yet, preserved?" It was a sorry day, indeed, when a married son, and a nearly thirty-year old spare were not enough for one's mama. "If something were to happen to you and Miles together—"

"That would be deuced unfortunate timing." He yawned and belatedly covered that show of his fatigue.

Too late.

His mother sharpened her gaze on his person and, if looks could burn, the thick snow lining the Brookfield estates would have been reduced to nothing more than a melted puddle. Rhys attempted to reason with her. "It is hard to imagine how such a tragic event would come about. We do not take the same carriages and, generally, if we ride, we do so beside one another." He winked once. "Certainly never on the *same* horse."

"Oh, you are incorrigible," she cried, tossing her hands up in maternal vexation.

"Very well. I would ride with him, were we in a situation where we happened to be together, stranded with the one mount—"

A shriek strangled in the dowager marchioness' throat.

A more honorable gent would have taken mercy. He'd long been without where his mother was concerned. If one wished to be truly precise… with any person, really. "I suppose there might be a freakish accident in which—"

"I am glad you find amusement in all this," she barked.

He inclined his head in silent acknowledgement.

"But if something were to happen to the both of you, I and your sisters will be at the mercy of a distant relative. Vile Mr. Pritchard."

He made a pitying sound. "Poor Mr. Pritchard." A distant cousin nearly ten years older than Rhys, he'd found the only thing vile about the man was his dreadful fascination with an intricately folded cravat.

"Poor Mr. Pritchard?" she squawked. "Poor me? I have not one, but two sons. And neither of you has produced any male offspring."

"Well, in fairness," he pointed out, lifting a finger. "If I had produced a male offspring in my current state, he would hardly qualify as a rightful heir given the rules of inheritance."

She slapped her palms over her face.

Ice-tinged snowflakes pinged the window at a steady little staccato, and he glanced over to the frosted panes.

A gust of wind stirred those flakes in a swirling blanket of white. Rhys stared longingly out. He'd take that cold. He'd relish a ride through the snow-clogged grounds of the Somerset countryside to an infernal lecturing on his wedded state. And as a rule, he avoided the blasted cold at any cost. Which gent truly wished to suffer through the blistering winds and pelting rains or snows?

But then, focusing on frigid weather was a good deal safer than the topic his mother had insisted on unearthing—

"I canna live in poverty. I want more for not only us... but for you..."

As if that Scottish beauty had truly wanted the best for *him*. He grimaced. Bloody hell. It had been years—many of them since he'd thought of her—Miss Lillian Hart. A flirtatious actress, she'd been as coy as she'd been stunning. And he, at the age of eight and ten had made the mistake of hopelessly falling for a pretty face, and venturing down the path to marriage.

Well, *very* nearly venturing down.

Miss Hart had proven to be an even more credible actress in real life than she'd been on the stage. When he'd been threatened with disinheritance by his late father if they wed, she'd made clear just what Rhys' value was—nothing. His *friend*, Lord Anthony Fielding, the Earl of Montgomery, however, had been plump enough in the pockets.

And one afternoon visit to the Earl of Montgomery's residence had ripped apart Rhys' very existence: he'd entered Anthony's study and found his *loyal* friend locked in an embrace with none other than Rhys' betrothed.

Rhys had turned and walked out of that townhouse sans one betrothed and one friend, and Rhys' heart shredded. That had been the last he'd ever seen either of them.

And years later, having seen himself saved from a miserable fate to a schemer, he was quite content to live the happy, carefree existence of a rogue.

And that existence most assuredly did *not* include any wife—particularly not a seven and ten-year-old child.

Glancing at his mother, still buried away behind her palms, Rhys drummed his fingertips on the wood arms of his chair.

With a slow, steady exhalation of air, the dowager marchioness matched his pose. "You need to marry her."

"Aria?"

"Of course, Aria," Mother said crisply. "She is Lady Lovell's *only* unwed daughter."

"She is a child," he said flatly. Surely with her devotion to logic over emotion, she could see the odiousness in a match between Rhys and that tender-yeared miss?

"Oh, hush. I was quickening with your brother when I was

Aria's age."

He cringed. Who'd have imagined that a discussion that sought to provide a death knell to his bachelor state could possibly worsen? And yet, mention of his late father and mother's young marriage and pregnant state had taken their discourse from distasteful to repugnant. Rhys tried again. "She is a seven and ten years old girl. I am—"

"You are just eleven years her senior. There are hardly a great many years between you, at all."

"Actually there is," he insisted. When Aria had been crawling about Rhys' then two- and-ten-year-old feet, he'd been stepping over her, racing from the room so he could fish and ride. "When I was at Eton she was just born. When I was at Oxford, she was in nappies. When I was—"

"You have made your point, Rhys." Fire flashed in his mother's eyes.

"As I was saying… at least eight years too many between us." It was an arbitrary number, fished from his mind, meant to stop the tide of his mother's questioning…. and had the desired effect.

"*Pfft.*"

One pence. It had long been a game he'd silently played with himself; earning an imagined pence for each one of those "pffts" of hers, to determine just the sizeable fortune he'd earn.

"Regardless, it is about more than the eleven years between us." *Lie.* "And more the fact that she's just recently left the school room," he attempted in a bid to reason with the reasonable-about-all dowager—except the marital fate and future of her children. As such, even his mother could not refute that.

"Two years ago," she countered, dragging her needle through the frame once more. "I'd have you know this is all your brother's fault. Marrying that woman," she muttered under her breath. "*Pfft.*"

Two pence.

"What was that?"

"Nothing at all," he demurred, having long been riddled with the troublesome habit of speaking to himself.

At last, she set aside that tedious frame, resting it on the mahogany inlaid table beside her. "Furthermore, if you are upset with your current circumstances, you've no one to blame except your brother."

Well, that was a recent and unexpected shift. Since his marriage to a woman who was not Lady Lovell's eldest unwed daughter, Miles had gone from the long-favored, agreeable son to... "Your brother", in discussions.

Most days, Rhys wasn't sure which had grated his mother more: the proper, dutiful son Miles had always been, tossing aside their mother's wishes and making the ultimate decision of his marital fate for his own. Or the woman Miles had made his bride.

"*Ohh*," he stretched out that utterance, deliberately needling. "I am content with my current circumstances as they are. Quite so." *Very much*. His greatest responsibilities were related to his business ventures. The latest, a partnership in steel with Daniel Winterbourne, the Earl of Montfort... and if he were being truthful with himself—to the mistress whom he sponsored in a given moment. Of which, he had been a deuced long in between. He'd rectify that soon enough. As a rogue, however, he'd draw the moral line at scandalous affairs during family house parties hosted by his sister-in-law, with young children in attendance.

"Well," she said cheerfully, gathering the teapot. "Then I suggest you become discontent very soon," she paused mid-pour. "Aria will be spending the fortnight."

He choked on his swallow.

Ambushed. Just like that.

Invited for the annual winter house party by Miles and Philippa, the last thing he'd ever expected was a happy celebration between the Brookfields and the Cunnings. For the plain truth was since the two mothers angling for marriage between their eldest children: Miles and Sybil—now married to other parties—there'd been only stilted tension between the leading matrons of Society. "But... but..."

His mother widened a triumphant grin. "Tea?" she offered, holding up a cup.

"Y-You are not even speaking to Lady Cunnings," he stammered.

Her lips formed a moue of displeasure. "Hush. Viscountess Lovell and I are as friendly as we've ever been."

Which might not be an untruth. Shrew-tongued harpies, they'd gotten on famously over the years. The fact that after a lifetime of friendship they still referred to one another by their titles was pointed proof of it.

Ignoring that offering, Rhys stood and walked over to the window. He contemplated the doorway and then the snow-covered grounds below. Which escape would be quickest? He was one for risk taking and, yet, he'd not wager his very life that the snow below was enough to break his significant jump.

Glancing about the White Parlor, he searched for a hint of a liquor cabinet.

Bloody hell, he needed a brandy.

Desperately.

It was going to be a long fortnight.

CHAPTER 3

Winchester, England

ALICE HAD BEEN WRONG ANY number of times.

The greatest case in point being the whole blunder with Henry Pratt's devotion.

And then there had been the disastrous decision to storm his offices in London… and *then* the wedding services, and object during Henry's vows.

But believing she could escape and find a joyful diversion this holiday season was the latest, and greatest, folly on her part.

She fought the urge to slap her palms over her eyes.

"I did not know," Lady Lettice blurted, ringing her hands.

After twelve hours by coach that day, and finally warmed in her guest chambers at the Marquess and Marchioness of Guilford's country estates, Alice had stood braced to exit those chambers with her friend, and chatter away about any and every topic that was not Henry.

"I never, ever, ever expected that *he* would come," Lettice rambled on. "He was not supposed to." The he in question was none other than the faithless Henry Pratt.

"Lettice?" she entreated.

How had such a blasted blunder been made?

Her friend's words rolled over one another as she spoke. "He is Nolan Pratt's brother."

"I know the connection," she said impatiently.

High color flamed her friend's cheeks. "Er right, right. Of course. His wife is a Cunning." She wrinkled her nose. "Sybil always was a nice enough young woman. A bit peculiar. Staid. Focused on her bluestocking pursuits."

Had it been any other time, Alice would have pointed out that she and Lettice focused on those same pursuits. But this was not just any other time. She pressed her eyes closed. This was the time she'd had it sprung on her that she would be spending the fortnight with her former betrothed and his recent wife.

Her stomach churned. She was going to cast up her accounts. Right here on Lady Guilford's pretty Aubusson floral carpet.

But then, that would certainly not be the least humiliating of acts for which she was responsible.

"…and Lady Sybil's mother, Lady Lovell, was a lifelong friend of my mother." Lettice was still rambling on with the blasted explanation of just how and why Henry Pratt was here of all places. "But that friendship was," Lettice made a macabre slashing gesture over her throat. "Over. We… my brothers and I believed that the friendship was done after Miles failed to marry Sybil and instead married Philippa." Lettice brightened. "Whom I quite adore, really."

Alice gave her a pointed look.

"Right, right. Mother and Lady Lovell. Well," she continued on a rush. "It would seem as though they are still friends for all the Cunnings are here to celebrate with my family and Lord Nolan clearly brought his brother and his w—" *Wife.*

Alice slid her eyes closed.

Lettice shrank back and slapped her palm over her mouth. "Mah gawd," that horrified curse came muffled from behind her friend's palm. "I didn't mean… I am so sor—"

Gripping Lettice gently by the wrist, she lowered her arm by her side. "It is," *a disaster.* "fine. It is fine."

"You are lying," Lettice pointed out. Having befriended her this past Season when everyone had avoided her like the social pariah she'd made herself to be, the other young woman had come to know her better than even her own brother in ways.

"A bit," she conceded.

Her friend folded her arms at her chest.

"Very well, a lot," she amended.

Think. Think.

Restless, Alice proceeded to pace back and forth across the room. Ever a faithful friend, Lettice matched those strides.

"Is he here?"

Lettice shook her head, knocking loose a ginger curl. "Not yet. He was to arrive earlier this morn." Her friend brightened. "Mayhap he suffered a carriage accident."

"Lettice!" she chided.

"Well, not a horrible one. Not one that left him," Lettice dropped her voice to a loud, not at all discreet whisper, "*dead*. Just one that…" She gave a little flick of her hand. "You know, detained him. For a fortnight," she said with a beaming smile.

Alice had ceased holding out hope for grand miracles where she was concerned. The last time had been the night before Henry Pratt's wedding as she'd lain abed, staring blankly at the mural above her bed, wishing and praying he'd alter his mind and abandon his employer's plans for a match between Henry and his daughter… and come to her.

She stopped abruptly and her friend collided into her. Lettice shot her hands out to steady herself.

"I cannot stay," Alice finally said.

As if in mockery to that resolution, a gust of wind violently rattled the frosted windowpane.

"Well, you cannot go out in *that*," Lettice countered, the way she might school a child on an unfamiliar lesson.

Alice stalked across the room. Reaching up, she flipped the lock. And then wrestling with the window lodged in place by its age and cold, she struggled to raise it. Grunting, she shifted and used her entire body to propel the wood up. Her arm slipped, sending her elbow crashing into the pane.

Craaaaack.

Both young women stared frozen, wide-eyed.

Oh, well bloody hell.

"Bloody hell," Lettice whispered, as the winter wind ripped through the gaping hole in the place where that pane had once been, sending snowflakes swirling about like tiny dust motes that melted as they struck the floor.

Now, she'd done it. She'd gone and broken her hostess' window.

Lettice cleared her throat, hurrying over. "Yes, well, I think that quite makes it a certainty. Can't go out there." She brought the window down hard—the remaining shards tumbled out of the pane and, together, Alice and Lettice leaned forward as one, and followed those pieces of glass' long, slow, silent journey below.

Alice pressed her palm over her eyes.

Could this day be any worse?

Or the damned Season? Or year? Or—

"As I said, mayhap he'll not arrive today as scheduled."

And then her friend reminded her that it could be worse—a good deal so.

For there could be only one certainty on this bloody terrible day in an otherwise only terrible year.

Mr. Henry Pratt would arrive with his blissful bride in tow.

And when he did, the last place she intended to be was hiding in these rooms.

BENT OVER THE BILLIARDS TABLE, with the blessed crack of the cue balls and silence his only company, Rhys positioned his stick for his next shot. He brought his arm back—

The door burst open. "I've killed my friend," his sister Lettice blurted.

The tip of his stick scraped the felt table, and he winced at the effrontery to that fine velvet.

And his solitude, she'd also killed that.

Readjusting his stick, he appraised the table, and slid the cue forward. "Did she deserve killing?"

At her protracted silence, he shot a glance over his arched shoulder.

Lettice tipped her head at a familiarly confused angle. She opened and closed her mouth like a trout in desperate want of water. "Deserve killing? What…? I don't…? No… She certainly did not… does not—"

He winked once.

Letting out a beleaguered sigh, she shoved the door closed hard behind her, rattling the doorframe. "Blast it, Rhys, this isn't a time for your droll humor or… or silly games…" She gestured to the billiards table, which he was, he supposed, to take to mean was one of the gentleman's pursuits his bookish sister took umbrage with.

He smoothed his features. "My apologies," he said with forced solemnity. He sketched a bow and then returned his attentions to his billiards game of one.

"Regardless of whether or not the lady deserved it, Mother will certainly take umbrage to a murder at her house party."

"Oh, you," she muttered, stalking forward. Just as he brought his arm back for his next shot, Lettice gripped the back of his cue and wrestled it from him.

Or attempted to.

He tightened his grip.

She wiggled again.

Rhys held all the tighter.

Lettice withered him with a glare, and Rhys, at last, abandoned his hold.

His youngest sibling stumbled back under the unexpectedness of that surrender. "This is certainly not a teasing matter, Rhys," she hissed, setting the stick down with a hard thwack. The cue rolled slowly to the edge, paused, and then clattered to the floor. Her voice fell in that exaggerated manner she'd used since she was a girl of four. "I very well might have *unintentionally* killed my friend."

Giving the billiards table a longing look, he also surrendered all hopes of a mindless game. With a sigh, he grabbed his half-empty snifter of brandy from the edge of the table. "What is it, Lettie?" he urged, using the nickname he'd called her since she'd entered the world a squalling baby, saddled with an unfortunate name that had never been good enough for her.

"My friend, Alice."

She lifted her chin.

He shook his head. If he were a better brother, he'd know precisely who the friend whose death his sister might or might not be responsible for, in fact, was.

And yet, he didn't.

Lettice hurled her hands up. "You are hopeless, Rhys. Hopeless."

Nay, he was far worse than that. He was a bastard of a brother who, since his parents had neatly and effectively broken his betrothal, had made it a point to take a wide-berth about his late father and still living mother. As such, his relationship with his siblings had been the true victim of his youthful folly. Regret tugged at him. "I am sorry, Lettie," he said quietly.

She rolled her eyes. "I'm not looking for feigned brotherly regret."

He frowned. It really hadn't been feigned. It—

"I'm looking for help."

And given that he'd been a rotter, it was the very least he could do to—

"I need you to go retrieve her."

He blinked slowly. "What?" he blurted.

"My friend," she went on in exaggerated tones as though imparting a common fact to a lackwit. "*Alice*," she added for good measure.

"Whom you might or might not have killed," he pointed out.

She skewered him with her gaze. "Hush, Rhys Brookfield. This isn't a matter to make light of."

He well knew that. She'd uttered it as much as three times since she'd stormed his sanctuary, stealing his peace. "I was not making light," he said anyway. "I was—"

"She indicated she wished to leave."

Clever lady, then. If his sister were truly a friend, she'd let her go and gladly rather than subject the chit to their nasty mama. "And you think she simply up and left without the benefit of a carriage, servant, or company?" he asked dryly.

Lettie gave a grave nod. "I believe that is precisely what she's done."

Given her earlier annoyance when he'd been speaking with seriousness about his remorse, it wouldn't do to point out that this had been one of the times he'd been making light. "I'm sure she did not leave."

A strong wind howled, as if in concurrence. With the storm quickening and the sun fading from the shorter day sky, the woman would have to be mad to embark into it. Even he wasn't so despairing of his mother's miserable company that he'd risk death by freezing.

"Bloody hell," he muttered.

His sister clasped her hands to her heart. "You are the very best brother, Rhys," she gushed. Rising up on her tiptoes, she planted a kiss on his cheek.

He wrinkled his nose. "Hardly."

"Yes, at best you are a close second behind Miles." A twinkle lit her eyes, blunting the seriousness of that jibe.

Grabbing his black wool jacket, he shrugged into it. "Tell me about your friend."

"Alice, Rhys," she corrected in tried tones that indicated he very well should know the lady. "Her name is Alice," she repeated, exasperation rich in her voice. And deservedly so. The young woman was his sister's best friend and Rhys didn't know her name nor could he identify her from a crowd. Shame reared itself. He'd been a self-absorbed bastard these years. Well, at the very least, he could retrieve the daft girl and bring her back.

Falling into step beside him, they took their leave of the billiards room and started through the halls. Maids and footmen bustled about; their arms laden with everyday décor that was being switched out in favor of vases with ivy and holly. "Well then?" he asked, as they dodged around a crimson clad footman, his face—and path—obscured by the three-foot gold urn overflowing with evergreen branches.

"Well, then, what?" his sister asked, lifting her gaze as they started the climb to his rooms.

"Was it a fight?" At her perplexed look, he clarified. "That sent…" He searched his mind. "Alison—"

"Alice—"

"fleeing," he finished over her. Rhys winced as she pinched him hard on his forearm.

"What manner of ogress do you take me for? It is nightfall. Of course I did not send my friend fleeing." She fell silent, and he glanced at her. Lettie worried at her lower lip. "Well, not *intentionally*," she said under her breath.

And as she went quiet—again—it occurred to him: she had no intention of telling him precisely why her friend had raced herself off into a storm.

Possibly.

"You are certain she has gone out?" he asked when they'd reached his rooms. Night had fallen, and no sane woman would ever dare venture out in—

Lettie nodded frantically, as always providing a very Lettie-like overabundance of information. "She claimed she had the start of a headache." It would seem the more and more his sister spoke, the more he found in common with the mysterious Alice. "And so I allowed her some time. But then when I went back a short while later to check after her, there was no answer to my knock." She spoke so rapidly her words rolled together. "So I let myself in and looked through the cracked window—"

His ears pricked up. "The cracked window? Oomph." He winced as she pinched him again.

"Do pay attention."

Grunting, he rubbed at his arm. "I should point out I was paying attention, and merely remarked upon—"

She silenced him with a glare that their shrew of a mother would be hard pressed to emulate.

"As I was saying, as I looked out, I caught sight of her cloak, disappearing into The Copse."

The Copse.

Those towering oaks and the heavy brush had long provided a shelter for the most mischievous of the Brookfields who'd been escaping whatever infernal affair their parents had been hosting. And even the troublesome Brookfields had never ventured out into a raging storm at nightfall.

Rhys shoved his door open.

"Rhys?" she called after him, in panicky tones. "You are going to retrieve her."

"I'll retrieve your blasted," *empty-headed*, "friend." Clever and spirited, his sister had never been one to keep company with wit-less misses.

She flashed a wide smile. "You are truly the best brother," she assured. "Even better than Miles."

And so it was, a short while later, his cloak draped over his shoulders, gloves in place, and black Oxonian hat pulled far forward, that Rhys slipped from his family's stone manor, and out into the blasted storm, to find the bothersome Lady Alice.

CHAPTER 4

HOW LONG DID IT TAKE for a person to freeze to death?

Surely a pelisse, velvet lined cloak, and leather gloves all delayed the process.

Or rather, her now damp leather gloves, that was.

Flakes of snow falling about, Alice beat her hands together.

Alas, after an endless swirl of time outside the Marquess of Guilford's grounds, she'd lost all chance to die with a proper answer to that question.

Her teeth chattered loudly. Not that she had any intention of dying out here.

And certainly not for him… *the bastard*.

From her position within the marquess' copse, Alice squinted into the distance as another black conveyance rumbled forward, the crest impossible to make out as anything more than a blur of gold emblazoned upon the door.

"Bl-black a-and g-gold," her muttering sounded inordinately loud in the winter still, and she immediately pressed her numbed lips tightly together. Yet another exactly-the-same color conveyance to amble up to the marquess' drive. Could nobody drive in anything different? Pink, pale blue, violet? Must all the carriages be the blasted same?

Her nose dripped, and she absently brushed the moisture back, all her attention trained forward on that exactly-the-same conveyance of another guest just arriving for the holiday festivities.

She stood there, motionless. The only hints of movement were the small tufts of white air escaping her lips.

Servants rushed about and then the door was opened.

Alice's heart threatened to beat a path outside her ribcage as the liveried footman reached up.

She perched forward on the balls of her feet. She was poised to flee, but needed to stay, just as confounded as she'd been since she'd discovered who would be spending the holiday season with her.

Nay, not her.

Such implied that Henry Pratt was something to her. When he wasn't. He was nothing more than a former betrothed, who belonged in name, body, and soul to another.

A familiar jolt of anger went through her and she embraced it. How much safer the outrage was than the pitiful sorrow that had gripped her for too long.

Would you get out of the blasted carriage, already?

After an endless stretch of time, with the help of a footman, the figure descended.

She groaned.

Lady Lovell.

One of Society's leading hostesses and also one of the most vicious gossips.

And here, she'd been so naïve as to believe the "looks" were far worse than anything else, only to be proven so blasted wrong. Alice pressed herself against the oak and knocked the back of her head against the jagged trunk. *Fool. Fool. Fool—*

A blanket of snow tumbled onto the brim of her bonnet, slamming into her shoulders. She gasped at the biting sting of it. Sputtering around a mouthful, she wiped an already hopelessly sopping glove over her face.

Alice whipped her head back with such force that her bonnet blew back, and she looked up.

The limbs overhead dipped under the weight of the snow, but for one now barren branch. She glared. A barren branch whose burden now rested on her bloody freezing person, and about her equally freezing feet.

Bloody hell. Yanking the strings free of her bonnet, she ripped it off and beat the snowy brim against her leg.

Could this day possibly be any—?

The slow rattle marking the arrival of another carriage, ripped across her useless self-pitying.

Alice froze; her teeth chattering uncontrollably providing the only slight movement. "Worse," she whispered. For she knew as she peeked out from her hiding place and spotted a pink carriage; that nauseatingly cheerful conveyance a vivid contrast to those elegant, black lacquer coaches.

Just as she knew with the same inexplicable intuition the day Henry Pratt's letter had arrived, breaking off their betrothal.

Still, as the carriage stopped and servants rushed about, one of the occupants stepped out. The sight that met her knocked the breath from her lungs.

With the aid of a servant, a bespectacled Henry descended. A black Oxonian perched atop his head gave him a boyish look—a boy playing with his father's regalia, when he'd never worn hats.

She cocked her head. He hadn't. Hadn't he? It was a silly thing to note as his young bride was handed down from the carriage and slipped her hand into his arm. Tall, statuesque, and in possession of midnight curls, she'd the look of a foreign princess.

Unlike Alice who'd been cursed with the same insignificant blonde hair as every bloody miss in England.

Just then, fate proved her hatred for Alice once more.

A gust of wind yanked at her red velvet cloak and set it whipping in the breeze.

Henry glanced over... at her thinly concealed hiding place.

Their eyes locked.

Heart racing, she dropped to her stomach, behind a slight drift. *Bloody, bloody hell.*

The cold, damp snow instantly penetrated her garments and a painful hiss slipped from her lips. She welcomed the stinging pain of it to the humiliation at being caught gawking.

Alice burrowed deep inside the folds of her wet cloak, again motionless on the ground. Frozen. Concentrating on the little puffs of white air blowing from her mouth with her every breath, Alice leveled herself up on her elbows. The iced snow crunched noisily under that slight depression as she stole a glance from her hiding place.

The gentleman with blindingly bright blond hair, alongside the Spartan-like beauty, climbed the steps of the marquess' family's estate. Free to study them unobserved, Alice stared blankly after *them.*

Flipping onto her back, Alice stared through the snow-covered limbs to the grey sky threatening more snow. Her lips chattered noisily in the winter quiet. She'd always loved the winter. One of the only benefits to having grown up a child without a mother, and an indifferent (now dead) father and previously hardhearted brother, was the freedom it had permitted. How many times she'd ambled through the snow-clogged hills of the English country-side, making snow angels and engaging in snowball fights with an imagined foe.

As much as she'd long loved the cold and snow, with it now soaking through her garments, she'd a newfound *un*-appreciation for the stuff.

A sharp gust of wind rippled over the countryside and set the branches swaying overhead. She glanced up and grunted, rolling out of the way as snow tumbled from overhead. It landed with a noiseless thump beside her. Picking her head up, she glowered at the now sloppy blanket of white. "Bloody hell," she hissed in the quiet. "Th-that is b-bloody f-freezing."

Raising shaking glove-encased fingers, she brushed the damp-ness from her numbed cheeks and nose.

Another gust of wind rolled through the countryside. Alice ducked out of the way as another batch of snow tumbled from the branches and landed with a wet thump in the drift.

Her numb lips turned up in a smile, just imagining the eulogy that would be delivered.

Poor Alice Winterbourne, died as she lived, unwed, surrounded by her former betrothed, who'd invariably chosen to make another woman his bride.

★★★Note, the bride was stunning in a masterful pink creation by Madam Lisette's.

CHAPTER 5

HOW LONG DID IT TAKE for a person to freeze to death?

Snow swirling about him, Rhys rubbed his glove-encased hands together in a bid to bring warmth into his chilled fingers.

He squinted, staring hard at The Copse where the lady had previously stood.

She'd flopped onto her back. His near frozen fingers awkward, he fished around for his timepiece, consulting it—nearly five minutes ago.

Though, if one wished to be more precise, the better question to be asked was how long would a lady stay hidden, before she allowed herself to freeze to death?

At first, curiosity had impelled the silent question from Rhys.

Then genuine awe.

And now concern.

Mayhap she'd already frozen.

If Lettice had been displeased before, she'd see him for pistols at dawn if he failed to return with her friend in tow—still alive. And though it wouldn't matter to most bachelors who made it a point to avoid familial obligations, he rather liked his sister. Clever, loyal, and not afraid to go toe-to-toe with their mother, any such person was deserving of loyalty, regardless of blood connection.

Nonetheless, he quietly cursed whatever squabble between Lettie and her mad friend had sent him out into the damned cold.

With the latest carriage of guests to arrive now unloading, Rhys started across the grounds.

After all, he was a rogue, but he wasn't a total bastard. Empty-headed miss or not, he wasn't one to leave a lady outside in the dead of winter.

Though, in fairness, there was something a good deal more comfortable in gadding about during a winter's storm than remaining to greet the parade of guests invited for the holiday season.

The wind yanked at his cloak and sent the black wool fabric snapping. Muttering under his breath, Rhys lifted his booted feet in a slow, deliberate pattern, turning up previously untouched snow.

The biting chill of the winter's air ripped through his garments and huddled deeper into his cloak.

Think warm thoughts:

Brandy.

A roaring fire.

A hot, eager widow.

Nothing would prove warming in this damned cold.

Rhys paused at the edge of The Copse and glanced down at the path made by smaller, more delicate footsteps. He did a quick search; his gaze instantly finding the splash of red sprawled on the earth in a puddle of velvet fabric.

Not breaking stride, he trudged the remaining distance. He stopped at the woman's side. Her skin pale but for the crimson splotches on her cheeks and the tip of her nose, the lady lay motionless, her eyelashes dusted with flakes of snow.

He balked.

"Good God, are you dead?"

The lady's eyes flew open and collided with his. Surprise, shock, and brief fear mingled in their brown depths. Those irises held him momentarily spellbound; the soft color of mahogany and—a shriek tore from her lips, ricocheting across the countryside, breaking that momentary lapse in sanity.

He whipped his gaze toward the most recently disembarked guests, a pup and his lady who glanced about searchingly.

Cursing, he flung himself to the ground beside Alison. Or Alex. Or whatever in hell her name was.

"Wh-what in bl-blazes do you think y-you are doing?" she demanded. "I-I am—"

A magpie. She was a blasted magpie. "Bloody hell, will you be silent," he hissed, layering himself to the snow-packed earth beside the loquacious woman. "The last thing I need this damned season is to be discovered in a compromising position with you."

The fear receded from the lady's eyes, to be replaced with a spirited glimmer of annoyance. "You are insufferably rude. *You* don't w-wish to be in a c-compromising position with *me*?" she muttered, pushing herself up onto her elbows.

Another black curse escaped him. Rhys caught the lady by the forearm and brought her back down beside him. "In fairness, I don't wish to be discovered with any proper miss," he breathed. "Particularly one empty-headed enough to go for a jaunt in a bloody blizzard."

She sputtered around a mouthful of snow. "I b-beg your pardon."

"As you should," he muttered. "Forcing me o-out t-to rescue y-you." Now his damned teeth were set to chattering from the cold.

"R-rescue me?" He may as well have stated plans to set her afire for warmth. "Wh-why you bloody—?"

"Unless you care for the latest guests to arrive to come exploring, with servants in tow, I trust you'll be quiet."

And miracle of all miracles this frigid night, the tart-mouthed spitfire went silent.

Though his intrigue had been unexpectedly piqued by a miss who freely let a curse fall from her lips, the fact remained Rhys still didn't care to risk discovery... this day or any day. He'd very nearly been trapped before. He certainly didn't have a wish to suffer that fate again and certainly not with a young miss who didn't have the common sense God gave an ant.

They remained shoulder-to-shoulder, gazes trained toward the drive, their position hidden by a blessedly useful snow bank.

The lady peeked her head up.

Rhys pressed a hand to the back of her head, gently forcing her back into place.

She shot him another glare. "Do you always freely handle a l-lady?" The lady brushed the back of her hand over her nose, shattering what would have been an otherwise scathing rebuff.

"Yes," he said unapologetically. "And they are a good deal warmer, more agreeable, and sensible," he added that last part under his breath.

Her mouth opened and closed. She opened and closed it again. "Well," she finally managed on a huff.

Rhys inclined his head a fraction, stealing another glance.

The young couple remained beside their nauseating pink carriage. Would they not leave already?

The spitfire at his side matched his movements, and he turned a silencing glare on her.

But where she'd previously been spitting and snarling, without a consideration of the potential risk of discovery, now she'd gone absolutely still. Her rosebud lips were so tightly clenched that white lines formed at the corners.

So she'd, at last, discovered the very real threat of being found together.

Rolling onto his back, Rhys settled onto the snowy earth and waited for the pair to be on their way.

"It was a mistake to come here."

It had been. As a rule, he'd made it a point to avoid any dealings with his mother.

An echo of his very thoughts, it took him a moment to realize the words belonged to another. The slip of a woman lowered herself into a like position beside him, and stared blankly up at the branches overhead. Gone was the spirited glimmer in her eyes, as a melancholy smile dipped her lips down at the corners.

"Indeed, it was," he said, wholly unforgiving. He'd come to rescue her, but he wasn't so chivalrous that he was above taking her to task for risking both of them to the cold and potential ruin. "What manner of woman runs off in a snowstorm?" It was a rhetorical question as much as one he truly wished an answer to.

"One who d-does n-not w-wish to be indoors," she mumbled.

It was a frustratingly unrevealing answer from a peculiar bit of a miss. For truly… which lady gadded about in the snow? The manner of women he kept company with wouldn't suffer through the discomfort of traipsing about in even a chill winter's day, let alone a storm.

He'd been ordered by his sister to return with her friend, however, she'd still remained perfectly clam-lipped about the source of contention between them. "A fight with Lettice?"

At the answering silence, he glanced over.

The young woman blinked slowly.

"Was it a fight with my sister, Miss…Alison?" he finished lamely, plucking the nearest name from his mind. For Lettie didn't have a malicious bone in her body or an unkind word on her lips. Which begged the question: just what conflict had broken out between them to send this one out into a storm.

The lady stared at him as though he'd sprouted a second head. "Miss *Alison*?"

He puzzled his brow. What in the blazes had her name been?

"Lady Alice Winterbourne," she said slowly. "M–my name is Alice."

Which had really been the least important part of questions he'd wished answers to. Except…he didn't cling to the lady's Christian form of address but rather, her surname.

"Winterbourne, you say?" He blanched. "Surely you're not the sister of *Daniel* Winterbourne, the Earl of Montfort?" Mayhap this magpie belonged to another family. *Please—*

She jutted her chin out. "I am."

Oh, bloody hell. Rhys scrubbed a hand over his face. Of course. It was to be *that* manner of day. A fight had erupted between Rhys' sister and the sister of his recent business partner. Montfort had already invested a sizeable sum in their steel venture. He decidedly couldn't let the lady go about freezing on his family's properties, *now.*

"Did you q-quarrel?" he asked bluntly.

"We did n–not."

The previously loquacious lady went quiet. If she'd been any other woman of Polite Society, he'd have accused her of coy games. This spitfire, however, was a mystery.

She stole another glance over the drift.

He arched his neck in a bid to see what held the lady so enrapt.

At last, the guests made a slow climb up the eleven steps to the portico.

The doors were flung opened and that pair sailed through.

At last.

Of course, this would not be a day when anything should go as expected.

The gentleman, a boyish-looking chap with spectacles, glanced back in their direction.

Rhys and Lady Alice Winterbourne instantly dropped to the ground.

He'd had any number of close calls: stolen trysts inside a host's empty parlor. An aging husband returning unexpectedly from the countryside, while Rhys had kept those discontented wives entertained.

Never before, though, in the frigid cold with the only blanket under him blasted snow. He turned his head to issue another warning.

But Lady Alice grabbed at Rhys' hand. "I-Is he g-gone?" she mouthed.

Frowning, Rhys peered quickly over.

The young gentleman continued a sweep of the countryside, lingering on The Copse, before the tall beauty at his side said something.

With a nod, he followed in behind her with, to Rhys' way of thinking, reluctant steps.

The door was shut, and they were gone... and Rhys and Lady Alice were safe.

Jumping up, Rhys bent down and scooped up the suddenly quiet spitfire, and set her on her feet. A startled squeak burst from her lips. "Come," he urged, dragging her by the wrist through the snow. Who was to know how many guests his family had invited for the holidays... and more precariously, when they would be arriving.

"Wh-what in the blazes are y-you doing?" She dug her feet in so that Rhys was forced to either stop or drag her down.

And for a long, long sliver of a moment, he entertained the latter.

"Did you hear me?" she demanded.

"It would be a demmed wonder if the entire house party didn't," he muttered.

She sputtered. "Wh-what was that you said?" The lady dragged her heels all the more.

Rhys sighed. Why couldn't he be the absolute blackguard his mother was constantly accusing him of being?

He released the tart-mouthed miss with such alacrity she went pitching forward.

Rhys shot his hands out to steady her but she tossed her arms wide and righted herself. That abrupt movement knocked loose her silly, floral bonnet, exposing a blindingly bright mass of blonde curls. A good deal of them tumbled over her brow and fell like a curtain over her eyes. His fingers twitched with the need to yank his gloves off and shove his fingers through those tresses to see if they were as silken soft as—

He recoiled. "Egads." The chill must have reached his brain. There was no other way of explaining his waxing on poetic about his sister's empty-headed friend's hair.

She shoved those strands back, robbing him of the pleasure, or saving him from that temptation. Either way, it was the same. "Wh-What?"

"What?" he echoed, frantically searching his mind for the reason for his question.

The lady took a step closer and peered at him. "*You* said '*egads*'. And—"

And she brought him blessedly back to the annoyance at hand—her. "Do you always chatter like a damned magpie?" he muttered. Grabbing her ornate bonnet, he jammed it back into place, swiftly concealing those luxuriant strands. There. No more worries about mooning over her damned hair.

"Wh-what in the blazes are you doing?" she demanded for a second time, as he took the long, satin ribbons and set to work tying them. "First you come upon me unannounced, and then proceed to chastise me—"

"You need a n-new milliner," he clipped out. "This bonnet is ghastly and these ribbons are entirely too long."

Whatever certainly stinging diatribe had been on her lips died. The stubborn minx folded her arms at her chest. "I-I like this bonnet."

Let the matter die. After all, it was both nonsensical and the height of foolishness, risking her ruin... for the purpose of continuing the debate on her bonnet.

"I am sure you do like it."

She pursed her lips; that red, beginning-to-chap, lush flesh he'd failed to note... until now. His gaze lingered, traced, and memorized each contour of those perfect bows. Yes, he'd failed as a rogue to appreciate only now the lady's tempting mouth. Lust bolted through him as he conjured all manner of wicked delights to enjoy with that tempting flesh.

"What in the blazes d–does that mean?" That tart, shrew–like tone would douse even the most unscrupulous rake's ardor, bringing him back to the moment—and the nonsensical debate.

He gathered one of the even–when–tied, entirely too–long ribbons, and twined it about his finger, again and again and again until his entire gloved index finger was draped with the fabric. "What I mean, love, is th–that a woman stupid enough to brave a bloody storm would be wearing such a monstrosity."

Her mouth fell agape. "Wh–why you've insulted me, twice," she breathed. The heated anger in that whispered realization, together with the fury in her eyes, was hot enough it could bring the storm to a raging stop.

"Just once. The other slight pertained to… this bonnet," he flicked the top of the article in question.

She shook her head back and forth in a slow, manner. "Who *are* you?"

Oh, blast, of course. Introductions and all that.

Rhys sketched a bow. "Lady Lettice's brother and I–I've been tasked with b–bringing you back." Before they both froze to death. He reached for her hand, but she again folded her arms.

The spitfire snorted. "I kn–know Lettie's brother." She scraped a gaze up and down over his frame. "And you, sir, are *not* him."

It was a simple misunderstanding that could be explained away with but a handful of sentences and, yet—her clear condescension rankled.

"I assure you, I am. Though I would vastly prefer if my more respectable brother saw to the honors of seeing you back."

The lady's arms fell to her sides, and her eyebrows made a slow climb until they disappeared under those golden curls. "You are the *other* brother."

The other brother.

It had been the proverbial story of his life.

The scapegrace.

The troublemaker.

The rogue.

The spare.

The other.

Not necessarily in that order, but that was generally the way of it in Polite Society.

"Yes, I am he. The 'Other' and…" The wind knocked about their cloaks, tangling her crimson velvet with his black wool. "I've been tasked with—"

"Bringing me back." She was already shaking her head. "I am not a recalcitrant child being tended to by a nursemaid."

Rhys closed his eyes briefly and prayed for patience… a marvel in and of itself as he'd never been the praying sort, and certainly not religious. But desperate times and all that. The lady he'd been tasked… sent to accompany, would try a saint on Sunday. Of course, this was the woman his sister would call friend.

With her spirit, his mother must certainly despise Lady Alice Winterbourne.

"Have I said something to amuse you?" she asked in tones more frigid than the winter chill that cut across the countryside.

He beat his gloved hands together, urging warmth back into his numb fingers. "My sister instructed me to bring you back and on any other day, I might gladly leave you to your own devices. But there is a bloody blizzard." And there was the inconvenient truth that the lady was, in fact, the sister of his newest business partner. Hardly a good foot to get off on letting the fellow's sister perish in the snow because of her stupidity and stubbornness. Growing annoyance pulled the words from him at a brisk clip. "It is snowing, dark, and cold. And even I would not be so callous as to leave you." He held his arm out. "So take my damned arm and let me escort you, back. *Now.*"

WELL.

In the whole of her life, no one had ordered her about.

Largely because she'd spent the better part of life invisible to all, from the father who'd no use for her the moment she'd entered the world to the brother who'd lived a shamefully rakish existence forgetting and uncaring about the sister out there.

It was a certainty that no one had ever spoken to her in that brusque, direct way… and if he weren't so insolent, and his annoyance directed at her, she thought she might have rather appreciated him for his frankness.

Alice angled her head, examining Lettie's brother through the swirl of snow. She sought to recall anything her friend had uttered about him.

… Rhys is the rogue of the family… he quite vexes Mother… and wisely stays away…

Beyond that, nothing much more had been said.

She inched her gaze up his six-foot, three-inch frame, heavy with muscle, before settling on the chiseled planes of his face, better suited for sculpture than real life. Her heart did a funny little leap.

A blond brow went winging up.

And at being caught staring, heat burned her cheeks. She gave thanks for the cover of darkness. Who knew it was possible to blush while having one's boots and skirts soaked from the snow, and one's entire body nearly frozen through?

And because it was far easier accompanying him than debating him after having been caught staring, Alice placed her fingertips atop his sleeve.

They fell into step. He adjusted his longer-legged stride to match her own.

The crunch of freshly fallen snow and the occasional ping of ice striking the earth filled the quiet as they made the long, slow trek back. Alice's teeth chattered, and she hunched deep inside her cloak, attempting to steal any remaining warmth from the soaked garment.

To no avail.

Her fiery exchange with Lettie's brother had concluded. A quiet silence was all that remained. Then reality intruded.

Henry and his bride's impending arrival.

Her flight.

Just like that, she'd abandoned her pride and risked running about in a winter storm because of him. Nay, to escape him. But it was all the same.

All over again, she'd gone and humiliated herself.

Shame soured her mouth. Removing her hand from his sleeve, she hugged her arms to her waist.

"It was not a fight then?"

At that unexpected intrusion into her miserable musings, she glanced up. "A fight?" she repeated dumbly. It had been far worse than that. It had been a broken betrothal and a public shaming that she'd brought upon herself, and—

"With Lettie?"

With Lettie.

Not with Henry.

How singularly odd and wholly welcome... she'd found the sole person in the whole of England who'd shown no inclination or interest in speaking about... her scandal. Did he truly not know?

Feeling his questioning eyes on her, she gave her head a clearing shake. "I'd never fight with Lettie," she said softly.

He snorted. "Then you have far greater patience than most."

She frowned. Lettice had been the only friend she'd had... ever. She was the one person who'd been unafraid of the gossip that came in any dealings with Alice, and hadn't been sorry-eyed whenever talk of Henry Pratt, "The Bastard", as Lettie had named him, was mentioned.

"I'm not disparaging my sister," he said, with an unerringly accurate read of her thoughts. He rubbed his gloved hands together frantically. He breathed against them, in what could only be a futile attempt at warmth. "She could put the greatest barrister in London to shame."

The shock of those words ripped through her. Alice tripped and went down hard on her knees.

With a curse, Lettie's brother stopped mid-stride and doubled back.

As he reached down to help her up, she searched the sharp planes of his face for a sign of deliberate cruelty. Brushing off his offer of assistance, she struggled to her feet.

"Are you all right?" he asked, glancing up and down her person.

She hadn't been fine in more months than she could remember. But he was the first who asked after anything other than The Scandal. "F-fine," she said quietly. "I am fine."

It did not escape her notice when they resumed their journey that he continued at a slower, more measured pace.

"So it was not an argument with my sister," he murmured, to himself. He cast her another look. "A row with dear Mama, then?"

That startled a laugh from her. How much more wonderful it was to laugh than to indulge the melancholy state she'd lived in for more months than she should.

He glanced questioningly at her.

Alice slapped a gloved hand over her mouth. "Forgive me." She measured her words. Well, blast, how to offer anything that would not be construed as an insult. "I just would not..." She went close-lipped. But then, mayhap word of her insult would reach the dowager marchioness and she'd order Alice gone... and then face could be saved. For then, it wouldn't count as fleeing.

Lettie's brother lifted an eyebrow. "Would not have taken the dowager marchioness as the maternal sort?"

Her lips twitched. Given the lady in question had insisted on being addressed only as "my lady" and nothing more at their first meeting, there'd never been a hint of anything maternal about the greying matron.

He winked once. A mischievous twinkle glinted in his steel-grey eyes. "You would be correct." He dropped his voice to a shame-fully loud whisper. "There is nothing warm or maternal about her. It is why I, to her greatest annoyance, call her Mama."

The tic at the corner of his right eye indicated she and this stranger... Lettie's brother had moved into dangerously somber territory, where all teasing stopped, and secrets dwelled.

Lettie's brother, whose name she still did not know. Alice peered into the distance. How far had she in fact traveled? The gentleman had been right in his earlier claims about her common sense.

He tapped a contemplative finger against his lip, bringing her gaze to that hard flesh slashed up in the hint of a smile. "Very well. You'll not tell me who your squabble was with, my lady?"

"There was no squabble," she persisted, hating the formality he'd erected through that proper form of address. Feeling his stare, she looked up. He lifted another pointed brow. "Alice," she corrected instead, giving him that name she so despised. "You may call me Alice."

The name was given to her not by a loving parent but by a servant after she'd entered the world. She was supposed to be a child meant to replace a beloved son her parents had previously lost.

"Alice," he repeated, as though experimenting with the feel of her name, his velvet baritone wrapping those two syllables in a silken caress.

She trembled; a little shiver that had nothing to do with the winter's chill that had left her numb with cold... and oddly more perilous for its effect. When he uttered her name, there was a beauty to it that she'd never before known. Not even from her betrothed, who'd been unable to divorce the "Lady" from her name when he'd spoken to her.

He is a rogue...

How matter-of-fact Lettie had been in describing her elder brother. And given that Alice had been the sister of a rake who'd only ever kept company with shameful and wicked scoundrels, she'd not paid much thought to Lettie's rogue of a brother.

But hearing mention of it and walking beside that same man, who managed to make one's hated name a soft caress, proved the dangerous power of those sorts.

"A-and d-do you have a name, as well? Or with her absence of maternal warmth, have you gone these many years without?"

A laugh escaped his lips, stirring little tuffs of white air. "My many years? Egads, Alice, you know how to wound a gent."

She knew nothing where gents were concerned. Alice had only learned of late just how little she knew about their entire species. "Is that a no?" she asked with a droll grin.

"Rhys."

His was warrior's name that so very perfectly suited a man of his command and ease. "After Rhys ap Thomas?" she ventured.

"Henry of Tudor's faithful supporter?" He doffed his hat and beat the snow-covered brim against his leg. "Alas, in addition to the dowager marchioness' lack of maternal warmth, there is also a woeful lack of appreciation for history." He waggled his brows. "Though, if she *were*, I trust it would be more likely Rhys ap Gruffydd, rebel, hanged for his plotting, that would have been a likelier muse."

Her mouth parted. As scholarly as her former betrothed had been, not even he possessed even the remotest interest in history.

He shot her a sideways glance. "Come, I am Lettie's rogue of a brother," he drawled, his boots kicking up snow around them as they walked. "Are you of an opinion that rogues should be slow-witted?"

"N-no," she said quickly, grateful for both the night cover and the brim of her bonnet for concealing her guilty flush. "Not at a-all."

They reached the bottom steps of the marquess' estate. Those stone stairs previously cleared by servants for the arriving guests were now dusted with a soft covering of snow. She hesitated. To enter together would expose them both to the very scandal he'd chided her over earlier.

Lord Rhys sketched a short bow. "I shall take the servant's entrance around back."

She chewed at her lower lip, and shot a glance down the expansive stretch of the marquess' properties, warring with herself. Lettie's brother had already journeyed out into the cold in the midst of a storm to assist her. Of course, she had not needed rescuing, as he'd so put it. But still, it was unpardonably selfish to be the reason he was still out trampling through the snow.

The wind howled mournfully about them.

Rhys dipped his head down, shrinking the space between them. Through the clean country air, made sharper by the winter, the sandalwood scent that clung to him filled her nostrils; that soft, warm woodsy smell oddly alluring. "Unless... you wish discovery, Alice?" he whispered, the dry amusement there shattering the pull, as much as the words themselves.

Whipping about, she sprinted up the eleven steps. Her fingers numb from the cold, she reached for the handle.

"I take that as a 'no'," he called, briefly staying her retreat.

She angled a glance over her shoulder. "A definitive 'no'," she whispered. After her disastrous taste of love with the faithless Henry Pratt, the last path she cared to venture down was the marital one.

As Alice let herself in, Rhys' quiet laughter rumbled after her.

"Unless I wish to be discovered, indeed," she muttered to herself.

With Lettie's brother... a notorious rogue with a ready quip on his lips. It was preposterous. It was—

"There you are!"

Alice shrieked.

Lettie grabbed her arm and dragged her forward. "Going out in the midst of a storm and in the dark of night," her friend whispered, with an outraged tone that would have impressed Mrs. Belden, their dragon of a headmistress. She glanced about, a frown deepening on her lips. "Where is my brother? I instructed him to return with you."

And he'd readily complied... in the middle of the freezing cold, at night. When, two years ago, Alice's own brother wouldn't have been able to pick her out of a ballroom full of ladies. As such, she'd an appreciation for a devoted brother. At her friend's probing look, Alice cleared her throat. "I'm afraid I do not know," she settled for. Which was, in fact, the truth. After he'd gone 'round back to the servants' entrance, she'd no idea where he might be.

Lettie grunted. "Where have you been?" she demanded.

A servant rushed over to assist Alice from her sopping cloak.

Originally, she'd taken flight with the sole purpose of hiding to sulk in her own misery. In that copse, however, with Alice's rogue of a brother, she'd gone from annoyed with Rhys' high-handed-ness, to laughing at a devastating wink and his ability to laugh and tease. In short, the dangerous combination that made up all rogues and rakes.

"Well?" her friend prodded as they made their climb abovestairs. With every step taken, Alice's boots left a sopping trail in her wake.

"I was walking."

"Because of him," Lettie lamented. She tossed her arms up in an exaggerated manner that only she could manage. "Pining for a man who was never, ever deserving of you."

They reached the main landing and several servants rushed all around.

"Hush," she whispered. "I was not... pining."

For she hadn't been. She'd merely wished to observe him and his perfect bride from a distance... and keep just that between them—a distance.

"Here we are," her friend murmured, bringing them to a stop beside a doorway. Lettie's expression brightened. "Given your window was broken, and there were no additional chambers in the guest suites, you've been given this chamber." She swept the door open. "Between mine," she motioned to the left of her. "And Rhys'."

Rhys.

Her *savior* in the snow. A teasing rogue who'd also quite freely ordered her about—or attempted to, anyway.

As her friend tugged her inside, Alice swallowed a groan.

Splendid.

CHAPTER 6

ℛHYS ADORED THE EARLY MORNING hours. It was that small sliver of time when all Polite Society slept on and the streets were largely quiet, the riding paths empty, and a man was free from bother.

Or a man was usually free from bother.

"Where in the blazes have you been?"

The following morning, that sharp whisper brought Rhys up short outside his chamber doors.

Given the owner of that equal parts furious and suspicious question and the unlikeliest use of blasphemy, he'd be foolish to not be suspicious.

With all the enthusiasm of one walking to face his hangman, Rhys forced his attention down the hall.

His mother stood, arms planted akimbo in a battle-ready position.

Oh, bloody hell. Here just one day and he'd already earned the Wrath of the Marchioness, as he'd taken to calling it over the years.

"Mama," he called out. The bane of her existence, he'd worked diligently since his boyhood days to needle her at every turn.

Her grey eyebrows shot up, and she raced forward. "Hush," she whispered, stealing a frantic glance about. "You will awaken the guests."

And moving at anything other than a sedate pace?

This did not bode well for him. At all.

"Considering they are an entire corridor and no fewer than one hundred paces between us, I trust we should be quite safe from discovery," he said drolly as he finished drawing the heavy oak slab closed.

He took a step.

His mother matched his movements.

Rhys feinted left.

She followed suit.

So he'd be forced into an early morning battle. Very well. Swallowing a sigh, Rhys rocked back on his heels. Given that the dowager marchioness had taken the whole of the years he'd known her to rising well after the sun had climbed high into the sky, these encounters were the worst for him and the wisest for her.

Unexpected moves from her that always saw him off-kilter.

By God, Wellington would have been wise to employ her all those years ago against Boney. The war would have not carried on for more than a month.

"I asked you a question," she demanded in hushed tones, stealing another furtive look about.

"No, you urged me to silence lest I wake guests slumbering more than… one… two… three…" He silently counted the remaining panels. "Twenty doors away."

She scowled; the wrinkled planes of her face deepening, highlighting her increasing years. The perpetual frown she wore made a lie out of all the words about one growing lax with age. "Do not try to distract me. I asked where you've been."

Rhys lifted his hands in false supplication. "Given that you've discovered me exiting my rooms, I trust it should not be a question to merit that volatile reaction."

The dowager marchioness alternated a suspicious stare between his door and the opposite end of the hall. "I know your flippant replies and shameful attempts at jest are meant to divert my attention from your… your… behavior."

His behavior. At any other time, she would have been well within reason to question his whereabouts and pursuits. "Given that you're personally responsible for all the guests," he drawled, "I assure you, there are no hidden widows or naughty lovers hiding about." He paused. "Though if you'd allow me to issue an invitation—"

She choked.

Rhys lifted his head in a mocking acknowledgement. "I take that as a no, then."

His mother's eyes bulged. "Y-you… y-you…" *Scoundrel.* "Scapegrace," she settled for. But then, she brought her shoulders back and gave a flick of her canary yellow skirts. "I'll not allow you to distract me." She proceeded to tick off on her fingers. "First, you disappeared last evening. Disappeared, Rhys, when… when…" He winged an eyebrow. Color fired in her cheeks. "Guests were expecting to see you."

"Guests?" he asked with feigned confusion.

"Aria arrived and you were nowhere to be found."

The lady his mother expected him to wed had arrived which added a level of very real peril to his circumstances that had been previously missing. He fought the urge to yank at his suddenly too-tight cravat, briefly eying the path to freedom beyond her shoulder, contemplating escape.

Her gaze bore searchingly into him; probing his face. "Do you have nothing to say for yourself?"

As much as he'd sustained himself through her company over the years with a false brevity to rouse her annoyance, now he wanted done with the whole exchange. Restless. "Lettie enlisted my services and, as her brother, I obliged," he said, with an unusual graveness.

"Enlisted your services?" she squawked. That break in her own calls for silence marked her rapidly spinning out of control temperament. "You are no servant, Rhys, no matter how uncouth and ill-mannered you so often are."

He opened his mouth to make mention of the vixen with a tangle of golden curls, but something quelled the words on his lips. Some inexplicable need to keep that surprisingly enjoyable and private exchange with Lady Alice Winterbourne a secret that belonged only to him. As such, he settled for his usual expected dry humor. "Oh, come, Mama. It is one thing to disparage me. But the Brookfield staff? They are the model of decorum and respectability."

His mother's eyebrows dipped. "Furthermore, when have you been the devoted brother? If it were Miles, I would trust there was something honorable at play there, but you?" She scraped a derisive glance up and down his person.

He frowned as her barb found its mark. Mayhap it was the early morning hour....or that the Christmastide season was nearly upon them. For the truth was... it was not her disgusted look or disparaging tone that struck uncomfortably close but rather her accurate claims about him as a brother. He had been a self-absorbed bastard these many years. His mother's betrayal aside, he should have been there for Lettie.

"You've gone quiet," she noted. "You are up to something." She took a step closer, jolting him back from his maudlin musings.

He retreated a quick step. His back knocked into the heavy panel, rattling the wood.

And it spoke to her determination that the dowager marchioness didn't give so much as a look or make mention about the noise. Going up on tiptoes, she peered at his face, the way only a leading gossip in Society could.

"Hmm," she said noncommittally, sinking back on her heels. "Very well, then," she said, with a surprising capitulation that only a fool would trust. And Rhys Brookfield was no fool... particularly where his ruthless mother was concerned. He'd born witness to the depths to which she would fall to orchestrate whatever ultimate end she wished her pawns-of-children to fulfill. "That will be all."

"Always a pleasure, Mama," he said in parting as he dropped a bow.

As he made a measured escape, he felt her gaze following him until he disappeared around the corner.

And feeling much like the troublesome boy whose knuckles she'd ordered his tutors to rap for misbehaving, he broke out into a quick run down the blessedly empty, quiet corridors.

He passed a young maid, exiting a room, with a cloth in her hand.

Her lips twitched, and she sank into a curtsy.

Not breaking stride, he winked, and continued on. Slightly breathless from his exertions, he skidded to a halt outside the breakfast rooms. At having his freedom once more, he whistled a naughty ditty, and entered.

"Babington," he greeted the senior footman on duty, catching the other man mid-yawn.

"Beg pardon, Lord Rhys," the fellow near in age to his own rushed.

The dowager marchioness' effects on the servants had proven lasting; a staff eternally afraid a wrong move would see them turned off without a character reference. Waving off that needless apology, Rhys gathered a plate from the sideboard. "Not a thing to apologize for. Not as though I'd come upon you tupping a parlor maid," he said in a bid at easing the other man's unease.

Babington blanched and shook his head frantically, his gaze all over the room.

Rhys added a heap of kidneys to his full dish, and then slapped the servant on the back. "No worries, my good man. Nor would you find yourself turned off if you were because of me."

The servant emitted a strangled sound, pointing a finger weakly beyond Rhys' shoulder.

He froze. Oh, bloody hell.

Babington winced, and gave a confirming nod.

"A lady?" he mouthed.

"A lady, my lord," the pained footman confirmed in like silence.

Bloody, bloody hell. Which guest would arise at this ungodly hour? Other than his mother to chastise and threaten him, of course. "My sister?" he ventured hopefully, still continuing their noiseless discourse.

The footman gave his head a regretful shake.

Shocking and scandalizing Polite Society was certainly not new for him, but even he drew the proverbial line at crass talk in the presence of respectable ladies.

Plate in hand, Rhys wheeled about slowly and faced the latest scandalized guest.

Of course.

Alice lifted her fingers in an insolent little waggle; her expression impressively deadpan.

Rhys unleashed a stream of curses in his head.

He *should* expect that a young woman who'd gone dashing about in a snowstorm would rise before the sun.

Rhys searched for the horrified shock and outrage over his ribbing with the footman. Instead, a wholly unaffected Alice popped a piece of plum cake into her mouth.

"Is it too much to hope you did not hear all that?" he called from the sideboard.

The young lady swallowed and then dabbed at her lips. "Which part? Your pardoning Mr. Babington's yawn?" A sparkle glinted in the troublesome minx's eyes. "Or your kindly overlooking any morning tupping he'd been doing?"

Babington dissolved into a fit of choking.

And Rhys, one of Society's most outrageous rogues responsible for blushing matrons, misses, and wicked wantons all over London, found his neck burning with color.

"Worry, not." Her eyes danced with mischief. "I've never been accused of being a proper miss." The young lady dismissively, grabbed a small—unnoticed until now—leather book propped open beside her plate and dedicated all her attentions to it.

His ears pricked up. "Oh?" Rhys was an excellent reader on those wicked ladies who were fair game and those virtuous ones to be avoided at all proverbial costs. He'd not been wrong before, but neither was he at all disappointed if the spitfire before him was, in fact—

"My brother is a rake," she said simply, the way she might have said she preferred the sugared pastries to the non-powdered treats.

"Ah," he was unable to keep the regret from tinging that utterance. Because really, what was a gent to say to that?

Alice scrunched her nose up, seeming content to carry on the conversation without further contribution from him beyond that one syllable utterance. "Or rather, he was a rake. He is—" She paused, sadness filling her revealing eyes. "Married. He is married," she softly amended.

And just like that, the teasing, mischievous lady of moments ago went dark, replaced once again with this solemn, downtrodden miss.

Drawn to the table, he abandoned his usual chair in favor of the one beside the young lady. Rhys waved Babington off, and claimed the high-back velvet upholstered dining chair. "Am I to take it you dislike said wife?" There could have been no missing her outward reaction, and one so visceral, at that. "What is it? Does she take umbrage to your being underfoot?"

"Underfoot?" she blurted like he'd gone mad. And mayhap he had. For what else was to account for sitting beside his sister's innocent friend, a respectable lady, and engaging her about her family. "No. I quite love my sister-in-law."

"Of course," he said slowly, as though he saw the reason for her effrontery. When in truth, he saw not an ounce of logic to, of, or about Lady Alice Winterbourne.

Giving her head another dismissive shake, she resumed her reading.

Yet—he drummed his fingertips upon the arm of his chair—she was not aggrieved over her brother's choice in bride, so what accounted for the downward tilt to her lips. Rosebud flesh that had far better uses and purposes than heart-rending frowns.

It hardly mattered whether she was sad. Or angry... or anything. She was nothing more than a stranger—albeit, Lettie's friend. That was, of course, what accounted for the need to chase back that melancholy and replace it with the earlier deviltry he'd spied from her.

"So you heard all of my exchange with Babington," he prodded, settling into his seat. A real gentleman would abandon the matter altogether and make pleasantries about the unseasonably chilled weather they were having.

Alice flipped the page. "Which part? Your words to Babington about his tupping a parlor maid?" Rhys' lips twitched. "Or your *generous* pardon if he were discovered in such a state."

The slight sound of the page being turned was drowned out by another bout of noisy exhalations from Babington.

Alice glanced up from her page, peering past Rhys' shoulder. "Though, I believe a far better question for Mr. Babington would be whether he is requiring a doctor to see to his persistent cough."

A grin turned Rhys' lips in a wide, easy smile. Not the affected roguish half-grins he generally donned with ladies, but a genuine expression of mirth.

That promptly faded as the lady returned her attention to her reading selection.

Accepting the proffered cup of coffee, Rhys blew on the steaming contents, and studied the young woman from over the rim—the wholly removed woman. Of course, it was always far safer when a virtuous miss was removed... particularly when that woman also happened to be his sister's closest friend.

One hand on the book, the other holding a piece of French baguette in hand, she awkwardly turned the page.

It was a sad day as a rogue when he'd been so dismissed by a lady, for a book.

He took a small sip and grimaced at the sharp sting of the acrid beverage. "I certainly see why my sister approves of you, Alice," he commented, matter-of-factly. Spirited, with a quick tongue and directness, she was unlike the simpering ladies who practiced an unspoken language behind their fans.

Alice paused, mid-turn. "I'm her friend."

He'd have to be deafer than a post to fail to hear her censure.

He gave her a questioning look.

"I'm not a piece of horseflesh or a pastry selection, Lord Rhys. I'm a friend," she said simply. Licking the tip of her index finger, she completed the page turn.

Rhys sat there, flummoxed, riveted by that innocent and yet wholly seductive for it, gesture. He had a sudden urge to draw that finger between his lips and suck.

He groaned.

The morning meal had been a horrid idea. And if the lady were given to rising early, he'd be better served avoiding the meal as long as she was here.

The young lady picked her head up. "Is everything all...?" As their gazes met, a becoming pink blush colored her cheeks.

So she was not wholly immune to him.

Around another sip of coffee, he grinned again and, emboldened by that delicate color, he stretched his legs out comfortably before him. "You still never did say what had you running all over the English countryside in the dead of night, Alice."

Had he not been watching her so closely, he would have failed to note the way she stilled. Her long, graceful neck slightly bent, straightened. "No, I did not."

He waited, counting the ticks of the clock. When after the tenth and another quick turn of her page, it became apparent that she intended to say not another word.

Rhys continued his study of her, taking a periodic drink of his now lukewarm brew.

The lady abruptly set her book down and dropped her elbows on a table that would have earned his mother's highest rebuke. And for it, she garnered his ever-increasing appreciation. "May I ask you a question?"

Given that he'd posed the same query to her more than four times since yesterday, and still hadn't received an answer, it was hardly fair play. More intrigued than proud, he inclined his head.

"Why do you drink it?"

His brow creased.

She pointed to his cup. "You've grimaced after every sip. Why drink it if you despise it?"

His mouth parted in brief startlement, which he instantly concealed behind an easy grin. "I'll explain my coffee indulgence when you explain what had you running about my family's properties."

She instantly went close-mouthed, and returned prompt attention to her book.

His intrigue redoubled. Had she been any other woman, he'd have accused her of playing coy in a bid to earn his attentions. Alice Winterbourne, however, had shown far more interest in her baguette and plum cake than she had in his presence.

And the only reason that irked was because he took pride in the image of rogue he'd cultivated. Yes, that was the *only* reason.

Shoving back his chair, Rhys climbed to his feet. Plate in hand, he wandered closer to the impervious miss.

She glanced briefly up, following his movements with quizzical eyes.

"May I take this seat?" he asked in quiet tones.

"Given they are all your seats, I trust you could take them apart and use them for kindling if you so much as wished."

"With my mother?" He snorted. "I'm fairly certain that would qualify as an offense punishable by exile."

She laughed. The sound was clear and bell-like, innocent… and one wholly unfamiliar with the women he kept company with. Not that he was keeping company with her. They were merely two guests forced together at a holiday house party, now breaking their fast. Despite all those assurances, her laughter was infectious and he joined in.

Footsteps sounded at the doorway, and they both looked up.

The bespectacled pup who'd arrived yesterday with his too-tall hat and furred cloak, stared back—stricken.

Alice's laughter abruptly cut out.

And as that pair silently looked at one another, a thick tension fell over the room, replacing the earlier cheer.

Rhys narrowed his eyes.

So this was the reason for the late night jaunt to The Copse—the too-stern looking Pratt fellow, doing a rather poor job in pretending he wasn't paying attention to the lady.

Surely she, a minx who freely cursed and boldly laughed, wasn't pining after a stiff, humorless pup like Henry Pratt, brother to the recently reformed rogue, Nolan Pratt?

And sitting back in his chair, Rhys cursed the unwelcome intrusion that had shattered his previous interlude with Alice Winterbourne.

CHAPTER 7

SHE'D BEEN LAUGHING.

Nor had it been the false expression she'd forced for her concerned family's benefit.

Rather, this had been Alice's laughter of old, pulled from her by a rogue, given to expert teasing. And it had felt so very good to laugh again... and mean it.

And then he'd arrived. *Henry.*

He remained rooted to his spot in the doorway. A hurt glitter lit his eyes.

Annoyance unfurled in her belly, and she swiftly yanked her attention back to her plate.

He was hurt? What reason did he have to be hurt?

Grabbing her knife, she carved up a sausage link. The tip of her utensil scraped along the plate and a chilling screech pierced the room.

Rhys leaned over and whispered. "Have a care, love. It's already been slaughtered."

Smile lines appeared at his eyes. "Now, if it were the roast at evening meal, *then* you'd have reason for your suspicions."

That gave her pause. "Truly?"

He lowered his lips so close they nearly brushed the shell of her ear. "Does my mother strike you as one who'd tolerate a roast that is still mooing?" His breath stirred the sensitive skin at her nape and, reflexively, her head tipped away. Rhys' gaze went to the elongated column of her neck.

A breathless laugh escaped her; a product of his nearness and reply.

Did she imagine the way his Adam's apple bobbed? When he lifted his gaze to hers, only the teasing glimmer remained, and his grin.

It was a remarkable smile that so beautifully revealed the flawless even rows of pearl white teeth. And yet it was not so much the perfection of it, as the honesty in his mirth. It was unrestrained, unapologetic, and with its freeness flouted Societal expectations to never display too much emotion.

And—

A loud crash from the sideboard split the quiet.

The diligent footman rushed over and, retrieving the silver server, proceeded to fill Henry's plate.

Porcelain dish in hand, without so much as a word of thanks, Henry made his way to the table and, with his usual devotion to propriety, waited.

Another servant rushed over to pull out his chair. And as he went through the pomp and circumstance of snapping his crisp white napkin three times and placing it upon his lap, Alice folded her hands together on her lap and clenched tightly.

Must he be here… at Lettie's… in this breakfast room?

Since his betrayal, he'd existed as more an amorphous figure to hate and resent. Now, he was before her, a tangible reminder of her folly and humiliation—a public humiliation she was responsible for, that would continue to be whispered about by Polite Society until the next scandal came along.

Or, mayhap, forever. Mayhap, all juicy morsels lingered and were dragged out for a retelling when the *ton* began to forget.

Rhys moved his lips close to her ear again and another rush of tingles raced down the sensitive column of her neck. "My mother finds it uncouth."

Fighting the dizzying pull of that whisper, she raised her gaze. "Beg pardon?"

"You asked why I drank coffee," he said, lifting his glass. "Long ago, I dedicated my life to earning my mother's disapproval whenever and wherever I could," he elucidated A thousand questions whirred. Rhys spoke of a conscious decision to agitate the dowager marchioness. What had prompted that vow? He lifted his half-empty cup. "And she quite disapproves of coffee. She claims the heathens drink it."

Her lips twitched. "She also advised Lettie that the heathens invented the waltz."

"Ah, if that is the reason a gentleman is allowed to take a lady in his arms and put his hands upon her waist, tangling his fingers with hers, then I have much to thank them for." He lifted his cup in salute.

Her heart did an odd little jump. She tried to laugh. His words, after all, were tossed in jest. And yet, God forgive her, he conjured an image of that waltz; one that was wicked and whispered of seduction, when she'd only ever seen it as a task insisted she master by her former finishing school instructor. Alice darted her tongue out and traced it along suddenly dry lips.

Rhys' thick, golden lashes, which would have been the envy of any lady for their lushness, swept down, but not before she caught his focus on her mouth.

Henry snapped one of the leather journals he'd come in with open, shattering the brief pull between Alice and Rhys, Lettie's rogue of a brother.

Instantly straightening, she grabbed her fork and knife and resumed dicing her sausage.

And this time, unlike before, as she popped that bite in her mouth, it didn't seem nearly so difficult to bring herself to swallow it down. Returning her focus to her previously forgotten book, Alice flipped through the pages, finding her place.

Her skin pricked. She glanced up.

Cup of coffee in his hands once more, Rhys spoke in his near silent words over the rim. "Is he the one?"

She shook her head.

Rhys gave a nearly imperceptible tilt of his head over in Henry's direction. Henry, as he'd been on so many occasions, was buried behind a leather folder, his nose deep in whichever case commanded his time. All of it.

"Your flight to The Copse?" he continued sotto voce.

Cheeks burning, she opened and closed her mouth several times. How in the blazes had Rhys gathered that... from *this*?

"Wounded eyes," he whispered. "Strained smile. Slumped shoulders. You have all the makings of a heartsick miss."

Immediately drawing her only slightly slumped shoulders back, she stole a glance about to determine whether Henry had overheard that pathetic catalogue. And furthermore… "I do not have wounded eyes." She paused, leaning close. "And by the way, what in the blazes is a wounded eye?"

He stuck up two fingers. "The pair of them."

"Well, it's silly," she said on a furious whisper. "Unless one's received a facer, eyes cannot be wounded. That is the kind of drip and drivel in those silly romantic novels." Those books she'd once favored which invariably saw love triumph. But that had been back when she'd been a hopeless romantic and believed in the power of love to conquer all and defy the odds. Mores the fool was she.

"Ahh." Rhys reclined in his seat, resting his elbows on the arms of his chair.

Do not ask it. Do not ask it. He's merely baiting me.

"What?" She'd always been hopeless when a challenge was issued.

"You once read romantic novels and now are reading—" Bold as the day was long, he picked up her forgotten volume. "Aristotle's History of Animals."

A loud scraping interrupted their discourse.

They looked as one across the table.

With stiff, hurried movements, Henry gathered the books he'd arrived with and then promptly quit the room.

Her faithless former betrothed forgotten, Alice snatched her book from Rhys' long, gloveless fingers. The olive hue of those long, callused digits may as well have been tanned by a summer sun for their deep coloring. "And you find it so very hard to believe that a lady should appreciate literature on wildlife?"

"I don't know you one way or another to say what you would be reading," he conceded. "I was merely assembling all the pieces to rationalize the very reason you were outside in a blizzard the evening prior." Coughing into his hand, he gave his head a less than discreet tilt in the empty seat previously occupied by Henry.

She shifted in her chair. And here she'd always taken rogues and rakes as self-absorbed sorts. Rhys, however, had gathered details the way a constable might the clues of a case. But then, a brother who went out in a storm at his sister's bidding and who noted the minutest details in Alice's words, bore little hint of those wicked sorts. "I… used to read them," she finally conceded.

He took another sip of his coffee. "It is a shame you stopped."

It was a shame? Curiosity piqued, she could not stop the question from coming. "In what way?" The young ladies she'd gone to finishing school with had all spoken of hiding those tomes away from mocking older brothers or disapproving papas.

"Reading the romantics suggests just that… a romantic spirit. It's entirely possible for a person to be both romantic in spirit and practical of mind. To exist, one without the other, leaves for a colorless soul."

A colorless soul. At that image he painted with his broad brush-stroke, her annoyance stirred. How dare he presume to form a judgment of her based on what she chose to read… and not read? She was not colorless… she was…

Flummoxed, Alice sank back in her chair.

Well bloody hell on Sunday. Since Henry's betrayal, she *had* been dispirited. Henry hadn't made her into a downhearted, morose figure, burying books and talks about the heart. She'd allowed herself to become just that. Unnerved by that realization and Rhys' piercing focus, Alice picked up her fork and dragged it around the barely-touched contents of her plate.

Quiet laughter filtered in from the hall.

The Marquess and Marchioness of Guilford strolled into the breakfast room. Arms looped, heads bent, they whispered to one another, the entire world seeming forgotten. There was a beautiful intimacy to their exchange. The young couple lingered in the doorway. Lord Guilford raised his wife's knuckles to his mouth, placing a kiss upon them.

Alice swallowed hard.

I wanted that… I wanted a devoted love, who saw me and no other…

But that had never been Henry. Even before he'd betrayed her. He'd been absorbed with his work as a barrister and his cases and earning sufficient funds to build them a fortune. Only, he'd never realized—she hadn't wanted a fortune.

But then, he had… and connections with his employer which his marriage had ultimately secured him. That is what had had been of most importance to Henry.

Feeling Rhys' eyes on her, she stole a peek.

He winked.

"Good morning, big brother," he boomed, and the pair jumped apart.

A pretty blush stained the marchioness' cheeks. "Rhys," she greeted, and then looked to Alice.

Alice hurried to stand and dropped a curtsy. "My lady."

"Lady Alice," the other woman returned with a warm smile that reached all the way to her eyes.

Her husband dropped a respectful bow.

Given the fact Daniel had attempted to seduce the young woman, and been bloodied senseless by the marquess in repayment, it spoke volumes to the marquess and marchioness' character that they'd be so welcoming of Alice.

Nonetheless… she gathered her book and, with another slight curtsy, bid the Brookfields a good morning, and made her escape.

"She's playing at matchmaker," his brother warned as soon as Alice had taken her leave.

Lingering his gaze on the doorway, an inexplicable regret filled him at the lady's hasty departure. Mayhap, it was merely the tedium of the countryside, but he'd been… enjoying speaking with her— again.

He forced his attention back. "What?"

"Mother," Miles clarified.

"Ah, yes. Of course." Doomsday could be approaching on the morrow and she'd be frantically trying to coordinate matches for all her unwed children. "I've gathered as much," Rhys muttered. A servant came forward and refilled his coffee. With a word of thanks, he blew on the contents. "She's been less than discreet and quite clear in her expectations."

"Aria," Miles stated as a matter-of-fact.

Rhys toasted the accuracy of that supposition with his cup. "Indeed."

His brother gave him a regretful smile. "Alas, I fear, the only thing that might deter her efforts is if you were otherwise betrothed." Miles' eyes glimmered. "And given the carefully crafted guest list, she's taken care with the ladies invited."

Married. All the women, he was otherwise not related to, were married.

Alice's heart-shaped visage flitted forward.

Well, not everyone.

His sister-in-law lowered her voice. "I'm sorry that you find yourself at the center of her…" She grimaced. "Efforts."

It had been, of course, the expectation that Miles would marry and secure the Cunning connection. Alas, the one time he'd shattered his role of dutiful son and instead wed Philippa, had seen those responsibilities shift. Not that Rhys would begrudge a single one of his siblings their happiness.

He inclined his head. "It was inevitable. Ultimately, we all find ourselves in her crosshairs."

"Uncle Rhys!"

He glanced over to the seven-year-old whirlwind of energy bursting into the breakfast room. Close at her heels, her three-year-old sister.

"We are under siege," he cried out, jumping to his feet.

Faith and Violet hurled themselves at him and he staggered back, feigning a fall.

Faith giggled. "You're too big for us to knock down."

"Mayhap at the last time we met." He hefted up his smaller curly-headed niece and dangled her over his shoulder, until great, big, snorting gasps of laughter escaped her. Again, he pretended to stumble, panting as he spoke. "You both must have grown a foot each and added two stones between you."

He set Violet, breathless with her giggles, on the floor.

The initial warm greeting now gone, Faith settled her hands on her hips with a look more terrifying than most matrons. "Where have you been?"

Over her mop of dark curls, he caught his sister-in-law and brother exchange a look. They proved little help as the little girl persisted.

"You arrived yesterday morn and didn't come to see us."

Violet held up two fingers. "Not even once."

Schooling his features into a somber mask, he stretched his arms wide. "I've been remiss. I must make amends." Mindful of Faith's partial deafness, he leaned down and, in an exaggerated whisper, spoke into her good ear. "Will this suffice?" He fished two small bags of peppermint from his jacket and held them over.

Violet's eager little fingers instantly grabbed her prize.

Faith stuck up a lone digit, more restrained than her younger sister.

"A ride on my horse?"

She waggled that gloved finger. "That is a *little* better."

"A battle in the snow?"

A slow, wide smile turned her lips up. "You are forgiven."

Frantic footfalls sounded from outside the breakfast room. In a remarkable break with her usual composure and decorum, the dowager marchioness spilled into the room, panting. "There you are," she gasped, clutching the doorjambs.

As she'd never been a devoted grandmother to Miles and Philippa's girls, he cast a hopeful glance over at Miles.

Miles shook his head. "Not me," he mouthed.

"Not him," their mother narrowed her gaze on Rhys' untouched plate. She pointed a finger at him. "*You*. You haven't concluded breakfast yet." She beamed; or as much as a ruthless harpie such as the Dowager Marchioness of Guilford could. "Aria and Lady Lovell will be breaking their fast soon."

Bloody hell.

Rhys pressed a hand to his heart. "Though it grieves me to disappoint you in any way…" Her eyes formed thin slits that swallowed up her irises. "I have a previous commitment."

Her spine stiffened. "But… who…?" She searched about. Did she think Rhys was hiding a mistress underfoot? "Surely not that—?" *Interesting.* The greater question was which lady did his mother so thoroughly disapprove of? It also explained why his mother had begun stalking his every movement since his arrival. "Who. Are. You. Meeting?"

An obedient son wouldn't take such delight in her tangible vexation. Rhys, however, had never been accused of that tedious trait. "Two someone others," he amended. Holding his hands out, Faith and Violet instantly slid their fingers into his.

Rhys left his mother sputtering in his wake.

A short while later, bundled with his nieces in tow, he made his way through the snow-covered grounds.

His youngest niece giggled, racing several steps ahead. Faith kept pace at his side.

"Mama and Papa said that Grandmother is going to make you get married."

"Did they?" he asked, beating his gloved hands together to bring warmth into the chilled digits. His niece had always proven an invaluable spy.

"Mm-hm. *And* they said Grandmother thinks you have to marry Miss Cunning because Papa married Mama instead."

Talk of giving up his bachelor state was a topic to avoided with all... chatty young nieces included.

"Well?" Faith persisted, refusing to let the matter go. "Will you marry Miss Cunning to make Grandmother happy?"

Given his niece's tender years he'd not point out that he hadn't done anything in the whole of his adult life to earn his mother's approval and he didn't intend to begin now.

"I have certain requirements before I make anyone my bride," he said solemnly.

Eyes a-goggle, Faith looked up.

He ticked off a list. "She must laugh and often."

Even as he said it, the unrestrained, clear expression of Alice's merriment echoed around his mind. Hers hadn't been the cynical laugh of the experienced widows and discontented wives he bedded. Nor a careful tittering, practiced and artificial. It had been real.

"Oh, yes," Faith said in solemn agreement, bringing him back. "I quite agree. Mama and Papa laugh often." She inclined her head. "What else?"

"She must be able to throw a flawless snowball."

Faith nodded. "I certainly agree."

"Of course, she must also swim," Rhys went on. "And if she cannot, at least be willing to learn how."

"And ice skate?" Faith put in, warming to the pretend list he compiled for his future bride.

Rhys stuck his index finger up. "Not simply ice skate, but twirl a perfect circle without even stumbling."

His eldest niece giggled. "Papa cannot even do *that.*"

"Then it appears I'm to remain unmarried, despite Grandmother's wishes." They shared a smile. Up ahead, Violet stopped to assemble a ball of snow.

Rhys started after the girl... when he registered the uncharacteristic quiet.

He glanced back. A troubled little frown marred his eldest niece's plump cheeks. Doubling back, he rejoined her. "What is it, moppet?"

Faith kicked the snow with the tip of her boot. "She doesn't like us."

He furrowed his brow. "Violet?" he asked quizzically. The little girl didn't have anything less than a smile for even the most miserable blighters—of which Rhys' mother was certainly the greatest.

His niece rolled her eyes. "Grandmother."

"Ahh." It had been inevitable. One as clever and quick-witted as his niece wouldn't fail to eventually note the dowager marchioness' coldness. Rhys shot a quick, longing glance back in the direction of the manor. This wasn't a matter for an uncle, but rather a devoted mama and papa.

Who would have figured that it would have been safer to remain in the breakfast room with his determined mama and the woman she'd hand-selected as his bride?

He opened his mouth to deliver one of his usual flippant replies, but called the words back. Ultimately, the dowager marchioness *didn't* like Miles' adopted children. She saw them as interlopers and strangers… but neither had she truly liked the children she'd given life to, either. As such, he'd been Faith and Violet, once. A child desperately wanting the approval and affection of one who could never give it. Rhys dropped to his haunches so he was at eye level with his niece.

"Sometimes… people are just miserable. It doesn't make it easier to forgive them for being such… rotters. Nor should you attempt to be anyone other than who you already are just to please those people." He paused. "Because they will never be pleased."

Her lips twitched, and she whispered loudly. "Are you calling Grandmother a rotter?"

He touched a finger to the side of his nose and blinked once.

She giggled.

Abandoning his teasing, Rhys gathered her hands and gave a little squeeze. "What is important is to surround yourself with those who are happy and able to smile."

"Like you?"

"Like me." It had ben vastly easier to force joy than give in to the pain of past heartbreak. Until…even he himself had come to believe in that happiness.

She looped her arms around his neck, giving him another hug.

A snowball collided with the back of his head. The frigid projectile dripped over the top of his head, from his brow into his eyes and mouth.

He licked the wet away and then carefully set Faith aside.

They looked to a giggling Violet, already at work on creating a new ball.

"It seems war has been declared." He let out a battle cry and then threw himself into the fight.

CHAPTER 8

A THUNDEROUS SHOUT SHATTERED THE COUNTRYSIDE; a booming echo that chased the kestrels from their branches and sent them into a noisy flight.

Seated on the wrought iron bench in the marchioness' now snow-covered gardens, Alice lowered her book.

She waited, straining her ears for a hint of another sound.

Then giving her head a shake, she returned her attention to her reading. She trailed a single glove-encased digit over the words written there. Rhys' slight admonishment lingered still.

How dare he presume to pass judgment on the type of works she read? Yes, she no longer read gothic novels and romantic tales but that didn't mean there wasn't value in the books on animals that she now devotedly read. The zoology works and talks she'd merely stumbled upon by chance when slipping inside the Royal Society of London to escape the whispers directed her way in the street.

That day, Alice had discovered the scientific disciplines… and, from there, a host of other once-neglected topics.

She'd also come upon Lettie that morning. Lettie, who she'd later learned, took to visiting lecture halls and museums and scholarly venues because she could be certain her matchmaking mama would never come for her, *there*. And so they, two ladies, avoiding gossip and marriage, had struck a very real friendship. Alice accompanied Lettie to her favorite history talks and Lettie joined

Alice everywhere. And along the way, Alice had discovered a world of academia, until then, that she'd not properly explored.

Science and history had proven to be an escape. After all, factual recordings and lectures on natural history had been infinitely safer than talks of Henry's betrayal and her mistakes and heartache.

Now, with one debate at the breakfast table with Rhys, he'd made her question those topics that had proven such a diversion to her. She chewed at her lower lip. Nay, not question them, as much as consider her motives in abandoning her previous interests. And sitting here, in the privacy of her own thoughts, she could acknowledge the truth—she missed reading romantic novels. She'd been so determined to bury all mention or hint of happily-ever-after and grand love because of the sharp ache left by Henry's betrayal.

Only... in time, the ache had dulled, but she'd been forever transformed.

Her gaze caught on her book. The winter wind tugged at the pages and she pressed her fingers to the corners, fixed on the words at the very left center page.

Of mollusks, the sepia is the most cunning, and is the only species that employs its dark liquid for the sake of concealment as well as from fear...

Alice paused.

... the only species that employs its dark liquid for the sake of concealment...

In short, colorless, seeking to escape and avoid notice.

Alice traced that inked text.

It had not always been that way for her. There had been a time when she, to her headmistress' shame, delighted in speaking freely and living boldly. She hadn't cared about Society's opinion or possible whispers. Nor had she deliberately sought to attract scandal as her brother had excelled at over the years. Rather, she'd simply... lived. For herself. For her happiness and freedom. It had been a part of her character born of being the forgotten child of a father who'd rejected her, blaming Alice for killing his wife in childbirth.

And then in one scandalous display, where she'd shamed herself before Henry and Polite Society that day, Alice had attempted to redefine herself... into the colorless figure Rhys had accused her of being.

It's entirely possible for a person to be both romantic in spirit and practical of mind. To exist, one without the other, leaves for a colorless soul...

In the distance, another shout went up.

Lifting her head, she did another search about.

There it was… *again*; a guttural cry pealed around the grounds.

Alice closed her book with a firm thwack and hopped up. With the snow crunching under her feet, she hurried out from the now deadened gardens.

She paused, straining her ears.

And this time, on the heels of that loud booming voice, was a flurry of cries. Ones that sounded like… a child's.

Intrigue sprung her once more into motion. Alice made her way down the path perfectly tended by the dowager marchioness' diligent servants and she made her way toward the distant shouts.

With each step, the shouts and cries grew louder.

And then, she stopped. The tableau before her, held her immobile.

Two little children ducked and darted around Rhys, hurling snowballs at him as they went.

Her heart fluttered.

I should leave. She was an intruder on a moment between Rhys and those two small girls.

And yet, her feet remained frozen as she stared on at the trio at play. Rhys' tall, black hat, long since lost in his snow battle, had left those too-long golden curls exposed to the sun's rays as he ran through the snow.

Alice's had been a solitary childhood. There had been a father who despised the mere sight of her. An older brother who'd been so busy whoring and drinking that he'd never bothered with a girl more than three and ten years his junior. Oh, he'd eventually noticed her… when her entire childhood had come and gone.

As such—Alice cocked her head—she'd never known a gentleman who spoke to a child, let alone engaged in games with one.

Just then, he drew back his arm, poised to launch another snowball.

"Uncle Rhys," the taller of the girls called out. She pointed a finger in Alice's direction, bringing his attention her way.

Arm still drawn, he turned. His gaze locked with Alice's.

Even with the fifteen paces between them, she detected the flash of surprise in his steel-grey eyes.

Her pulse leapt.

She lifted her hand in a hesitant greeting.

He returned her wave with his spare hand—

A snowball slammed into the back of his head.

He grunted. Dropping the snowball in his fingers, he whipped around.

Alice cried out a warning—too late.

The other child hurled another ball of snow at his chest.

The two giggling girls with their impressive aims, raced off.

Alice slapped her hands over her mouth to bury a laugh. Her own brother had always been too cynical as a young man to ever do something as frivolous and fun as to play child's games in the snow.

Rhys cupped his hands around his mouth and called over. "I trust when you started on your jaunt, Alice, you didn't expect to stumble upon a battle on my brother's properties."

She matched his movements, framing her lips. "A war."

The sun formed a soft halo about him, giving him an other-worldly magnificence. "Beg pardon?"

Alice pointed beyond his shoulder.

Rhys whipped back and took another well-aimed missile in the face. He sputtered around a mouthful of snow as the little girls again darted off.

"It appears an outright war has been declared," she shouted.

Dusting a gloved palm over his face, Rhys smiled. His even, white teeth flashed in a devastating half-grin that upset the ordered beat of her heart.

Again, she urged her legs to move so Rhys might return his attention to the two minxes darting about.

Alas—

Swiping his hat from the ground, Rhys jogged over; his long-legged steps languid, and sleek despite the heavy snowfall that lay around them.

His breath stirring faint puffs of white, he stopped before her. "Lady Alice…" His gaze went to her hands.

Alice followed his stare.

"Ah, you've taken your reading outside."

Reflexively, she curled her fingers tightly around the book, holding it close. Again, he'd pass judgment and with reason. Of all their exchanges thus far, she had been hiding… from something, more specifically, someone. "I merely sought some... quiet," she said after a long stretch of silence. As soon as the words left her mouth, she cringed. What had become of her that she, the bane of her nursemaid and governess and then finishing school instructors' existence craved... quiet.

Rhys instantly shuttered his expression and she mourned the death of that previous lightheartedness. He adjusted the brim of his hat. "Forgive me, I will leave you to your reading, madam."

Good. It was as it should be. Those two little girls now paused in their games, stared curiously back at their uncle and Alice. Propriety dictated that she let the family to their gayness while she—

She dropped her stare to the book still clenched in her fingers. "I wasn't suggesting you leave," she said quickly, her voice ringing loudly in the empty country quiet. Alice recoiled. *Oh, bloody hell.*

Rhys spun back.

She cleared her throat. "That is... what I *meant* to say..."

Another one of those neat golden eyebrows went up.

"I was merely explaining why I was here." Not announcing herself, watching him. Alice gave thanks for the bite of the frigid air that left her cheeks chilled and no doubt reddened, concealing the blush her admission had cost her.

"Uncle Rhys!"

They glanced across to the pair trotting over, hand-in-hand. With every step that brought the dark-haired girls closer, the curiosity in their gazes deepened.

"Hullo, moppet and poppet," he intoned with such affection for the pair, that it sent another dangerous warmth spreading through her chest. "May I present my nieces, Lady Faith..." The taller girl dropped a curtsy made sloppy by the uneven snow. "And Lady Violet."

Not bothering with the formality of a curtsy, Violet tripped over herself in her haste to reach Alice. Tilting her head at an impossible angle, she met Alice's gaze. "Who are you?"

She sank to a knee. "My name is Alice."

"Are you a friend of my Uncle Rhys?" the older child put to her, refocusing Alice's attention beyond the small girl's shoulder. Curiosity brimmed from Lady Faith's expressive eyes. "Or are you another one of those wicked wid—" Rhys covered the loquacious child's mouth with his palm, burying the rest of that scandalous query.

Heat burned a path from Alice's toes up to the roots of her hair.

Outraged eyes peeked up at her uncle's. "What?" Faith groused, her words muffled. "I overheard Grandmuffer—"

"A friend," Alice squeaked, and all eyes went to her. And then she rather wished she'd allowed Rhys to handle his inquisitive niece's questioning.

"You are a friend of Uncle Rhys'?" the toddler beside her piped in.

"No," Alice said too quickly.

"You are... not a friend, then?" Violet asked, scratching at the top of her head. "Why not? Uncle Rhys is good fun." Not allowing Alice a word edgewise, she ran through a quick enumeration of her uncle's attributes. "He brings us peppermint and gives us rides on his shoulders. And he sneaks his dessert onto our plates during dinners when we're together."

A smile tugged at Alice's lips and, unbidden, her gaze wandered over to the devoted uncle in question. So as to not offend the child, she schooled her features. "Your Uncle Rhys sounds like a wonderful uncle." And he did. From his willingness to romp about with two small children—nay not a willingness but an enthusiasm, he was a manner of gentleman that she'd not believed existed among Polite Society. Why, ever polite and dignified Henry had maintained a careful composure with all—Alice included. She certainly couldn't imagine her stiffly proper former betrothed running about in the snow. "What I meant to say is that I'm a friend of your aunt, Lettice."

"Ah," the little girls said in unison.

"Aunt Lettice knows how to throw a snowball," Faith said matter-of-factly. She took several steps closer. A probing glimmer lit the girl's cornflower blue eyes. "We believe it is important a young lady knows how to throw a snowball. What do you say to that?

Having been herself a master of mischief, Alice well-knew there was something more at play here.

An odd, strangled sound from the gentleman brought Alice's gaze briefly over. "Oh, undoubtedly so," she said somberly. "I trust proper snowball skills are near as important as fishing and riding."

"Splendid." Lady Faith beamed. "Would you care to join us?"

"Would I...?" She touched her spare hand to her chest. A yearning stirred inside. When was the last time she'd raced around the countryside freely laughing and playing, without a care for what a soul said?

"Oh, you must join us," Violet put forward excitedly. "You can be on Uncle Rhys' side because he was doing very badly on his own. And I will be with Faith and—"

Rhys coughed loudly. "I trust Lady Alice would far rather return to her reading than join us in our ruthless match."

Disappointment filled her. Something in Rhys' words hinted at one who believed Alice wholly incapable of doing anything lighthearted and frivolous. Which, in fairness to Rhys, had been the case for Alice these past months. But she hadn't always been that way. There'd been a time when she'd moved about every aspect of life with complete abandon.

I miss that... I wish to be that, again...

Alice let her shoulders sag. "Yes," she said softly. "Yes, of course. I should let you continue your battle."

"But—"

"Come," Faith interrupted her younger sister's protestations.

After the pair had scampered off, Rhys lingered a moment, hovering before Alice. Then, he lifted his hat, in parting, revealing a magnificent tangle of curls. "Lady Alice," he murmured, that satiny smooth baritone set her belly aflutter. Those husky tones possessed the quality of warmed chocolate or the sun now beating down on them.

"Lord Rhys," she murmured.

"Uncle Rhys," his eldest niece shouted.

Turning on his heel, he trotted off.

Alice stared after his retreating form and a wave of wistfulness stole through her. How many times in her own life had she been the one rushing off to revel in life's simple pleasures? What a sad day indeed that she now stood here morose and downcast while Rhys Brookfield partook in a snowball fight. Since her scandal she'd allowed herself to be bound by constraints. And for what purpose?

Alice tucked her book into a pocket. Dropping to her haunches and, hastily assembling a snowball, she rose and hurled it.

Her small, but perfectly rounded projectile hissed through the air. The snowball slammed into the back of Rhys' hat, knocking it forward.

It landed on an untouched portion of snow and skidded across the icy layered top.

He turned; standing shoulder to shoulder with his suddenly silent, slack-jawed nieces. At the thick, pregnant pause, Alice clenched her hands into fists.

"Did you just hit Uncle Rhys?" the youngest of the two girls whispered.

"Uh..." She tugged at the laces of her bonnet, feeling very much like the oft-chastised child who'd delighted in her nursemaid's misery.

"And it was a good one," Violet breathed in reverent awe.

"I..." She smiled. "Why, thank you." From the corner of her eye, she stole a glance at Rhys, attempting to decipher anything from his deadpan expression. Coughing into her fist, she dropped a sloppy curtsy. "I should really leave you now to your..." fun. "battle," she settled for.

And yet, fun is precisely what it was. And Alice had been so morose and miserable that she wanted the revelry to continue on... with her a part of it.

She lingered, wanting Rhys to invite her on to join him and the two little imps.

An offer that did not come.

"Lady Alice," he said, with another slight inclination.

Oddly bereft at being cast out as the interloper, she fished the small, leather tome from her pocket, and started back for her abandoned seat.

Suddenly, a snowball collided dead center with her back.

She gasped, the icy cold faintly penetrated the thick fabric of her velvet cloak, and sent her book tumbling from her fingers.

Alice whipped about.

Rhys, an arrogant grin on his well-formed lips, waggled his eyebrows.

Her lips parted. Why... why... he'd tricked her. And worse, she'd allowed herself to be tricked.

The two little girls flanking his sides alternated wide-eyed stares between Rhys and Alice.

It was Alice who broke the impasse. She retrieved her book and tucked it back into her pocket, once more. "It seems all out war has been declared."

And hastily assembling another snowball, she launched her next attack.

CHAPTER 9

ℛHYS HAD BECOME SOMETHING OF a master at sneaking about.

Through the years, he'd honed his skills as a rogue. He would move furtively about the parlors and offices as he'd meet wanton widows in the middle of balls and soirees for an assignation.

Why, when he'd been a young man, recently betrayed by the woman he'd given his heart, and intended to give his name, too, Rhys had become particularly adept at meeting lovers in gardens. And off riding paths.

Always out of sight, always escaping notice.

Never before, however, had he sneaked about in a wooded copse with the purpose of hiding from a lady.

His back was pressed against one of the ancient, gnarled oaks. Rhys scanned the area around him.

Snow tumbled to the ground, landing several feet away. He stiffened, looking up.

A squirrel, its fur a bright splash of color upon the stark white landscape, scurried overhead. Not pausing, the creature jumped to the next mangled branch. It continued its quick pursuit, before scrambling into a yew tree and disappearing within the thick evergreen.

Silence reigning around him, Rhys bolted to the next ancient oak and stopped mid-stride.

Alice, a wicked smile on her supple lips and mischief in her

deep brown eyes, stood there, not unlike any of the women he'd
previously taken to his bed. And yet, at the same time, Lady Alice
Winterbourne was wholly unlike every one of those ladies.

"Caught," she whispered and drew her arm back.

Belatedly, he feinted left.

Her missile found its mark at his chest, the snow exploding with
such force that it splattered upon the already badly dampened garment and sprayed his face.

With a clear, unfettered laugh, Alice darted off. Her battlefield
partners giggling, raced after her.

"Traitors," he called after them, and his nieces only laughed all
the more.

Rhys dusted off the front of his cloak and gave his head a wry
shake.

Yes, in all his years purported to be a rogue—and with justifiable
reasons—not a single lady had been running away from him.

Except, in those instances, they'd been engaged in erotic games
that had involved the thrill of the chase. Ultimately, they'd ended
with a round of passionate lovemaking.

Desire bolted through him as he imagined Alice. Only not the
innocent hunt between them but one that saw them together,
entangled in one another's arms and—

Alice darted out from her cover, once more, and hit him square
between the eyes with another snowball.

Breathless, she stopped, little puffs of air spilled from her lips as
she spoke. "Your snowball fighting skills leave something to be
desired."

None of the women he'd taken as lovers had ever called into
question... any of his attributes or skills. Rather, they'd been
fawning. How much more he preferred Alice's realness to all that
empty praise. "Indeed," he drawled. Nor, for that matter, would a
single one of those scandalous widows have cavorted in the snow
with two small children, with no purpose but play in mind.

"She really is correct, Uncle Rhys," Faith lamented. And then in
her usual display of loyalty, added, "Though you aren't *always* this
dreadful."

Lips twitching, he rejoined the three ladies. "Thank you for that
high praise," he murmured with false solemnity.

Still too innocent to detect sarcasm, Faith bowed her head.

Violet tugged at his gloved hands. "Sh-she can throw a s-snow-ball," the girl whispered, teeth chattering.

"Indeed, she can," he murmured, approvingly. The only other woman to do so had been his sister, Lettie, and, even now, he could not remember the last time she'd done so.

Alice's cheeks already reddened from the cold and her sprinting about, flushed all the deeper. He'd always taken care to avoid innocents and respectable ladies of any age. What, then, accounted for this hungering to take Alice Winterbourne's chilled frame in his arms and discover the taste of her?

He tamped down a groan.

Violet scrubbed the back of her gloved hand over her dripping nose. That innocuous gesture brought him back from all improper musings about his sister's innocent friend.

"Come," he urged his nieces, continuing over their protestations. "If we remain out here any longer, you'll turn to ice." He shuddered. "And then, I'd receive a stern scolding from your papa and mama."

"Oh, fine," Faith muttered. Then, grabbing her sister's hand, she dragged Violet along at a quick clip through the snow.

Rhys and Alice fell into step at a more sedate pace until the manor drew into focus.

Gone was the boisterous, cheerful minx of a few moments ago. In her place was the quietly contemplative woman he'd first stumbled upon last evening. It was as though she'd allowed herself a fleeting reprieve from whatever sorrow held her in its grip. Surely, that bespectacled, stern-faced pup at the breakfast table wasn't the cause for her melancholy? And why did the possibility needle at his chest?

With her spirit, she was one who should always have a laugh falling from her lips and a smile in her eyes.

Now, her attention remained riveted on the two children at play twenty paces ahead of them. She followed Faith and Violet's every movement the way a scientist might examine his subject. "I was not always serious."

For a moment, he believed that hushed, barely-there admission had been nothing more than a product of the gusty winds and his own imaginings.

Silent, Alice remained riveted by the girls at play. The wistful smile that dimpled her cheeks was heartbreaking for the sorrow there.

"I used to dash about and make mischief and…" Her voice dissolved into a whisper and then faded to nothing on the winter's breeze.

His mind reflexively balked at those unfinished thoughts Alice left dangling. Whatever accounted for the lady's despondency belonged to her and her alone. As a rule, after having had his heart shredded by a faithless woman, outside of lovemaking, Rhys had disavowed any and every connection with women.

After all, sex offered a physical release and nothing more. There was no risk to one's heart. There was no shattered pride. There was simply mindless bliss, and nothing. Rhys craved that nothing. He hungered for it. He'd built himself into someone who was stronger because of it. Now, this lady, his sister's friend, no less, challenged that order he'd established for himself.

Shaken, he trained his eyes on his nieces up ahead. "The serious fellow at breakfast?"

He winced. Where in the blazes had that probing come from?

Except… even as that query defied his rules on engaging a person in talks of the heart, he didn't want to call it back. Mayhap, it was that he himself had been hurt by love. Mayhap, it was an inexplicable wondering about the woman at his side. But he did want to know what accounted for her misery.

Silence marched on for a long while, and then she spoke. "His name is Henry." It didn't escape Rhys' notice that, for a second time, she didn't counter his supposition.

Henry.

It was a perfectly stodgy name for a somber fellow who didn't make his own plate and wouldn't sit without a servant pulling out a chair for him.

And more… it spoke of an intimacy between the man and the lady with whom Rhys had been dashing around the English countryside a short while ago.

Something uncomfortable slithered around his chest. It was something he couldn't identify and didn't care to begin exploring.

Alice collected her bonnet strings in a white-knuckled grip. "We were betrothed." He fisted his hands. She was to have married the gentleman. "He…" She drew a deep breath and spoke on a rush.

"He married another."

His gut clenched as, at last, her palpable glumness made sense. Her quiet despondency was one he could understand. One he had experienced… before he'd devoted himself to becoming Society's leading rogue. "I see," he said softly.

She stopped in her tracks and glanced up at Rhys; her eyes filled with wariness. "And just what do you see?"

He saw the reason for her melancholy. He saw why she remained outdoors in the middle of a storm, in the dark of night.

His nieces' laughter pealed around the air; the joyous sounds spilling from their lips at odds with the somberness of his and Alice's exchange.

In the end, he didn't give her flippant assurances or a roguish retort. "I see why you would avoid the gentleman." Looping his hands at his back, he rocked on his heels. "That, in being around him, you're continually reminded of what could have been and what your life would be like even now had… things gone differently."

Alice stared at him with stricken eyes. "Oh," she whispered, touching a hand to the clasp on the front of her cloak.

"Did you expect me to make light of your revelation?" he drawled, unable to keep disappointment from creeping in. But then, he was the affable rogue to all and certainly not one to listen to a young lady share her most private heartache. What reason did she have to trust there was anything sincere about him? The only one who knew that he, too, had been gutted by love, his mother, would sooner turn over her title of Dowager Marchioness than share Rhys' scandalous hopes for a future with an actress.

The lady studied her gloved fingers a moment. "No. Yes." She shrugged. "I don't know what I expected you to say. I was captivated by Henry because he was reliable, bookish, serious, and yet…" Her throat moved. When she looked at Rhys there was such hurt in her eyes, he ached to chase it away and restore the smile that had been there a short while ago. "That *honorable* gentleman betrayed me." It was a bitter pain that he knew all too well and, though she was more stranger than anything, he hated that she should know that hurt. A wry little laugh shook Alice's frame. "And yet, there is my brother, once a rake with a rotted reputation, who has proven to be a devoted husband to his wife and loyal and…" She plucked at the black velvet ribbon that hung from the heart-shaped clasp. "I've learned it is best to simply look at a person not as a title or category they might fit in to, but rather for who they are."

He searched his gaze over her wind-burned cheeks and an appreciation for both those words, and the woman who'd uttered them, stirred. In a world where rank drove all, including, in Rhys' case, his parents' affection—or lack thereof—Alice saw more. "And what do you see when you look at me?" His body jerked and he wanted to call the query back. What did it matter what she believed or her opinion?

Alice took a step closer. The crunch of snow under her boots was inordinately loud in the morning stillness. She continued moving forward and then stopped, a mere foot apart. Head tipped back, she studied him. "I see a rogue."

He curled his lips into their customary position of indolence. "One requires but a glimpse into the scandal pages to ascertain as much," he drawled.

"There's the grin," she murmured. She stretched a fingertip close to his mouth, a breath of space from touching. His amusement faded. There was something vastly more erotic in the hint of Alice's caress than all the bold touches and embraces that had come before from wanton widows. "A practiced smile. One that is carefree. Bored. Arrogant. Your smile says all those things."

Her accusation was certainly not the first time he'd been called such, and he'd certainly been called far worse. So why did her words rub at a nerve he'd never before known was exposed?

"But, do you know what I've come to find, Rhys?" She trailed her gaze over his face.

"What is that?" he asked gruffly.

"There are many types of smiles and after one has been hurt, one dons a safe grin."

Her stodgy betrothed. "You speak as—"

"As one who knows?" she interrupted. "Yes. A smile, I've come to find, is often used to deceive. It's not reserved for rakes, rogues, or scoundrels but a tool used by all who've been hurt. I am just as guilty. It is how I know that one is false. Most rogues, they are not rogues because they were born condescending, cold-hearted dastards." She angled her head, lifting her gaze to his.

Panic welled in his chest. His mind thundered for her to stop. He wanted to silence whatever utterance was about to spill from her lips… because she saw too much.

And it scared the bloody hell out of him.

"Smiles hide hurt. I'd wager you've known your own." The lady lifted her shoulders in a little shrug. "Or I could be wrong, and you really could be this arrogant, content-to-shock scapegrace who sets Polite Society to talking."

Regret filled him. Regret that, at the moment he'd come upon her in The Copse, vulnerable and hiding from a man who'd never been worthy of her, Rhys had been irreverent and rude.

"I am sorry," he said quietly.

She shook her head. "I don't…?"

"Yesterday, when I came to… to…"

"Retrieve me?" she dryly supplied.

Rhys winced. "Surely I didn't say—?"

"Oh, you did," she said, more of the cheerfulness from their snowball fight before restored.

He tugged at his collar. "I was an unmitigated arse." Who'd allowed his previous experiences with women of all stations to cloud his judgment.

"Yes," she concurred. "But I was also pitiable, sulking about outside… in a storm." Her eyes twinkled. "Shall we come to an arrangement, then?"

Again, his mind danced down the path of wickedness. "What manner of… arrangement?" he asked, his voice hoarse to his own ears.

She flashed an innocent smile, absent of coyness and wickedness. That act hinted at one wholly unaffected by him, effectively shattering his lust.

"I shan't be the downtrodden, sad-eyed creature hiding about and you won't be dismissive and presumptuous."

He winced, wanting to debate her on that scathing assessment. And yet, he'd lived a life dismissive of all because… well, it had simply proven to be more safe.

"Well?" Alice stuck her gloved palm out.

He stared at those long digits, encased in gloves, wanting to tug the thin, leather fabric back and feel the heat of her palm. Rhys quickly took her hand in his. Even through the fabric of their damp gloves, an electric surge shot at the point of contact, traveling up his arm.

Let her go… release her…

And yet, he remained, fingers curled around her smaller ones, unable to relinquish that hold. Not wanting to shatter the connection.

Alice's smile froze, and then slowly faded as her gaze went to their joined hands and then back to his. Her bow-shaped lips parted.

But she did not make any move to draw back. Instead, she curled her delicate palm, lightly squeezing his—

A loud squawking from across the snow-covered lawns, broke the pull.

They looked as one to the stone terrace, cleared in the early morning hours by meticulous Brookfield servants.

His mother, arms akimbo, watched on.

With a gasp, Alice snatched her hand back and he silently cursed the blasted interruption.

The dowager marchioness was flanked by Ladies Lovell and Guilford. Even with the distance between the ladies and Alice, there could be no doubting the ire in the two matrons' like expressions. Faith and Violet rushed onto the terrace, jamming their fingers excitedly in Rhys and Alice's direction.

He swallowed a groan. His mother had taken to following after him… outside, in the dead of winter? It was a mark of her determination.

The ever-jovial Lord Lovell hovering just beyond his wife's shoulder, waved in greeting. "Rhys, my boy, a pleasure," his booming voice echoed around the countryside.

Oh, bloody hell. "Likewise, Lord Lovell," he called out that lie.

And by the loud snorting that left the other man, he'd gathered the fabrication there.

Alice adjusted her bonnet, drawing the brim low over her brow. As they joined the gathering on the terrace, Rhys found himself longing for the stolen moments in the snow he and Lady Alice Winterbourne had just shared.

CHAPTER 10

THE ONLY THING MORE OMINOUS than the Dowager Marchioness of Guilford's too-obvious matchmaking attempts was her silence.

Since he'd returned, with Alice at his side earlier that morn, Rhys had been greeted by scores of it from his mother. Great, big stretches of unending silence and dark glares. He had enough unfortunate experiences with the woman who'd given him life to trust that taciturnity.

As such, Rhys had taken the safest—and certainly the most cowardly path—to safety. He'd retreated.

Or, if one wished to be truly precise, he'd hidden.

Which was no small task or unimpressive feat in a household brimming with guests and servants.

Alas, desperate times and all that.

Standing before the bevel mirror in his chambers, Rhys lifted the collars of his shirt. With a murmured word of thanks, he accepted the black silk cravat from his valet, Fischer, who hurried off to gather a jacket from the armoire.

Except… he paused, fabric dangling from his fingers.

Was it his mother he'd been hiding from? Or Alice who'd seen entirely too much?

Unnerved, he looped the satin scrap around his neck and leveled the sides of the material. Quickly going through the motions, he wrapped the fabric once, and then drew it through the main knot creating a haphazard display.

"My lord." Pain stamped in his face, Fischer reappeared, a black tailcoat with black velvet trim in hand.

Rhys snapped his collar down.

"Cheer up, Fischer." Rhys plucked the jacket from the other man's hands. "You look even more miserable than me."

Fischer held his palms up, imploringly. "Might I?" Agony contorted his features. "May I…" He reached for Rhys' neckwear.

"I assure you, my knot is fine." Or fine, enough, anyway. In the sense that he had one on.

The stout valet swallowed loudly. "But, my lord, last time Her Ladyship followed me to the servant's dining quarters and scolded me on your deplorable dress," he whispered. "She suggested I take my services elsewhere."

Rhys gnashed his teeth. Interfering, miserable harpie. It was as much a part of her as the perpetual scowl she wore and the coldness that spilled from her person.

Ah, the dragon had that effect on all. She always had. "Do you take me as one who'd sack you because of a cravat I'd gone and rumpled myself?"

"No, my lord," the other man said, his voice threadbare.

Rhys smoothed the lapels of his tailcoat. "That is correct. I wouldn't."

Rhys then looked around the room. "My boots, if you would."

Fischer cringed. "But, my lord… *boots*?" Rhys may as well have ordered the other man to steal the dowager marchioness' jewels for the horrified shock in that whisper. Swiping a hand over his face, the valet shuffled off.

Returning his attention to the mirror, Rhys readjusted his silk cravat, smoothing the knot.

There was a firm knock at the door. That rapping was solid and powerful, unlike his mother's vexing scratch. "Enter," he called out.

The door handle was already twisting, and his brother stepped inside. Immaculately attired from his snowy white cravat to his strapped, gleaming, black shoes, he exuded refinement and a deference to Polite Society's fashion dictates.

Miles did a quick once over of Rhys. It was a perfunctory search employed by one who sought to verify that Rhys was suitably attired for the dinner party.

Rhys arched an eyebrow. "E tu, Brute?"

"I don't know what you're speaking about." The guilty flush staining his brother's cheeks marked him for the poor liar he'd always been.

Rhys snorted. "Were you sent to verify whether I was joining the dinner party? Or to drag me to the table if I weren't?"

Miles grinned. "Both?" he asked, sheepishly.

"Ah, at last, honestly." Taking pity on Fischer, who stood shifting back and forth on his heels, he dismissed the servant. The portly fellow dropped a bow, and another deferential one for Miles before making a hasty retreat.

"She was fearful you wouldn't join us," Miles confessed after they were alone.

He chuckled. "What rubbish. Mother hasn't feared for anything outside the marquisate title."

Miles' lips turned down at the corners. "You know that isn't true," he said somberly.

Of course, the optimistic counterpart to Rhys' cynicism, his brother had long rushed to their mother's defense, if for no other reason, Rhys oftentimes suspected, than to spare the family conflict and tension.

"She is also equally concerned with each of her children's marital states," his eldest sibling intoned. There was such an unexpectedness to that droll reply, it pulled a sharp, bark of laughter from Rhys.

"Which, I trust, is the reason for your visit to my rooms?"

This time, his brother nodded. "She also asked that I... speak with you. Brother to brother."

Rhys tensed. "Oh?" he ventured cautiously.

Hands looped behind him, Miles wandered over to the garish rognon desk. Its ornate rosewood trellis marquetry and ormolu mounts suited to the tastes of the woman who'd outfitted the manor twenty years earlier: ostentatious, glimmering, the décor of this place exuded wealth and prestige. Letting his arms fall to his sides, his brother examined the open ledger. With a distractedness to his movements, he caught the corner of the page between his fingers and lingered his focus there.

Rhys stiffened, braced for a disapproval that came from all members of the peerage for one who *dabbled in trade.*

At last, Miles shot a look back. "A... steam engine?" he murmured.

He sought to make sense of the meaning in those three words strung together and punctuated by a slight pause. Rhys rolled his shoulders. "It has been around for more than a hundred years now," he felt compelled to defend. "An inventor named Newcomen. Watt merely improved it."

"Hmm," Miles replied, again his thoughts carefully schooled. His brother returned to studying Rhys' books. Near in age, they had been close as young boys. Where many spares to the heir resented the role as second and forgotten child, Rhys had never coveted the title. Instead, he'd welcomed the freedoms it allowed him to escape their parents' notice. Yet, Miles had never been one of those aloof, unfeeling brothers either. Rather... he'd been a friend until, with the passage of time, responsibilities and life... for each of them had replaced the friendship they'd once enjoyed.

At last, his brother released that page and faced him. "I had no idea of your business interests."

"Yes, well, there is much we don't know about one another." Lillian. Rhys' business ventures. So much. That hadn't always been the case. There had once been a time they'd shared secrets and stories. Regret filled him at the natural gulf that had been brought by time and their responsibilities.

"You are right," Miles said, sadness stealing into his tone. "Mother asked me to speak to you about the Guilford line."

He laughed. *The Guilford line?* "Married as you are and she's still not content?"

"Faith and Violet will be the only children Philippa and I will ever have," his brother said with a quiet somberness that killed Rhys' dry amusement.

Rhys' jaw went slack. He struggled to force words out. A question. A platitude. And he, glib with words, found himself at a complete loss with this.

His brother coughed into his fist. "It is a decision that belongs to Philippa and me, and is a product of..." Miles' eyes darkened. "My being unwilling to risk her life for the sake of an heir."

"I didn't know," he said lamely. *I should, though. I should know about my brother's life and Lettie's friends...* while all along, he'd been so self-absorbed that he'd kept a careful façade in place and shut everyone out. How odd that after a handful of meetings, one young lady had so carefully detected that mechanism within him, and made him see the truth of how he'd lived his life these past years—safe. For he hadn't wanted to speak on what was hard or painful... for him... his family. It had been easier transforming himself into the careless rogue Alice had described.

Miles skimmed his fingers over the ledger. "I'm telling you this to try and explain mother's relentless determination where you're concerned. To her..." His brother paused. "To all... *you* now represent the line."

Rhys dissolved into a paroxysm of choking, until tears streamed down his cheeks.

His brother quickly crossed over and banged him on the back.

"I... I..." The last thing he wanted, desired, or needed was the obligation of the Guilford title. And yet, with everything his brother had shared, the dowager marchioness' determination to see Rhys wed made sense.

At least as far as ruthless matchmaking mamas were concerned.

Miles flashed a wry grin. "You're taking this a good deal better than I'd suspected." That hint of amusement instantly faded to a mask of solemnity donned by his brother. "I'm..." He hesitated, seeming to search. "Sorry that her attentions have shifted to you and that my inability to carry on the line should see those responsibilities pass to you."

They'd grown, and grown apart. That divide was a sadly natural gulf as a product of life's responsibilities. Miles' murmured regrets, however, spoke to a brother who'd always known Rhys... even with the passage of time.

"Do you believe I'd resent you or Philippa for that?" He scoffed. Striding over to the gleaming, black boots at the foot of his bed, Rhys sat. "If that is the case, then you don't really know me," he chided, tugging into first one of the articles, and then the next.

Miles steepled his fingers, tapping the tips of the gloved digits together. "I thought I'd explain Mother's determination... and the situation the Brookfield line finds itself."

The muscles of his gut clenching, Rhys stared at the boule mantel clock in an act of cowardice, unable to meet his brother's gaze. For what his brother now alluded to thrust forward long buried possibilities: Rhys married... with a family of his own. Those had been silly, romantic dreams he'd allowed himself as a young man; dreams he'd never before shared with another. After all, gentlemen didn't willingly cede their independence for marital constraints. The hopes, however, had been there. He hadn't sought a proper Societal wife; stiff, dull, and vapid. Rather, he'd longed for a spirited one, capable of laughter and who'd flout Polite Society's conventions along with him.

A lady such as Alice—

Rhys jumped up. "We should go," he blurted, his heart thudding inside his chest.

What sickness afflicted his head that a proper miss should keep wheedling her way inside his mind?

Miles gave him a probing look. "Are you all r—?"

"Fine. I'm fine." He wasn't. He was madder than King George himself.

Rhys reached for the handle when a hand on his shoulder stayed his movements.

He cast a questioning look back.

"Mother wished me to speak to you about your doing right by the line," his brother said with a somberness that sent Rhys' muscles tensing. "I, however, wanted you to know that I would never expect you to marry because of the Brookfield line or to please Mother or me." He held Rhys' eyes. "Or anyone… except yourself. As one who deeply loves his wife, I would hope that you will one day know that."

Rhys' rubbed the back of his neck. Even with everything his brother had revealed about his own life, Rhys still could not bring himself to share the folly he'd made in his youth: giving his heart to a woman who'd broken their secret betrothal all for a sack of silver like the Judas she'd been, to stay away from the Brookfield spare to the heir. Once, such a truth had devastated him. Now, nothing but embarrassment at his own folly lingered. "I…" he finally brought himself to say. "Thank you," he finished lamely. "We should join the dinner party," he continued on a rush.

"Of course," Miles murmured. He stared at Rhys for a long moment, having the look of one who wished to say more.

And as they started from the room, Rhys' mind returned to thoughts of the dinner party… and the minx he'd spent the better part of the day hiding from.

CHAPTER 11

THE DOWAGER MARCHIONESS DESPISED ALICE.

There was no other accounting for her placement at the dining table.

Alice peeked between the gold candelabras unfortunately placed and the garish tremblent to where her friend sat.

"I'm so sorry," Lettie mouthed. She cast a too-pointed glance to the miserable blighter Alice had been partnered with.

At her side, laconic as he'd always been, Henry spooned some of the white broth into his mouth. While at the opposite end of the enormous, rectangular table, his wife, regaled those around her with talk of their honeymoon trip to Paris. That talk was definitely loud enough to reach Alice's ears.

Colorful tales of the Continent that should hurt Alice. Nay, the telling should gut her. After all, at this very moment, had life continued on the path she'd expected, she would be seated here as Mrs. Henry Pratt.

She stole a sideways glance at her former intended. He attended his bowl the same way he had his books.

Alice nibbled at the tip of her finger.

Had he always been this quiet? She searched her mind for the discussions they'd had. What had they spoken of and about? Aside from his career and his aspirations as a barrister, there had been remarkably little else of import… and never had he delved into her interests or hopes or dreams.

No, he'd *always* been so serious. He had certainly never been, nor would ever be, one who'd dash about throwing snowballs at a lady and two children. Why... even his laugh had been restrained and... respectable.

Unbidden, Alice's gaze traveled to the gentleman seated on the opposite side of the table, three seats to the right of her.

His dining partner, was none other than Miss Aria Cunning. A hauntingly dark beauty, who wore a ready smile. Gesticulating wildly as she spoke, the young woman earned a deep, rumbling laugh from Rhys and those seated around her.

I was once ready with stories and jests... and freely smiled. But never had she been one to charm. Not the way the stunning creature held those around her enrapt. Rhys nodded at something the lady was saying and then, whatever his return reply, he earned a pretty blush... and a husky laugh better suited to a wicked widow than a darling debutante.

Stop staring. Except, she remained horrifyingly riveted to the pair in the midst of their discourse, an interloper watching through a glass at people who did remember how to laugh.

Only, Alice hadn't forgotten, as she'd believed.

In these two days here, she'd laughed more than she had in the time since she'd been thrown over for another. More precisely, she'd been brought to laughter by Rhys.

Another throaty expression of mirth filtered from Miss Cunning's perfectly formed lips.

Just as he'd managed to elicit the same response from that lady. It was what rogues excelled in; charming and tempting and—

Gritting her teeth, Alice grabbed her spoon and dipped it into her bowl. A little too forcibly.

The clear broth spilled over the edge and splattered the table, leaving a small mark upon the white satin tablecloth.

Bloody hell.

Alice's skin pricked with the feel of those looking her way. She was a Winterbourne, however, whose family had been prone to far greater embarrassments than spilled broth.

Alice tipped her chin up and the curious onlookers returned to their discourse and meals.

All except for one. From her seat near the head of the table, the dowager marchioness gave her head a disgusted shake before she, thankfully, shifted her miserable attention over to Lord Guilford.

Alice made to retrieve her spoon and stopped. Unrepentantly, with a boldness only a scoundrel could muster, Rhys stared back.

God help Alice for being a miserable rotter, she hated the grin on his well-formed lips that met his steel-grey eyes. For it wasn't one of those false expressions they'd spoken of earlier. This was real and sincere and dangerously alluring… and all because of the young beauty who just then said something else that brought his focus back.

Her place properly tidied, Alice forced herself to reach with calm, measured movements for her spoon. This time, she took a careful bite.

What business was it of hers whether Rhys, master flirt, engaged the young debutante in repartee?

Because it means your two stolen exchanges were nothing more… they were merely a rogue's game, freely played with whichever lady was at hand.

Mayhap. it was because she'd been thrown over before. Or mayhap, it was something more… that ultimately rogue or barrister, respectable gentleman or wicked lord, Alice had never truly mattered. Not in the ways that she, once dreaming of love, had longed to matter.

Bereft, she set her spoon down with fingers that trembled.

A quiet cough brought her head up.

Using the gold brocade napkin in his fingers, Rhys dabbed at the corners of his mouth. "Smile," he soundlessly commanded.

Alice blinked slowly.

Rhys articulated each word, slow, mute. "No sad eyes." Angling his head ever so slightly, Alice followed that gesture…

To Henry.

Henry?

Her lashes stopped their movement altogether.

Henry.

Rhys had erroneously assumed she'd sat silent and morose because of the arrangement that had placed Alice precisely beside the bounder who'd broken her heart. She glanced at her former intended and found him boldly studying her from over the rim of his wine glass.

Alice started.

There was a greater directness to the gaze that met hers than ever before. "He's a rogue, you know."

At having been caught silently engaging Rhys from across the table, her cheeks burned hot. "I beg your pardon?" How dare this man, of all people, publicly speak to her on what Rhys was or was not?

One hand gripped his spoon, while his other held firm to the edge of the table. "Guilford's brother." He flicked his fingers and returned them to their previous position. "I've seen the way he's flirted with you." He paused, some simmering emotion revealed through the lenses of his spectacles. "It's the same way he's flirting with Miss Cunning even now."

Outrage flared in her breast. "Either way, you have no reason to speak on it," she said coolly, as her bowl was cleared.

Alice gave thanks for the interruption, eager to have done any talk at all with the blackguard beside her.

The gold-clad liveried footman placed silver platters of roast fowls and chicken, stewed peas, and French peas about the table. Then, they proceeded to serve the guests.

Alice murmured her thanks, and reached for her fork and knife.

"And why shouldn't I speak on it?" Henry intoned, freezing her movements. "Should the fact that I marr—?"

Uncaring for the guests around them, she leveled him with a hard glare. "Careful," she warned. First, he'd thrown her over, and now he'd casually make mention of it in passing at a dining table filled with guests? Was he blasted simple or emotionally deadened?

Henry blushed but, relentless, he leaned forward, whispering close to her ear. "My circumstances should not drive you to carelessness where that one is concerned." He flicked his chin at a near imperceptible tilt toward Rhys.

Alice followed that insolent gesture to Rhys… who stared boldly back through thickly-hooded, golden lashes.

The candle's glow sent shadows dancing on the harsh, angular planes of his face. It was timeless in its masculine beauty the manner of which artists and sculptors lauded in their works.

She forced her gaze back to the hated figure at her side, latching on to two insolent words dropped from Henry's mouth: That one.

"Dearest, Henry, I was just sharing with the others, the magnificence of Paris' street lighting." Those seated offered the black-haired beauty the attention she coveted. When all eyes were trained on her, she beamed. "What was the name of them, dearest?"

"Street lights," Henry mumbled, earning a slight frown from his young bride. "They're called street lights." Mumbled words, when Henry had always spoken in his crisp, decisive, barrister tones as Alice had teasingly once referred to them.

"Yes, street lights," his wife parroted. "They line the Passage des Panoramas and…"

As the other woman prattled on, Alice reclined in her chair and, blessedly, Henry didn't utter another word.

She peeked over at Rhys. Silent, he now contemplated the contents of his wine glass, while the effervescent Miss Cunning chatted with her brother-in-law.

Alice willed him to lift his gaze; mourning the earlier connection shattered by Henry.

When at last the meal had come to an end, she sent a prayer skyward.

"Well, that was a lesson in torture," Lettie muttered at her side. "Street lighting? Street lighting?" she repeated incredulously. "The woman went on for at least an hour—"

"It was an hour and three minutes," Alice whispered. Such details, she'd obtained courtesy of the tortoiseshell bracket clock.

A snorting giggle exploded from her friend, that mirth-filled sound bouncing off the walls.

The dowager marchioness, arm in arm with Lady Lovell, leading the ladies on to one of the too-many-to-count parlors, stopped. The other followed suit.

Lettie's mother glanced back. "Lettice, if you'll accompany me?" Disapproval glittered in her always-cold eyes.

Lettie groaned, but quickly disguised that misery as a cough. "Always escape notice. Always escape notice," she breathed, that litany rolling from her lips in a regretful mantra.

"Go, I assure you I'll be quite fine at the back here."

"You are just glad you don't have to join me with them at the front," Lettie said under her breath.

"Lettice," her mother called out again, warningly.

Alice winked. Muttering to herself, Lettie quickened her step and, skirting the other small gathering of ladies, joined her mother.

As soon as the party had continued on, Alice ducked around the corner. The footfalls and discourse of the ladies grew increasingly distant. Nonetheless, Alice lengthened her strides, hurrying on.

A booming laugh sounded from over her shoulder.

With a gasp, Alice slammed her hand to her chest and searched the empty halls.

Then it came again.

Approaching steps; heavier footfalls and deeper voices and...

She groaned.

Blast and damn. It was the gentlemen.

Ducking into the nearest room, Alice did a sweep of the haven she'd found.

Only...

The space doused in light, gleamed from the mahogany billiards table and well-stocked sideboard.

She slapped her hands over her face. The billiards room. Of all the bloody, rotted rooms to sneak in to, she'd chosen the most masculine of all sanctuaries. Alice forced her arms back to her sides and fought to regain control of her panicky thoughts.

After all, just because she'd found herself in a billiards room did not mean the marquess and his guests would take their drinks here. There were parlors and libraries and—

Approaching footsteps—too many of them to discern a precise number—reached her ears.

Heart hammering, Alice did a frantic search. She settled her gaze on the floor-length doors leading to the stone terrace that ran the length of the impressive estate. Her skirts whipping about her ankles, she raced for the double-doors.

"Alice."

She gasped, whipping about.

Her heart sank.

Framed in the doorway, Henry stared back. Then he moved his gaze away, touching his eyes on each corner of the room. "What are you doing here?" he asked with an insolence that set her teeth on edge.

Her annoyance was short-lived, as the footsteps and voices in the hall grew increasingly closer.

Henry pulled the door closed.

"What are *you* doing?" she whispered, grabbing for the gold handle.

He shot a palm up. "Please, wait," he implored. "They are

adjourning to Lord Guilford's libraries for bran—" Color raced up her former betrothed's cheeks.

"Brandies?" she supplanted. It was hardly shameful and simply customary of Society, and, yet, with his usual display of propriety, he couldn't manage to utter that word. And with silence falling between them in this cavernous room, Alice caught a glimpse of the life that would have been hers had they been married: polite, staid, safe. In short... dull. Such would never be the existence one would have if married to a man such as Rhys. Jolted at that musing, she gripped the door handle hard. The gold metal bit sharply into her palm. "You should leave, Mr. Pratt," she said tightly.

His throat muscles convulsed. "You once called me Henry."

Yes, she had. And they'd once been betrothed. "I asked you to leave."

"I'm not leaving until I speak to you."

She clenched her jaw. Her faithless, former betrothed wished to speak to her. After offering her marriage, then jilting her, wedding another, and stealing the privacy she'd sought to take for herself... he'd ask for anything from her? How had she failed to see his selfishness? "There is nothing to say." And when he folded his arms at his narrow chest, rooting himself to his spot, Alice pressed the handle. She'd rather brave the elements of the winter's night than his company. She let herself out.

The cold air slapped her face and invaded her lungs, sucking the breath clear from her.

Teeth instantly set to chattering, she drew the door shut with a firm click. In a desperate bid to bring warmth to her trembling limbs, Alice rubbed at her arms. She'd rather take her chances with the bloody cold than deal with—

Henry joined her on the terrace.

Alice tossed her hands up. "Wh-what do you w-want?" Why would he not go away? Her frustration had nothing to do with the pain at being near him, but a deep-seated annoyance.

"I-I had n-not finished speaking of that gentleman... Lord Guilford's br-brother." With every exhalation, Henry's breath fogged the lenses of his spectacles. With an aberrant curse flying from his lips, he yanked those wire frames from his face and proceeded to rub the slight fog from them. "He's a r-rogue."

"A-and?" she asked tightly, hugging her arms close.

"A m-man such as h-him is d-dangerous for l-ladies to be around," he finished weakly. Was it the hypocrisy of his passing judgment on any person's character? Or simply the cold that had robbed the remainder of that admission of breath. "I've h-heard stories of his reputation. Y-You w-will only be hurt if—"

"How dare you?" she seethed, taking a step closer. "First, you attempt to lecture *me* in the midst of a dinner party."

He cringed, but proved wiser than she'd credited, for he remained silent.

"And then, you would presume to disparage Rhys Brookfield. Wh-why?" she demanded, advancing again.

Henry backed away.

"Because you've heard gossip about him?" Alice snapped, her fury spiraling with each question she leveled at her former betrothed. "Let me tell you something, Henry Pratt. Rhys might be a r-rogue…" He was. There could be no disputing that was precisely what Lettie's brother was… and likely would always be. Henry's eyebrows dipped low at her use of the other gentleman's Christian name. "But he's a loyal brother!" One who'd gone out in the midst of a storm to rescue his sister's friend. "He's the sort who encourages a lady to read and use her mind, and also urges her to embrace her passionate spirit." Unlike Henry, who'd cringed whenever he'd come upon her reading romantic novels and gothic tales.

Her former betrothed blanched. "P-Passionate spirit…?" He may as well have swallowed a plate of rancid kippers for all the horror there.

A sharp gust blew through the countryside, buffeting the windows, and stealing several curls from her previously neat chignon. She went on as though he hadn't spoken. "So do not presume to disparage Lord Rhys or me, or anyone else when you've proven to be nothing more than a faithless, spineless, traitorous bastard."

Henry's body jerked. With stiff movements, he perched his spectacles on his nose. "I've offended you," he said tightly, adjusting the wire rims behind his ears. "However, I w-will not sit idly by wh-while you f-fall prey to a r-rogue." Yanking at the front of his jacket, he stalked off, closing the door quietly behind him.

As soon as he'd gone, Alice growled. "The bloody insolence of h-him. The conceit of him. The—"

A slow, quiet clapping cut across the terrace.

Her heart jumped into her throat.

Alice shrieked.

From the shadows, a towering, heavily-muscled figure stepped forward. A faint glow shone from the tip of the cheroot clenched between his teeth. Rhys strolled over, beating his gloved hands together.

"Brava, madam," he murmured from around the scrap of tobacco. "Brava."

Alice briefly closed her eyes, grateful for the shroud of darkness.

Bloody, bloody hell.

CHAPTER 12

¶IT HAD BEEN AN IMPRESSIVE display.

And not simply because not once, in the whole of his first mischievous and then roguish existence, had a single person—loyal siblings included—come to Rhys' defense.

The sight of Alice as she'd been, eyes flashing, cheeks burning with both the cold and her tangible fury, produced the look of a warrior woman, who'd bow to no man, and certainly not a pompous pup like Pratt.

The wind howled, knocking the ashes from the tip of his cheroot. He took another draw from his smoke and unabashedly studied her.

Hugging her arms close, she rubbed at the cream white flesh. "I-Is it t-too much to hope you d-didn't hear all of that?" she asked, in a teasing echo of their earlier exchange that morning.

"Which part?" He blew out a small puff of smoke. "Pup Pratt's ill-opinion of me?" Rhys flashed a grin. "Or your spectacular defense?"

"I t-take that as 'all of it', then," she muttered, her breath stirring the winter's air and mingling with the remnants left by his cheroot.

They shared a smile. That wide tilt of her lips transformed her from ordinary to spectacular in her beauty.

The minx eyed the scrap of tobacco in his fingers.

Rhys held it out in silent challenge. Without hesitation, Alice accepted the cheroot and, with the ease of one who'd been smoking them the whole of her life, inhaled deeply, and then breathed out a long, slow stream of white smoke.

His lips twitched as she took another draw. "Given Lettie turned green and cast the contents of her stomach onto my slippers after she'd tried her first cheroot, I trust you're quite familiar with them."

A little twinkle sparkled in her gaze, as she took another pull. "I t-told you, I've never been accused of being a proper miss." She said it without apology and absolute pride and, God help him, in that instant, there was an odd shifting in his chest.

Alice passed the cheroot back and their hands brushed. Fingers shaking, Rhys took another deep inhale, letting the smoke fill his lungs, calming.

Alice remained there, rubbing at her arms. "I-I should return."

"Yes," he murmured.

They both should. As one who appreciated the material comforts, any other time he would have finished his cheroot, found a bottle of brandy and a roaring fire. He'd have set himself up there, studiously avoiding all his brother's esteemed guests. Standing outside beside this woman, in the dead of winter, chilled through as he was, Rhys found himself—frozen, wanting this moment to go on with her, determined for it to continue.

Clamping his cheroot between his lips, he shrugged out of his jacket. "Here," he murmured.

"Wh…?" her question faded off, as he draped the garment over her shoulders.

The double-breasted coat hung on her slender frame, and there was something so very right in seeing his jacket wrapped about her shoulders.

His skin pricked with the heat of her gaze on him. She had clever eyes that probed and likely saw far more than was safe. Taking the small scrap of tobacco away from his lips, he said, "I believe there is a rule that expressly forbids a person from abandoning an unfinished cheroot."

"Ah," she demurred with a weighty somberness to that utterance. "No doubt, the same rule was issued about gentlemen honoring the customary brandy after dinner?"

As if on cue, the echo of voices from within the billiards room filtered through the crystal windowpanes.

They swung their gazes as one.

Silently cursing, Rhys dropped his cheroot and stomped on it. Grabbing Alice by the hand, he tugged her unceremoniously down the stone terrace, the heels of their shoes churning up snow. "Years of meeting scandalous ladies and *this* is the manner of stealth you're g-given to," she muttered under her breath as he dragged her along.

He shot her a silencing look and forced them into an even quicker pace.

To the lady's credit, her eyes glimmered with an impish amusement and not the histrionics most innocent misses would have been given to.

A mournful wind battered at them. The noisy gusts battered her skirts against his legs. With each step, that frigid air robbed the breath from his lungs.

Reaching the end of the stone patio, Rhys and Alice bolted down the steps, not stopping until they'd reached the base.

Dropping her hands atop her knees, Alice bent over, gasping.

Rhys dragged a hand through his hair. "Bloody hell," he muttered, pacing back and forth. They'd almost been discovered… and by every last male guest invited to his family's estate. And in this instance, instead of the horror that should bring, he was transfixed by the flyaway curls that had come free during their hasty flight to the gardens. It conjured a tempting image of those same waxen curls cascading over his pillows, in a silken waterfall. His breath came hard and fast, for reasons that had nothing to do with their exertions. And yet… this time, she truly had been mere moments away from ruin at his hands.

For Polite Society wouldn't care that not so much as a kiss had been shared. They'd only see the appearances of ruin… and amongst the *ton*, there was no other reality that mattered more. "Forgive me," he said gruffly. "After, Pratt took himself off, I should have allowed you to return." Selfishly, he'd wanted the spirited minx to remain for reasons that had nothing to do with a desire to seduce and everything to do with one simple fact—he enjoyed being with her.

Her breath settling into an even cadence, Alice lifted her head. "And gone and broke the rules surrounding a good cheroot?" she whispered, punctuating her question with a saucy wink.

A bark of laughter escaped him.

The minx touched a fingertip to her lips. "Hush, I have it on good authority the last thing you need this damned Season is to be discovered in a compromising position with me."

Yes, it was any rogue's greatest fear—the parson's trap. Something, however, told him that whichever gent found himself wed to Alice Winterbourne, said gent would never be without a smile or laugh. "It is not just you, Alice."

The lady snorted. "Lah, sir," she gave an exaggerated flutter of her lashes. "With compliments such as that, it's no wonder you've the reputation you do."

His heart knocked around his chest at an uneven beat. Had he truly believed her passably pretty? The breathtakingly fierce warrioress who'd so effortlessly dismantled the Pratt fool had the beauty and spirit of Boadicea. *Look away... she is an innocent young lady. Your sister's friend... a proper miss...*

He swallowed loudly, that sound lost in another gust. That sharp wind tossed Alice's locks across her eyes.

"Blast and damn," she gritted out, wrestling with her hair... all the while wholly immune, wholly unaware the effect her mischievous grin and spirited show had on him still.

"Here," he murmured.

"Wh-what...?" Her voice trailed off as Rhys pulled free the shell-comb and placing it between his teeth, proceeded to gather the stubborn curls in his fingers.

And despite the frigid cold of the night air, he ached to shed his gloves and test the softness of those strands. Concentrating his gaze on the top of her head, he drew each errant curl back, tucking it into place until all the tresses had been gathered in a loose chignon.

Unbidden, he worked his eyes over her face. Her slightly-parted lips stirred little puffs of white, the scent of mulled cider, peppermint, and cheroot a quixotic pull at him, filled him with a need to taste the allure of that sweetness.

"Is it a-all right?" she whispered.

Lowering his head, Rhys hooded his lashes. "There could be nothing more right," he breathed, bringing his mouth closer, ever closer.

Alice pressed her gloved hands to the ruby heart hair comb, patting the knot he'd made. "Thank y-you for arranging them."

Thank you...? He'd received a similar response from well-pleasured ladies after an evening of lovemaking, only this steady, distracted murmur of gratitude hadn't come from a sated lover.

Rhys' eyes locked with Alice's saucer-round brown ones.

And then reality slammed into him—hard, fast, and humbling.

He jerked his head back with such force, the muscles down his neck strained in protest. "Uh—you're w-welcome," he finished lamely, hoping she'd credit that slight stammer with the effects of the cold and not the blow done to his ego as Society's most wicked rogue. "We should return," he forced himself to say. She was a siren. There could be no other accounting for it. How else to explain braving the cold, without even a jacket for protection, that he'd rather remain here, engaging in their back and forth repartee of moments ago.

Alice angled her head, glancing past his shoulder. He lingered his stare appreciatively on that long, graceful column. "I trust you've an idea that includes an alternate entry inside?"

He mustered a smile. "I've long excelled in sneaking about these very p-properties," he assured, holding his elbow out.

The fearless minx immediately tucked her arm in his and allowed him to lead her onward. Unlike the frivolous women he'd largely kept company with through the years, Alice did not jump to fill voids of silence with inane banter. As effortless as she'd been since their first meeting with her cheeky retorts, was as at ease as she presented herself with silence. Perhaps, it was that realization that drew forth Rhys' question.

"Was it previously arranged?"

She cast him a quizzical glance.

"Your meeting with Pup Pratt," he clarified. "Or was it an unexpected meeting?"

Her answer shouldn't matter. Nonetheless, it did. Just as he'd been consumed by an inexplicable urge to throttle her dinner partner, the bloody fool who'd let her go and then proceeded to ogle her through the course of the entire damned meal. For a long moment, he believed she intended to ignore him. As she should. He was nothing more than her friend's brother... Rhys and Alice, strangers until now.

Rhys forced himself to look at her.

Alice chewed at her lower lip, her gaze trained contemplatively forward. "He courted me. I was betrothed to him. When he first began courting me, he would arrive at the same exact time, each day. Not one moment earlier, not one moment later. At first, I..." She paused. Her brow furrowed deep with the lines of her contemplation. "I admired that dependability. My brother and the rakes he kept company with couldn't be bothered to show up on time to a single event." Alice grimaced. "My brother didn't even remember to come fetch me from finishing school when my term there had ended."

Her brother, the man Rhys had recently entered into a business partnership with, had forgotten her. Rage held Rhys in its grip.

Alice's wistful smile pulled him back from his spiraling fury.

"And yet, there was Henry," she murmured. "Punctual. A gentleman. And he was so very unlike those scoundrels a lady is warned away from, but are drawn to because they represent the forbidden. Men such as..." Her gaze went to Rhys.

Men such as him...

The word hung there as though she'd spoken it aloud. Odd, he'd relished that role until now. Being so casually lumped in beside a sea of amorphous, like fellows, deemed worthless and indolent, stung.

Alice cleared her throat. "Yes, well, each time he visited," she went on, not breaking in her story, "we would read together."

"Your romantic novels?" he ventured.

She nodded.

Of course, because, then, she'd not suffered a heartbreak that left her jaded.

"And your Pratt?" He cupped his hands and blew into them, the warm sough of his breath fleeting. "Do not tell me. He'd likely be an ardent admirer of Sir Edward Coke's, *The Lion and the Throne*."

"An enlightened work on how man might help procure liberties and freedoms for the people?" Alice snorted. "Henry would hardly read anything even half so interesting." She was surely the only woman in the whole of England who'd not only heard of the preeminent jurist but who'd also read that two centuries' old works on the late Tudor and early Stuart era. "He could never be found without his copy of *An Introduction to the Principles of Morals and Legislation*."

He winced.

Alice laughed. "That w-was precisely my th-thoughts after I myself read it."

A sharp gust ripped down the graveled path with such ferocity, Rhys gritted his teeth to keep them from chattering. "Y-You read it?" he asked, shock creeping into his question. Who was Lady Alice? Bluestocking? Minx? Siren? *Or rather, mayhap, she's simply an extraordinary blend of the three.*

Hugging her arms close, Alice sent an elegant, golden eyebrow arcing up. "Have *you*, Lord Rhys?" she shot back.

Flummoxed, he opened and closed his mouth several times.

"Just because I'm a woman, doesn't mean I can't or don't have diverse literary tastes," she said with a frankness he appreciated.

"Touché," he conceded, lowering his head in apology. He felt the sharp sting of remorse. How many times had he himself been so judged? His parents and siblings had never seen past the spirited boy who'd ridden his mounts too fast and reveled in outdoors pursuits. "As a boy, I read any book within my reach." The admission came slowly and he braced for her mockery. The world, after all, had been content to see an idle gentleman who didn't take anything, outside of his pleasures, seriously. Curiosity seeped from Alice's eyes, encouraging him on. "One day I came upon Bentham's title in my tutor's possession. I filched the book and didn't return it until I'd read the whole volume through. Now, fair turnabout," he murmured, steering her back to her own interests. "How did you find yourself with that tedious work?" His own former betrothed couldn't have been bothered with even feigned interest whenever he'd attempted to speak of authors and books he'd been reading.

They reached the end of the graveled path and stopped before the rear entrance to the conservatory. His fingers numb from the cold, he struggled a moment with the handle. The latch gave with a satisfying click. As he let them in, she explained the relevance of that text. "We'd sit there, on opposite sofas, across from one another, never beside each other."

If Alice had been Rhys' betrothed, he'd have kissed her often and deeply, so that when their wedding night had come, there would be few secrets and only anticipation simmering between them. "Pratt was a demmed fool," he murmured.

"Oh," she whispered, touching a hand to her chest.

It was hard to say who'd been more stunned by that admission. Alice's eyes went soft, those deep, brown pools a window into a mind that suggested Rhys was something more than he was.

And then she spoke, Pratt's name falling too easily from her lips and shattering that connection. "At first, I wished to know what held Henry so riveted." She lifted her shoulders in a little shrug, hopelessly endearing in Rhys jacket. "But then," she strolled about the indoor garden sanctuary kept by Rhys' sister-in-law, "after I'd begun reading it, I desperately wished to know how anyone could rationalize sacrificing other people, regardless of number, for the happiness of most." Alice stopped, standing beside a stone table littered with fir branches. "And that is when I truly knew…"

He placed his palms on the edge of the table and leaned forward, hating the space she'd placed between them. "What?"

Relinquishing that branch, she clasped her hands as if in prayer. "I learned, just what manner of person I was betrothed to. Oh, at the time, I fought the realization, calling myself faithless for my ill thoughts. But he proved himself one who could unflinchingly set aside…" Alice studied her interlocked fingers.

Rhys stretched a hand out, covering hers. "Your happiness," he finished for her, in somber tones.

She remained with her gaze locked on their joined hands. "My happiness," she murmured, as two competing emotions vied for supremacy within him: the desire to bloody Pup Pratt senseless for having hurt her and the need to drive back her sorrow. At last, she lifted her eyes to his and anguish spilled from their depths. "And do you know why he threw me over?"

Because he was a damned bloody fool. There was no other reason for it. "The Pratts are impoverished," he ventured, reluctantly forcing his arm back to his side. All of Society knew the financial woes of the former roguish, now wedded, Lord Nolan Pratt. The gent had wedded Lord and Lady Lovell's eldest daughter, Sybil Cunning. But the Cunning fortune was not great enough to have sufficiently eased that family's debts.

"My dowry is sizeable," Alice explained. "Henry would have had a fortune upon our marriage." With the tip of her index finger, Alice trailed some invisible, nebulous outline on the corner of the stone table. She gave all her attentions to that distracted movement and then stopped. "Henry aspired to the role of partner within

his firm," she lifted that same long digit and spoke in a remarkably like impersonation of Pratt's stiff, concise tones. "Monies are
fleeting but his reputation as a barrister is forever. He couldn't rely
upon anyone but himself to restore the Pratt name to its onetime
greatness."

All Rhys' muscles went taut. "Good God, surely he wasn't so
sanctimonious that he'd said all *that*?"

Alice shook her head.

The tension left him.

"He wrote it."

Wrote it?

She expounded, moving an imagined quill through the air. "In
a note."

Rhys fought the growl working its way up his chest. "My God,
he called it off in a bloody letter?" The desire to thrash the pup
senseless filled him once more. Not only had young Pratt proven
himself faithless, but he'd shown he was a coward, as well.

"Indeed," she murmured, lifting a fir branch. That delicate movement wafted the fragrant evergreen scents.

He searched his mind for a suitable reply. And yet, to tell her
she was better without that cad in her life, to remind her Pratt
had never been deserving of her, was the same rubbish Rhys had
been fed by his mother after Lillian's treachery. In the aftermath of
a broken heart, all one knew was the agony of regret, of what had
been, of what almost was, and all that would never be.

In time, Alice would come to appreciate that she'd been spared.
Just as Rhys had eventually reconciled Lillian and Anthony's
betrayal in his heart and mind. But no person could force that
acceptance upon another. His former best friend served as life's
testament to that.

Alice cleared her throat. "I should leave."

"Yes," he acknowledged. The guests would be rejoining soon for
the evening's parlor games and their absence would be noted.

Did he imagine the lady's reluctance? Did he simply see that
which he wished?

Alice turned to go.

"Alice?" he called out, staying her.

She cast a questioning glance back.

"Stretching his hand up to reach the stars, too often man forgets the flowers at his feet."

Her lips parted, the softness there filled her eyes. "Thank you," she whispered.

And then she was gone.

CHAPTER 13

The HOUSE GUESTS HAVING LONG ago sought their chambers and the sprawling house quiet, Alice sat in Lord and Lady Guilford's libraries.

Sleep had proven elusive.

As such, she'd gathered her book, abandoned her chambers, and sought out a distraction that had always come from literature.

That same leather volume, however, now rested beside her, forgotten and useless.

Her knees drawn close to her chest, Alice rested her cheek atop them, and stared absently into the impressive flames that still raged in the hearth. Rhys' parting words echoed around her mind.

Stretching his hand up to reach the stars, too often man forgets the flowers at his feet...

Just seventeen words from Bentham's work... and they'd thoroughly transfixed her since Rhys murmured them in his silky baritone hours earlier. Four hours, if one wished to be truly precise. And since they'd parted, he'd retained hold of her thoughts with an unrelenting tenacity.

Alice rubbed her chin along her cotton robe.

Who *was* Lord Rhys Brookfield?

Conversing so freely with her on Bentham's works one instant, and bringing her to blush with nothing more than his crooked half-grin, the next? He was equal parts scholar and equal parts charming rogue. And together, they made for an alluring gentleman who robbed a woman of sleep.

And for a brief moment when they'd been alone outside, she'd believed he was going to kiss her. The burn of his grey gaze had sent heat racing through her, driving back the winter's chill. And she'd wanted his kiss. Yearned to know the crush of his mouth against hers.

Her betrothed had never kissed her. At first, she'd marveled at him for being unlike the rogues and rakes whispered about in Society. Henry Pratt was a gentleman in every way. Alice, however, had quickly tired of politeness. After weeks of his courtship and then their betrothal, she'd yearned for his embrace. Only, it hadn't been a wild, burning passion that filled her; a need to feel his arms about her. Rather, it had been a frustrated curiosity to have her first kiss.

Having grown impatient, it had been Alice who'd taken matters into her own hands—both literally and figuratively. With him across from her reading poetry one visit, and her maid deliberately sent off for refreshments, Alice joined Henry on the sofa. She had looped her arms about his neck and pressed her lips to his.

Slightly damp, soft… and cold, there had been an absolute emptiness to Henry Pratt's kiss that had left her hollow. Wishing for more. Yearning for a glimpse of the thrilling excitement written of in those romantic tales she'd read since she was a girl. All through that exchange, she'd told herself that all women surely felt the same way in a man's arms. That the fluttering sensations and quickening of one's heart captured on those pages of romantic novels was just that… words of fiction. And when Henry had jerked away, ending that sloppy embrace, a deep-seated shame had consumed Alice.

Not because of the wanton display that had earned a stinging rebuke from a blushing Henry, but because she'd been so very glad the embrace had been over.

That kiss she'd stolen had been her first… and her last…

Something told her, despite her conclusion that no embrace could stir a woman to grand passions, that being in Rhys' arms would be altogether different. Somehow, she knew with a woman's intuition that when Rhys kissed a woman, that lady would plead for more, and give over her reputation and pride just for the thrill of that embrace. All the while, knowing that one could never be anything more to him. She picked up her book, fanning the pages distractedly. No, with their every exchange, he'd reiterated time and time again that the last thing he desired was a respectable match.

Why, his failure to rejoin the party for parlor games was proof enough that even the exchange that still held her enthralled hadn't been so very important to him. And the truth of that left her... bereft.

The faintest groan of a floorboard slashed across her pathetic musings.

Her heart did a funny leap.

It was as though she'd conjured him with her thoughts.

Still in flagrant disregard of proper dress, Rhys entered the library, similar to how she'd last seen him—sans jacket. And sitting as she was, in the corner, Alice hunched her shoulders in a bid to make herself as small as possible, using the opportunity to study him. A new, less rumpled, but equally crisp white shirt had replaced the previous article he'd donned. The garment hung loose. She stared on unabashedly at the olive-toned skin exposed, the hint of tightly coiled curls upon his chest. As he started across the room, she dipped her appreciative gaze lower, to his narrow hips and buttocks.

He stopped at the sideboard, moving a hand over the collection of decanters.

Cravatless, shirtless, shoeless, he was every last inch of his remark-able frame the forbidden rogue that young ladies such as herself were so often warned of, and schooled to avoid.

Alice gulped. *Announce yourself...*

She would... eventually. Later. Soon.

Or mayhap she'd simply remain tucked in the corner, and he'd fail to notice that she'd been here admiring him like some emp-ty-headed ninny. For the truth remained: he was a remarkable specimen of chiseled male perfection.

Her gaze worked over his broadly powerful frame before linger-ing on his bare feet. For the masculine strength that spilled from his heavily-muscled physique, there was something also so very tender in the sight of him so.

"Would you care for a brandy, Alice?" he drawled.

Shrieking, Alice jumped up. Her book sailed to the floor, landing indignantly on its spine with a near-deafening *thwack*.

His hip perched on the edge of the mahogany piece, Rhys lifted his snifter… and then his eyes caught on her gaping night wrapper. Thick, golden lashes, most women would have sold their souls for, swept down, hooding his gaze. She gasped and swiftly belted the garment.

"N-No," she squeaked, humiliation bathing her cheeks in heat. "No brandy that is. Thank you," she spoke quickly, her words rolling nonsensically together. "You must be wondering at my silence." *Hush now, Alice Winterbourne. Hush.* Her tongue, however, moved without a care for her silently pleading logic. "I intended to call out a greeting, but I was…"

Ogling you.

He lifted a single, elegant brow.

Alice winced, wishing the Aubusson carpet under her feet had a hidden passage so she might disappear within. Even with the length of the room, a knowing glitter sparkled in his eyes. "Reading," she lamely settled for. "I was engrossed in my book," she repeated as he joined her.

Belatedly, Alice rescued the forlorn volume and held it aloft. "Do you see?" she blurted. Good God. She cringed inside.

The ghost of a smile teased the corners of his lips. "I do… *see.*" And something in that slight emphasis suggested, he very much did. That he'd seen entirely too much. Rhys dipped his eyes to the lace trim that ran the length of her wrapper. "First, meeting over snowballs, then over cheroots, now brandies." Rhys motioned for her to sit.

She chewed at the inside of her lower lip. Having been alone with him several times before, she'd risked scandal. To remain closeted away in this room, with him in flagrant dishabille and her in her night garments, would have her dancing with ruin that no lady could ever recover from.

"That is probably the wise decision," he murmured. "Your leaving."

There was a challenge contained within that statement. Alice set her jaw.

With stiff movements, she reclaimed her seat. Placing the book on her lap, Alice folded her hands primly atop the leather volume.

Taking a sip of his brandy, Rhys settled his broad frame into the peculiar pale green upholstered mahogany chair. Women's figures carved into each arm, it was a strange seat at odds with the simplicity of the other décor.

With one hand lazily cradling his glass, Rhys draped his spare palm along one etched beauty. His fingers grazed the décolletage, and there it was again… that wild fluttering in Alice's chest. Compelled by his every movement, she stared transfixed by his long fingers stroking back and forth along the swells of the woman's breasts.

Back and forth.

Back. And forth.

From over the rim of his glass, Rhys' unswerving gaze met hers.

If he expected her to hastily avert her eyes, he knew her not at all.

That distracted caress kindled a yearning low in Alice's belly. The stirrings of desire she'd accepted solely as false words printed in books, now proven wrong by Rhys Brookfield… and an engraved armchair.

The wondering that had slithered forward earlier that night reared itself once more. What if Rhys, in fact, had assignations planned with another lady and Alice was nothing more than an in-the-way distraction? A stone pitted in her stomach.

Alice caught a lone curl and twisted it around her finger distractedly, until his gaze caught on that movement. She abruptly stopped. *During your exchanges with gentlemen, be nonchalant. Never show emotion.* Miserable Mrs. Belden's frequently echoed lecture rattled around Alice's mind. Who would have believed a single lesson from the old harpie would have proven useful? "Do you know, Lord Rhys, it occurs to me you also happen to be missing from all the planned festivities." Also conspicuously absent had been Miss Cunning. Alice's stomach muscles clenched. "Why is that?" she asked, dropping her elbow onto the arm of her chair.

Contrary even in drink, Rhys swirled the contents of his glass in a counterclockwise circle. "Truthfully?"

"I'd rather you did not lie to me, if that is what you're asking."

He grinned and then leaned forward, conspiratorially. "I was… avoiding certain guests."

An odd lightness suffused her breast as the tension went out of her. "Your… mother?" she ventured, hating the hopeful edge she was unable to conceal.

"My mother?" he snorted. "She is, of course, a given." His expression tightened. That affable demeanor lifted and, in its place, came the cynical, hardened shell of the person whose company she'd come to enjoy these past days.

Wounded eyes... strained smile... slumped shoulders... you have all the makings of a heartsick miss...

Her heart tugged. Rhys presented a flawless image of indolent rogue to the world. Until now, she'd failed to see that Rhys, too, had known hurt. She, just like everyone else in Society had seen the surface and never searched for anything more of him. Shame filled her at her own self-absorption. What secret pain did he carry?

When silence marched on and it became apparent he intended to say nothing else, Alice prodded him to continue. "So there is another you're avoiding..."

Leaning back, Rhys stretched his legs out so the heels of his feet brushed her toes. An electric charge tingled at the contact; a thrilling shock like when she'd run in her bare feet across the carpets at Mrs. Belden's.

"My mother is matchmaking at this house party."

"Yes." As a motherless girl, Alice lamented the absence of a caring, loving mama in her life. And then she'd born witness to the ruthless manner in which the dowager marchioness sought to maneuver Lettie into a respectable match. From that moment on, she'd acquired a whole new view on mothers and daughters. "She is always matchmaking," she pointed out.

Rhys steepled his fingers, resting them on his flat belly. "She has now hand-selected my bride," he muttered, that terse utterance at odds with his languid pose.

Alice's leg jumped and the book again tumbled to the floor. Heart racing, she bent to retrieve the leather volume. All the while, her mind swirled.

He hadn't been speaking about the dowager marchioness matchmaking Lettie with one of the gentlemen present. He'd spoken of himself. Her chest constricted.

Miss Cunning.

"Yes, well, my mother has never been circumspect in her attempts with any of my others siblings. I trust she wouldn't change now for my benefit," he drawled.

Cheeks burning, Alice jerked upright. She'd spoken aloud. She swallowed a groan.

Rhys sipped his drink. "The young lady is my mother's god-daughter." And breathtaking and able to make him laugh. Those two thoughts made her want to suddenly cry. "It was expected my brother would marry Lady Lovell's eldest daughter." The Baroness Webb... Henry's sister-in-law. "And since the connection was never made between our families..."

"It falls to you," she whispered. Why did the idea of him wedded to that dark-haired beauty clutch at her insides, scraping them raw?

He lifted his glass up, toasting that statement. "My mother certainly hopes so."

Nonchalance, Alice. You must be nonchalant. Alice fanned the pages of her book. "And you do not see yourself marrying her?"

He blanched. "Little Aria? Egads, no."

Little Aria? Tall, splendorous in her beauty, she had the look of the damned fertility goddess Diana painted upon the urn in her uncle Percival's office.

"She is a child. Seven and ten years of age." He furrowed his brow. "Almost eight and ten." He knew that intimate detail about the young woman. It spoke to that close familial connection; one that the dowager marchioness was determined to solidify.

"She's not so very young," she said haltingly. At seventeen, Alice had given her heart to Henry... and now, she was just two years older than Miss Cunning.

Rhys downed the remaining contents of his drink in one long swallow; the muscles of his throat worked rhythmically. He grimaced, and then set the glass down on the table beside him. "She's certainly too young for a man nearing thirty."

In a Society where ladies married men two decades their senior, the eleven years Rhys spoke of was insignificant. Nonetheless, she'd not debate him on the lady's suitability as a bride for him. For shamefully selfish reasons... even as she would never trust her heart again to any man, she abhorred the idea of Rhys married to the stunning beauty.

"We make quite the pair, don't we," she brought herself to say, instead. "Two individuals brought together because one," she motioned to herself, "is avoiding her former betrothed, and the other," she pointed to him, "his future intended."

Rhys laughed. That booming, masculine sound was filled with amusement. Jumping up, he collected his glass and returned to the sideboard. The soft clink of crystal touching crystal, and then the steady stream of liquid pouring filled the library.

It did not escape her notice that he hadn't refuted her latter claim. Alice curled her fingers over the arms of her chair, leaving little half-moon marks upon the ivory upholstery.

Rhys stilled and then slowly turned, a bottle and glass in hand. "That is it."

That is it.

Bitterness made her tongue heavy at that dismissive end to their discussion. "Of course." She glanced to the gilt bronze and marble mantel clock. "It is late and it wouldn't do for us to be seen together. Particularly given your mother's intentions for you," she forced out.

Before she took a step, he set aside the burdens in his hands. "Not the evening, Alice. Our arrangement."

She puzzled her brow. "We don't have an arrangement." Except… "Other than the one where I promised to not be the downtrodden, doleful miss you accused me of—"

"Not that arrangement," he cut in.

"Oh."

He grinned, that smile dimpling his left cheek. "Why, I'm going to court you."

Her pulse accelerated. "Court me?"

His smile deepened and he was across the room in five long strides. "It is perfect."

"Perfect," she breathed. Alice knew she sounded like a lackwit parroting back his words, and yet… she sought to muddle through his every pronouncement.

"There's Pup Pratt."

Alice whipped about, searching for the stodgy person in question.

"And then there are my mother's matchmaking plans for me," he went on. "A pretend courtship would be mutually beneficial."

And just like that…

Of course. He spoke of a false courtship. Nor should she even entertain a true one with him… or anyone for that matter. The last thing she wanted, desired, or needed was a gentleman in her life…

and a roguish one at that. So, what accounted for the disappointment that now filled her? Rhys stared expectantly back; smug,
entirely too pleased, he had the look of one who'd discovered the
true meaning of life.

Needing distance between him and her tumultuous thoughts,
she wandered around the sofa. As she paced the length of the ivory
seat, she trailed her fingertips along the scalloped top. "And just
how will a *faire semblant de faire la cour* benefit me?"

Rhys continued forward and, standing at the opposite end of
the sofa, he matched her pacing. "Pup Pratt has every intention of
protecting you from my unscrupulous advances." He held her gaze
squarely. "But if my intentions are honorable, a gentleman who
adheres to propriety truly cannot make a nuisance of himself."

It was a silly plan and yet...

Alice came to a slow stop.

She didn't wish to be bothered anymore with Henry thrusting
himself back into her life and looking after her as though she had
ever truly mattered to him.

A warm, strong hand settled on her shoulder. She gasped, glancing up at Rhys.

How was it possible that a man of his sheer power and size could
move with such stealth?

"And there remains the obvious truth," Rhys whispered against
her ear, delicious shivers tingled down her neck. "My courting
you, his seeing us together, will drive him mad with jealousy."

Odd, he spoke of her stirring envy in another man. Yet with her
back brushing against his chest, their bodies touching with the
hint of intimacy, she could not so much as dredge forth a memory of Henry's face. She could only think of the man beside her,
the one whose presence stirred an unfamiliar yearning low in her
belly. Alice fought her body's pull. "What happens when the house
party is over?"

He lifted his shoulders in a too-casual shrug. "Near the end, you
can break it off."

Her lips twitched. "You want me to throw you over?" When
most gentlemen's pride were too big to endure a public humiliation, it spoke depths to his confidence.

Rhys waggled his golden eyebrows. "There is a first time for
everything." Those teasing tones startled a laugh from her.

She swatted at him. "You are incorrigible."

"Oh, quite," he demurred. Rhys tapped the side of his mouth. "Before the end of the house party," he continued with all seriousness, "you shall realize I'm not the reverent gent you desire. You'll create the scandal of your choosing."

Her amusement faded. "I've already made a scandal of myself before, Rhys," she said quietly. "I have no desire to travel that path again."

"You care too much about what the *ton* thinks," he murmured, dusting his knuckles over her cheek in a butterfly caress. "Even so, the only guests present are my siblings and their families who'd fight the king himself to protect one another—my roguish self included. And lifelong friends of my mother's who desire a match between me and their unmarried daughter." Miss Aria Cunning.

No, with Lord and Lady Lovell's aspirations for their Diamond of a daughter, they'd certainly not breathe a complaint against Rhys, not when there was still a chance of their daughter marrying him. Her stomach muscles contracted.

Rhys moved his mouth closer. He was so close that, as he spoke, his lips touched the shell of her ear over and over; tiny, too-fleeting kisses. "You want to say yes."

Delicious thrills of awareness raced through her. Alice's head tipped sideways as she reflexively opened herself to him. "I want..." *you. I want you...*

His long lashes swept down. "What do you want?" he enticed, like the Devil himself with that forbidden fruit cradled between his fingers.

Somewhere along the way, they'd ceased speaking about games of pretend and reality had stepped in. "I want you..." Those three words came garbled, heavy with her need for this man.

"Yes, Alice. Tell me what you want?" he breathed against her mouth.

"To c-court me," she blurted out the safer thought. Did that throaty whisper belong to her? The wanton, sultry tones, unfamiliar to her own ears, brought Rhys' lashes down all the more, concealing those grey irises. But not before she caught the glitter of desire there.

Desire for me. He desires me.

Since she'd been jilted, Alice had believed herself undesirable; a woman easily thrown over, and hardly one to rouse a man to true passion.

And there was something so very heady in this newly discovered woman's power.

Rhys' hot, piercing gaze lingered on her lips. Then, cupping her nape, he covered her mouth with his, kissing her as she'd always dreamed, kindling a desire she'd believed she could not feel.

There was nothing hesitant or searching in this kiss. He slanted hard lips over hers again and again, laying claim to her mouth with a primitive possession that weakened her knees.

Melting into him, Alice gripped Rhys lawn shirt hard; the heat of him penetrating that fabric and burning her fingers. A growl of masculine approval rumbled from his chest. Sliding his arms around her, he filled his palms with her buttocks. She moaned as he drew her between the "V" of his legs. The hard length of his sex prodded her through the thin barrier of her night shift.

Rhys swept his tongue inside her mouth; hot, tasting of brandy and cheroots.

Hungry for him, wanting this moment to stretch on forever, Alice met each bold thrust and parry of his tongue. Heat exploded in her belly, spiraling quickly through her like molten lava. Her hips began to move and, unlike with Henry, there was no shame in this moment, in her response, in her simply feeling. There was only a primal hungering to know every last mystery of Rhys' embrace.

He drew back and a soft, shameless cry burst from her at the sudden loss.

But he only shifted his attentions elsewhere. Touching his lips to the corner of her mouth, he trailed them lower to her jaw-line. Then finding the delicate shell of her ear, he took that flesh between his teeth and gently suckled.

"Rhys," she moaned, his name both a prayer and a plea.

Tangling her fingers in his loose curls, she luxuriated in the satiny softness of those strands. He was a fallen angel, cast from the gates of paradise, and now master tormenter to mere mortals.

"So beautiful," he breathed, dragging his hot mouth down her neck. He lightly nipped and suckled at the place where her heart wildly pulsed. She dimly registered him working his hands between them, loosening the ties of her wrapper.

The cooler air was a sough upon her heated skin. He freed her breasts, cupping the mounds in his palms, drawing them together. The sensitized tips pebbled from the cold, from the anticipation.

And then he took one of those tips between his lips, suckling her.

Alice's cry reached to the rafters; the desperate, aching sound of unfulfilled desires echoing in her ears. Of their own volition, her legs fell open in a wanton invitation.

He switched his attentions to the other, neglected peak.

Her legs gave out and he caught her under her knees. Effortlessly carrying her to the ivory sofa, he lay her upon the velvet squabs and followed her down. Resting his weight on his elbows he continued worshiping the swollen nipple. Flicking his tongue over the pebbled bud, circling it, before taking it in his mouth, once more.

Rhys dragged her skirts up, slowly until her legs lay naked. Reaching between them, he palmed the soft thatch of curls shielding her womanhood.

"Please," she begged, not knowing what she pleaded for. All she was had been reduced to a bundle of nerves incapable of anything but feeling: a desire that was both excruciating and exquisite.

PLEASE.

It was a single word that had fallen from the lips of all Rhys' previous lovers.

Only this breathy, pleading, one-syllable utterance was different and for very many reasons.

Sweat beaded on Rhys brow, and a single bead rolled a path down his cheek and fell like a lone teardrop upon her breast.

Alice's long, golden lashes swept up. "Rhys?" she whispered, the uncertainty underlining his name wrenched at him.

He clenched his eyes tight.

Wishing he could be the wicked scoundrel the world took him for.

For if that were the case, he would toss aside Alice's white linen nightgown, a scrap of fabric that exuded innocence from its cut to its color, and lay between her shapely thighs. But not only was she the sister of his business partner... she was also an innocent.

"I cannot… forgive me…" he said, his incoherent apology hoarsened by unfulfilled desire.

Alice's stricken eyes met his. Her body went taut under his and she angled her face away. "I see."

He'd hurt her.

Leave it that way. It was far safer, wiser to let her believe whatever unintended slight he'd delivered.

His chest rose and fell in harsh spurts. Rhys cursed himself to hell. Cupping her cheek, he brought her gaze back to his. "Since the moment I came upon you in The Copse, I wanted to take you in my arms." Her mouth parted and he brushed his thumb along the slightly fuller flesh of her lower lip. "I wanted to know the taste of you and the feel of you. So do not ever think for one moment that my stopping has anything to do with you." It had everything to do with him clinging to the last shred of honor he had left in his miserable blackguard body.

"Is it because I'm Daniel's sister?"

He grunted. The other man would be well within his rights to call Rhys out at dawn and put a ball through his heart. "There is that."

Alice rolled her eyes. "I assure you, my rakish brother is hardly the one to pass judgment on my actions."

Of course, Alice, the spirited minx, would never be contented with even that. Rhys dragged both palms over his face. For the truth remained, it didn't matter how many women Montfort had tupped to earn his reputation, a young lady was altogether different. He let his arms fall. "Because I don't dally with innocents." Except, even as that admission left him, there was an inherent wrongness to it. Having Alice in his arms hadn't felt like a mere empty meeting of two lovers. There had been an explosion of feeling and desire that consumed him still. He made to stand, but Alice shot a hand up, gripping his shoulder.

"But what if I want you to?" Her whisper was temptation itself and Rhys had an appreciation for the battle Adam had waged before his great fall from grace.

He closed his eyes, fighting for resolve.

As if sensing his weakening, her satiny soft palm glided down his cheek in a caress that forced his gaze back to hers. "Rhys, I'm ruined."

"You weren't discovered in a compromising position, Alice," he said gently, needing her to see the difference. Rather, she'd been jilted and by a pompous arse who'd never deserved her. What a bloody injustice that she should find her reputation in tatters for Pratt's crimes. Averting his eyes, he swung his legs over the side of the sofa. Planting his feet on the floor, Rhys dropped his elbows on his knees.

The soft rustle of Alice's modest lawn nightshift and the faint creak of the sofa spring indicated she'd moved.

She touched his shoulder. "I shared but one kiss with my betrothed." Red hot hatred for Pratt coursed through Rhys' veins as Alice painted an image that was all too real of that bastard with his mouth on Alice's, the way Rhys' had been moments ago. "I was the one to initiate it," she confessed; the shame tingeing that admission knifed at him.

"He was a fool," he clipped out. If Rhys had been betrothed to Alice, he would have reveled in the right and pleasure of taking her in his arms so that, come their wedding night, there would have been no secrets between them.

A wistful smile curved her lips. "I do not disagree with you there. But that is not why I told you…" Her cheeks pinkened. "About Henry."

God, how he abhorred the effortless way Pratt's name fell from her lips.

Alice came up on her knees beside him. "After his betrayal, after," she grimaced. "The Scandal, my reputation was destroyed, and do you know, Rhys? I didn't care," she whispered. "It didn't matter to me that I'd never marry. I loved and lost in the most humiliating way." *Humiliating.* Not devastating. Not heartbreaking. Did Alice realize that key distinction? "I came to accept that love and desire were rare gifts for some and I was not to be one who knew either." Alice drew in a slow breath. "I won't marry."

He scraped a hand through his hair. "Your brother would rightfully skewer me at dawn."

"I'm a woman," she said simply. "Why should I be without choice?"

"Because it is the way of Society." His protest came weak to his own ears.

Alice smiled wryly. "And you've always done what Society

expects?" No, from his work as a self-made man to the woman he'd once offered marriage to, he'd reveled in flouting those conventions.

"This is different," he said reluctantly. "This isn't about my reputation." Or the Earl of Montfort's. It was about Alice's. "You've been hurt before and have given up on the idea of love and marriage. But that does not mean, in time, you will not desire those very things." An image flickered to his mind's eye of some nameless, faceless gentleman laying her down, parting her thighs, and giving Alice the pleasure Rhys longed to. A growl started low in his belly.

"Don't presume to tell me what I want," she said matter-of-factly. "Or decide my future. If we make love…" Oh, God. He faltered, as those four words painted erotic images that would tempt and torture him long after this moment. "That is *my* choice. Just as you've chosen to live a bachelor's existence, I would live now, not for Society or propriety but for myself." Alice grasped his hand and drew it to her chest. He swallowed hard as she laid his left palm against her breast. His palm cupped the swell, reflexively.

"Alice," he implored, in one last, desperate bid to do what was right.

"I want to feel, Rhys," she breathed. "Make me feel again."

And with those four words, the battle was lost. He would not take her virtue, but he would give her the night of pleasure she sought.

Rhys tangled his fingers in her silken tresses and brought her mouth to meet his.

Alice kissed with the same beautiful abandon she went through every aspect of life: fierce, unapologetic, bold. She parted her lips and their tongues met in a passionate dance. All the while, he worked his hands over her as he'd ached to these past days; exploring the curve of her flared hips, her buttocks.

She pressed herself against him; her breasts crushed against the wall of his chest. Through their thin linen garments, the heat from their bodies melded. Lifting her skirts once more, he bared her before him.

He touched his gaze on muscled legs that spoke of a woman who rode.

Guiding her back down, he palmed the soft thatch of curls

between her thighs.

"Rhys," she hissed, her hips shooting up.

His shaft swelled, straining against his trousers, as the aching need to take that which she offered wrought havoc on his honorable intentions. "You are so wet for me," he rasped, slipping a finger inside her wet channel.

Alice whimpered and he thrust another finger inside her.

The glow cast by the fire bathed her face in a soft light, playing off the moisture that dampened her brow. Then, he began to stroke her. In and out. In and out. That primitive echo of lovemaking that fueled his desire.

Her speech dissolved into incoherent, gasping pleas.

With his other hand, he freed her breasts from her night shift and refocused on the perfect, pink crests. Lowering his head, he took one tip deep in his mouth at the same time he quickened his fingers in her sodden center.

Her body stiffened, the tension spilling from her slender frame; all the muscles of her heart-shaped face were taut, and then a scream tore from her. He swiftly covered her mouth, taking that beautiful shout of release as she bucked her hips into him.

And then she collapsed, her breath coming hard and fast.

His body throbbing from the ache of unfulfilled desires, Rhys dropped his head against her chest.

Of all the times for him to become... honorable. He tamped down an agonized groan.

"That was wondrous," Alice murmured, her breath fanned his cheek.

He lifted his head from her breast, studying her.

Her eyes closed, a contented smile on her lips, she had the look of the cat who'd gotten into the cream. Male satisfaction filled him.

The loud creak of a floorboard slashed across their stolen interlude.

Surging to his feet, he glanced to the door.

"What is it?" Alice whispered, hurriedly sitting up.

Rhys held a finger up and trained his ears for a hint of sound.

The fire in the hearth continued to hiss and crackle but, otherwise, silence reigned.

"You should return to your rooms," he said in hushed tones as he set to work righting her garments. Her loose, golden curls hung in a tangled mass down her back. "Here," he murmured, guiding her around. Wordlessly, he sifted his hands through those strands, putting them to order.

When he'd finished, she faced him.

An awkward pall fell between them.

She cleared her throat. "Thank—" He narrowed his eyes, and that insulting expression of gratitude died on her lips. A word of thanks made this exchange nothing more than an empty meeting. And yet, mayhap, it was the late hour or, perhaps, it really was some peculiar hold this minx had claimed from their first meeting—this interlude had felt like so much more.

"Good night, Alice."

She bowed her head. "Good night, Rhys."

Long after she'd left, Rhys remained standing there, staring at the door she'd slipped out, unable to shake the ominous feeling that with the pretend courtship they'd agreed to, Rhys had made the greatest of mistakes.

CHAPTER 14

Splendorous.
Magical.
Wondrous.

LAST EVENING, IN RHYS' ARMS, Alice had discovered that passion and desire were real… and more, that she was capable of feeling. That one stolen moment could never be enough. Now that she'd tasted the thrill of Rhys' embrace, how could she ever be contented?

And yet…

That had also been the last she'd seen of him. When she'd arisen early as she always did, humming a joyful ditty under her breath, she'd rushed to the breakfast room to find it empty of anyone—except her former betrothed.

She'd suffered through the morning meal, casting eager glances at the doorway, anticipation coursing through her for the moment he arrived.

How was a woman to be around the man who'd awakened her to the beauty to be found in lovemaking?

Alas, after she'd quit the breakfast room and taken a morning walk, the answer proved elusive.

He was avoiding her.

There could be no other explanation for it.

"I suggested hanging the Brookfield gems from the edge… shall we…?"

Alice blinked slowly and glanced over to the young woman standing beside her.

Lettie held up a spectacularly garish bough, adorned in gold, crimson, and velvet ribbons. "Of all the wonders, she listens," her friend drawled. "You've been distracted since we began. You're woolgathering."

Alice promptly grabbed for the forgotten soft blue ribbon she'd selected for her bough. "I am not… woolgathering," she whispered. *Liar! You've thought of no one and nothing except Rhys Brookfield since he discovered you in The Copse.* Her fingers shaking, Alice devoted all her attention to tying the ribbon about the aromatic green.

"Pining, then," Lettie put forward, persistent as she'd always been. Where she'd loved her friend for that determination that had steered Alice away from the doldrums many times, now that attribute was a blasted nuisance. With an exaggerated tip of her head that could never be considered discreet, her friend motioned to the opposite end of the room.

As one, they looked across the rectangular oak table.

Henry, standing beside his young, loquacious bride, stared back through the lenses of his spectacles. A frown hovered on his lips.

Alice and Lettie swiftly returned their attention to their boughs. "I am most certainly not pining," she whispered furiously. Except, in a way, she had been. Just not for the gentleman her friend believed she'd been thinking of.

Lettie paused in tying yet another tiny ribbon to her greenery. "Alice," she said gently in hushed tones that barely reached her ears. "You've done nothing but pine since the moment I met you."

Yes, she had. She'd been the mournful, sad-eyed creature Rhys had called out for being that morning in the breakfast room. Only, these past days with Rhys, aside from her telling of the failed betrothal, she'd not given thought to Henry.

She faced her friend. "I am not pining for him," she quietly assured. "Not anymore." *Never again.*

Lettie puzzled her brow and, squinting, she peered at Alice. "Truly?" She continued before Alice could speak. "Because you kept looking to the door and I assumed you were plotting your escape but…" Her eyes flared wide as she glanced to the door and then back once more to Alice. "You are looking for someone," she blurted.

"Hush!" Cheeks ablaze, Alice glanced around at the other guests assembled about the table. The ladies and the handful of gentlemen present remained fixed on their discussions and greenery projects.

Alas, there could be no quieting Lettie when she'd gotten something into her mind. "These past days, I believed you were sneaking off because you were hiding; after breakfast, then again after dinner, this morn... while all along you're smitten with some gentleman." With her ability to ferret out information, her friend would be better served in the Home Office.

"I am not," Alice said weakly. For she wasn't. They were largely strangers; two people who'd come to a mutually beneficial agreement last evening.

In his arms last night was not nothing. That voice at the back of her mind continued to needle. *You came undone in his arms, shamelessly and with abandon, and wish to do it again.*

She stole another furtive glance at the doorway—the still *empty* doorway.

From where she sat at the head of the table, the dowager marchioness glowered in Alice's direction until Alice squirmed in her seat. The other woman couldn't know that, even now, Alice searched for Rhys. Lady Guilford, seated beside the miserable harpie, gave Alice a reassuring smile.

"Don't mind her," Lettie said, gathering a string of gold beads and winding them around the bough. She paused in her efforts. "Mother, that is," she clarified, resuming her work. "Not Philippa. She's quite lovely. A loving sister-in-law and devoted mama..."

While her friend carried on, Alice picked up a thin fir branch and her mind wandered.

By Rhys' conspicuous absence, the magic of that exchange had clearly meant far less to him than it had to Alice. She had, after all, been the one begging him like a shameless harlot; pleading for him to continue when he'd pulled away. Alice cringed, and all the breath stuck sharply in her breast. With her entreaty, she'd behaved in the same desperate manner she had after Henry had broken it off.

Lettie gasped, snapping Alice to the moment. "My God, you are *still* daydreaming."

"I am certainly not daydreaming," she gritted out, peeking about the room. Again, Henry watched them. Only this time, he made no effort to hide his open assessment.

Dismissing him outright, Alice attended her branch. No, she certainly hadn't been daydreaming about Rhys. Rather, she'd been lamenting her own pathetic response to his rejection.

"You were looking at the entrance of the room," her friend persisted.

Had she been? "I…" Alice's words froze on her lips as Rhys filled the doorway. Clad in a navy wool tailcoat and buckskin trousers, he was a model of male elegance and… *he is staring at me.*

Rhys' stare, however, was not the casual, indolent stare of a rogue. This was the hooded, hot, piercing gaze that belonged to a scoundrel, whose eyes made silent, scandalous promises that any respectable lady would gladly shred her reputation for.

His lips, those same ones that had been on her, all over her not even twelve hours earlier, curved up in a dangerous half-grin that set her heart to racing.

He inclined his head. "Lady Alice," he silently mouthed, either uncaring or not noticing the room full of guests noticing him. But then, that was the unfettered way he moved through life. And amid the wild fluttering in her breast, there beat an appreciation for the gentleman who'd given Alice her first taste of passion. When nearly all members of the *ton* cared overly much about the opinions of others, Rhys had a go-to-hell attitude, and it was hard not to admire that confidence and strength.

Emboldened by that, she returned his soundless greeting. "Lord Rhys."

He shoved from the doorjamb and strode slowly, with languid steps better suited to a panther stalking its prey.

"Oh. My. God. In. Heaven," Lettie exhaled that blasphemy in a too-loud whisper. "It is… Rhys," she squawked. "You…and… Rhys and…my God," she repeated.

Alice wanted to tell her friend all. She wished to unveil the scheme crafted last evening by Rhys, so there could be no falsities surrounding Rhys' intentions.

But the words would not come. For with every step that brought him closer, there was a realness to his hot steel-grey stare. No man could fake such a response.

Ultimately, it was the dowager marchioness who shattered that pull.

Dragging along her goddaughter, the stunning Miss Cunning, the dowager marchioness stepped into Rhys' path, forcing him to a stop.

The branch she'd been holding snapped and the greenery dangled, two forlorn pieces, between her fingers.

Lettie swung her clever gaze between that trio and Alice. "Will you say something?" she hissed.

She couldn't. Instead, Alice remained riveted on Rhys and Miss Cunning.

"And do not say I'm merely imagining… this," she waved another garish gold bow in Rhys' direction.

Cursing under her breath, Alice snatched her friend's wrist and forced it back to the table. "Will you at least be discreet?" she implored.

Lettie merely folded her arms. "Well?"

In the end, Alice was saved from answering.

"My dearest sister," Rhys boomed, dropping a reverent bow that sent those golden curls tumbling over his brow.

With an inelegant snort, dearest sister crossed her arms at her chest again. "You want something."

He pressed a hand to his chest, staggering back. "I'm insulted." Rhys grinned. "May I relieve you of your partner?"

With the gaze of every last guest present trained on them, Alice's body burned with a blush that started in her toes and ran to the roots of her hair.

"Only if *my partner* wishes it."

Brother and sister stared at Alice.

Oh, bloody hell. She shifted back and forth. For with that unspoken question on her friend's part, she demanded an answer to her earlier query about Alice and Rhys.

Lifting a golden eyebrow, Rhys extended his elbow.

Alice hesitated a moment before placing her fingertips on his sleeve and allowing him to guide her down the length of the table, further away from Lettie and even further still from his mother and prospective bride.

Rhys brought them to a stop at the unoccupied station. Angling his shoulder, he shielded them from the stares trained on them. He placed his lips close to her ear, his breath stirring the sensitive skin. A giggle tumbled from her lips. "That is splendid, love," he whispered.

Love.

It was just one word and, yet, spoken in his melodic baritone, it rolled off his tongue like an intimate caress.

"Mmm," she murmured incoherently, swaying closer.

Raising her hand to his mouth, Rhys brushed a lingering kiss upon her knuckles and her skin burned from that slight contact. "A heated stare, a stolen interlude is all it takes for the world to see precisely what it is they are expected to see." Those casual, too-matter-of-fact words brought reality crashing into her with all the force of a fast-moving carriage.

The agreement they'd struck.

Their pretend courtship.

Why, Rhys hadn't come in here eying Alice as though she were the only woman in the world because he desired her. Rather, his entrance had been part of a scheme to thwart his mother's plans for him.

Her heart sank to her belly and sat heavy there.

What did you expect? That any of this show was, indeed, real?

"Is he looking?"

Is he looking? What was he on about? She struggled through her miserable musings, trying to make sense of his query.

"The pup."

Henry.

Her stomach churned. Why… he was speaking so casually of her former betrothed. And why shouldn't he? The other end of their pact had involved Alice making Henry outrageously jealous and thwarting his efforts to see her.

She forced herself to dip her gaze around his shoulder.

An ashen-faced Henry didn't even make an attempt to hide his scrutiny. His frank observation now was the only time in the course of their never-ending betrothal where he'd ever done anything as outrageous as to gawk.

Henry's gaze locked with hers… and Alice felt… nothing.

There was no thrill of satisfaction at his upset. There was no regret for what had almost been with them. No, there was no victory in any of this. Rather, she was filled with a hollow emptiness for the game of pretend she'd entered in to with Rhys.

Which was madness, feeling any such wistfulness for a man she'd only just recently met.

"Tsk. Tsk. This will never do."

Unblinkingly, she glanced up. "What?" she asked cautiously, more than half-afraid with his rogue's intuition that he'd gathered the tumult he'd wrought in her.

"It won't do for him to see you woebegone. It has all the markings of a broken heart."

He'd come to the erroneous conclusion that her upset came from her pining after Henry. She gave silent thanks for that misunderstanding. "And you know so very much about broken hearts," she muttered.

He fell uncharacteristically silent and she glanced up.

A shadow darkened his eyes. She drew in a silent breath.

Of course.

How had she failed to completely understand it before now? It was why he'd so easily recognized the product of Alice's misery. She'd had an inkling of it before, but now she was sure. "You had your heart broken," she quietly ventured.

His body stilled. "We aren't talking about me. Smile," Rhys urged in another tantalizing whisper.

It didn't escape her notice how effortlessly he'd steered them from the intimate query she'd put to him. Alice drew in a shaky breath. Damn Rhys Brookfield and the effect of his nearness. And damn her for her own weakness. She forced her lips up, stretching them into a smile until her cheeks ached. "Are you happy?"

"I am." He snorted. "But there can be no confusing your smile as anything more than an ill-concealed grimace."

Her lips twitched.

"That is a slight improvement." Rhys waggled his golden eyebrows. "Not a convincing I-love-you-and-only-you-Rhys-Brookfield smile, per se, but it will suffice."

A sharp bark of laughter burst from her lips and her melancholy lifted. "You're insufferable, Rhys Brookfield."

"Oh, I've been told many times from my dear mama," he shared, gathering a fir branch. Then, sifting through the decorations that had been set out by servants, Rhys collected a pale blue satin ribbon and a string of silver beads. He sat and proceeded to loop the ribbon around the branch.

Alice opened and closed her mouth several times. "What are you doing?" she blurted.

"I believe we were decorating boughs."

"*You* decorate boughs?"

Pausing in his task, he dropped his elbows atop the table and looked up at her. "I join you wherever you are, madam."

Again, his being here was a product of their pact.

The feeling of moroseness swiftly returned. Alice sat and began work on a bough of her own.

Rhys leaned down. "I may have some experience with decorating garland," he confessed.

She snorted.

"My sisters enjoyed it. Each Christmastide season Lettie and Rosalind would challenge me to a snowball throwing contest. If they won, I would join them in creating decorations."

How very different the relationship he painted with his sisters than the one she herself had known with Daniel. She'd been invisible. Forgotten. And then there had been brothers such as Rhys who allowed himself to be cajoled into child's games. She hadn't known there were brothers such as the one he'd been to Lettie and Rosalind. She hadn't known there were any men such as him. "And if you won?" she asked, her curiosity piqued.

Rhys tied his ribbon off at the end of the garland. "Why, I never won, of course."

Her pulse tripped several beats. "You let them win," she breathed. Despite the end result meaning he'd be forced to join two younger girls in decorating the sprawling household, he'd ceded those victories.

He winked and resumed knotting another ribbon to his strand of garland.

And as they shared a secretive smile, a little sliver of her heart fell for Rhys Brookfield.

CHAPTER 15

SHE'D SEEN THE TRUTH.

When his own siblings had been oblivious to the heartache he'd suffered at the hands of Lillian and his closest friend all those years ago, Alice had gathered the secrets he'd kept.

And it scared the bloody hell out of him.

It terrified him because the women Rhys kept company with, the ones he'd taken as lovers and mistresses, had been content to see him as an empty-hearted rogue, capable of bringing them pleasure.... and never delving any deeper, and never wanting anything more.

And so, he'd retreated from Alice. Retreated, even when it went against the arrangement they'd struck, to a place she could never enter without bringing down a small scandal in the household—the billiards room.

A cheroot clamped between his teeth, Rhys leaned over the felt table and positioned his stick. With one fluid movement, he slid it forward.

The satisfying thwack of his cue ball striking the red ball, filled the room.

"Good shot," a voice sounded from the doorway.

Rhys stiffened. Taking the cheroot between his fingers, he exhaled a circle of smoke. "You sound surprised," he drawled, facing his brother.

"At your billiards skills?" Miles chuckled. "Hardly. You were always a master of the table. Far more skilled than me." His eldest sibling drew the door shut behind him.

Rhys put out the remainder of his smoke on the edge of the table. Oh, bloody hell. So it was to be one of those visits.

"May I join you?" Miles was already striding over to the wall and collecting a stick.

"Be my guest." He motioned to the table. Whether his brother either heard or cared about the drollness of that invite, he gave no outward reaction.

Setting his stick down on the edge of the table, Miles gathered the three displaced balls and meticulously arranged them. Wordlessly, he looked to Rhys.

Rhys waved him on.

Positioning the red ball on the billiards spot, Miles led his play with the safety shot. "You were missed at dinner," he remarked after the balls had all settled.

"Yes." Rhys walked a path around the table, considering his move. "Given Mother's intentions, I trust I was," he said drolly, positioning his stick.

"I didn't refer to Mother," Miles murmured, as Rhys let his shot fly. "Rather by a lady. Lady Alice, that is."

The leather cue tip scraped the felt, widely missing the ball.

Miles grinned and, in one fluid motion, he took his shot. His cue connected with the yellow ball.

"You've never been one to play dirty," Rhys groused under his breath. Grabbing the chalk, he rubbed it along the tip of his cue stick.

"And you've never been one to court a lady."

There was truth to that. Even Rhys' secret betrothal had been to a Covent Garden actress.

"And is that what you believe?" he asked, training all his focus on the table, deliberately avoiding Miles' probing stare. "That I'm courting the lady?" He thrust his cue forward.

His shot just missed the baulk line.

Resting his stick on the edge of the table, Miles abandoned his poor showing of nonchalance. "Playing in the snow with Lady Alice?"

Over the course of his adult life, Rhys had been discovered in any number of compromising positions. This, however, was talk of Rhys and Alice, whose stolen interludes had been far more intimate than any moment before. He loosened his suddenly tight cravat and tossed it aside. "Faith and Violet?" His loquacious nieces couldn't keep a secret even if it meant they'd secure triple portions of dessert for the remainder of their lifetimes.

Miles lifted his head. "The very same."

"Traitors," he muttered without inflection.

"Outside on the terrace last evening?"

Rhys choked on his swallow. "You—?"

"Saw your flight to the gardens below?" A devilish grin played on Miles' lips. "Indeed."

Rhys slapped a hand across his eyes. God help him. Discovered by his eldest, always proper brother? Rhys' reputation as a rogue was officially in tatters. "Did anyone else… see?" he managed to force the question out.

"No," Miles assured. He paused. "Except for Henry Pratt. The gentleman rushed over to the window and set up camp there while the other gentlemen drank their brandies." He lowered his voice. "You've never dallied with innocents. That is why I trust there is, in fact… something more between you and the lady."

Rhys and Alice's courtship was a pretend one. As such, Rhys should be relieved that everyone had formed the exact erroneous conclusion he'd hoped they would. So why did his brother's questioning leave him so confounded. "Was there a question there?" he asked belatedly.

"It was an observation." Miles came 'round the table.

Rhys stiffened, bracing for a renewed lecture on respectability and the lady's reputation. His eldest brother stopped beside him and slapped him hard between the shoulder blades. "I wanted to speak to you," Miles began somberly, "and say it brings me joy knowing that you are, at last, happy."

That he was, at last, happy? Rhys tried to muster a suitable quip. A laugh. A half-grin. Anything. But God help him, with Alice, Rhys had been happy these past days; far happier than he'd been since Lillian's betrayal. Terror snaked around his chest.

Tiny footsteps pattered in the hallway. The door burst open and his youngest niece stormed the room. "Papa!" she cried, flying over to him.

Miles easily caught her about the waist, hauling her up. "Little

Bloom," he greeted, that endearing nickname.

After the curly-haired girl squished his face between her small hands. "I've been looking for you," she scolded. "I wanted you to read the story."

Rhys stared on, an interloper to the tender exchange between father and daughter. Although Rhys and his siblings had shared a bond, there had been an absence of the tangible warmth of Miles' young family. It was a dream he'd once carried for himself and long ago abandoned.

Now, with the pair before him quietly chatting, Rhys allowed himself the whisper of that dream, once more. In his mind's eye, Alice flickered forward as she'd someday be; a young mother, chasing her spirited children about.

And for a dangerously tantalizing moment, he saw himself as the equally joyous papa.

"Uncle Rhys?"

All the blood rushed to his ears and he jumped. "What?" he croaked.

Violet scrunched her brow up. "Are you sick? You look sick," she went on before he could speak. "Is that why you weren't at dinner? You didn't come play parlor games, either. Aunt Lettie and her friend, Alice, did. But I think she was sad that you weren't around. Why weren't you there?"

Flummoxed by the rapid-fire questioning, Rhys looked hopelessly at his brother.

Miles' eyes twinkled and he took mercy on his brother. Setting his daughter down, Miles ruffled the top of her head. "Come, we have a story to read."

"But Uncle Rhys—"

"Had an upset tummy but is better now," Miles assured, holding his hand out.

Violet nodded. "Very well." She pointed at Rhys. "But I expect to see you tomorrow." The little girl slid her fingers into Miles' and the pair started from the room. But Violet suddenly stopped in the doorway. "And Lady Alice. She wants to see you tomorrow, too."

A sharp bark of laughter exploded from his brother, as he urged his daughter on. "My apologies," he mouthed.

Rhys gave a flick of his hand, staring after the pair until they'd gone.

It would seem he'd done a rather convincing job at his pretend courtship of Alice. So convincing that he himself had gotten his thoughts about the lady all jumbled.

He started over to his cue and stopped, feeling her presence before he saw her.

"Alice," he called, collecting the stick.

Framed in the doorway, in an ice blue wrap front gown, her gleaming blonde tresses swept back, she had the look of a thawed ice princess. They stared at one another, time ceasing to matter. Rhys drank in the sight of her, his mouth dry. The imposed distance he'd kept between them that evening, proven wholly ineffective.

Her lips quirked up in a smile. "Tsk. Tsk. We had an arrangement, Lord Rhys."

Lord Rhys. It didn't escape his notice that she reverted to that formality when displeased.

"Were you looking to the empty doorway for me, madam?" he murmured, as she started forward.

"I may have been," she acknowledged. That directness was contrary to their Society, and his appreciation for Alice Winterbourne swelled. The lady picked up Miles' discarded cue and balanced it in her hands.

As his brother and niece had just shared, Alice had been searching for him. A lightness suffused his chest. "And I trust Pup Pratt noted your frequent glances about?"

Her smile faltered and it was like the room had been doused in cold. He mourned the loss of that camaraderie. "That is why you didn't come to dinner or join in the parlor games," she said flatly.

As much as he admired her frankness, he battled with himself to share that same honesty. For with every exchange and interaction, she kicked down the protective walls he'd carefully erected about himself. "No. That wasn't why," he quietly acknowledged.

"Is it…" Alice fiddled with the cue stick "Because of what I'd asked earlier, about your broken heart?"

Rhys stiffened. How could she, this woman he'd only known a few short days, have such a terrifyingly accurate read on him and his thoughts? Fingers shaking, he rescued his thoroughly rumpled jacket from a nearby sofa and fished out a cheroot. Presenting his back to her, he used a nearby sconce to light the tip. He took a long, slow inhale, letting it fill his lungs. "I didn't say I'd ever had my heart broken," he said carefully after he'd exhaled.

"Yes, you did." Alice positioned the cue and expertly slid the stick forward. The cue ball struck its mark.

He searched his mind.

"Just not directly," she clarified, straightening from her shot. Abandoning her stick, she circled back around and stopped a mere handsbreadth away. "It's how you know," she said softly, searching her clever gaze over his face.

"Know what?" he asked cautiously, taking another draw from his cheroot.

"Wounded eyes... strained smile... slumped shoulders," she said, a repetition of the charges he'd leveled at her days earlier. Alice turned her delicate palms up. "You recognized all the signs of heartbreak because you yourself *experienced* it." Hers wasn't a question, but rather a statement that left him raw; splayed open before her.

When no one ever delved beyond the surface of the façade Rhys had presented before the world, this woman had gathered the secrets he kept.

Contemplating his response, he flicked his ashes into the rose medallion tray at the end of the table. "I did."

"What happened?" she asked quietly.

Rhys studied the burning tip of his cheroot. "I was young, nine and ten, nearly twenty when I... met her." He stared beyond the top of Alice's golden curls, to the opposite end of the room. "You fell in love with Pratt for his love of books and seriousness. I fell in love with Lillian for her smile." In the end, that artful expression had proven nothing more than a trick she'd employed upon the stage. "She was quite the actress," he murmured to himself.

"She lied to you?" Alice ventured haltingly.

"There was that." He took another puff of his cheroot. "But it was also what she did. Lillian was a performer, one of the most acclaimed actresses in Covent Garden."

Alice's lips moved but no sound came out. And then... "You fell in love with an actress."

Knowing the tenacious lady before him would never be content with only that partial telling, he hurried on with his accounting. "My father and mother discovered my intentions to wed Lillian. They threatened to cut me off. I told them to go to hell, that I was marrying her anyway."

Alice clenched a hand at her breast. "What happened?"

The memory of that day came rushing back; the shock, the agony, the absolute... numbness. "One afternoon, I paid a visit to my friend's residence. We were to ride that morning and he never arrived. I was shown to his study. I came upon Anthony and Lillian locked in an embrace."

Horror wreathed Alice's features. "Your friend?" she choked out.

He nodded. Odd, how now those remembrances didn't threaten to rip him apart. When had they ceased to hurt?

Alice let fly a black curse that singed even his ears.

Rhys grinned, a lightness filling him at her fury on his behalf.

He finished his telling. "I turned around and walked out. Lillian never knew I was there. Anthony, however, came rushing after me and explained why he bestowed his attention upon her. It was a bid to save me from myself. My mother had put him up to it and he acted on my behalf."

"Oh, Rhys," Alice whispered. Stretching a hand out, she brushed his fingers.

"It was just a kiss. But it didn't matter. It was what that kiss represented. Betrayal. The end of a dream. The death of a friendship." And a new person had been born that night.

Warm, delicate fingers covered his.

It was the first time he'd spoken of that night... to anyone. And there was a catharsis in this moment. "I was better for it," he acknowledged to the both of them. "I know that now." He hadn't at the time. Just as Alice would someday come to find herself fortunate to have escaped marriage to Pratt.

"That doesn't make it easier. It doesn't make the shame and regret go away," she said gently. Alice worked her gaze over his face. "Their betrayal is the reason you became a rogue."

He lifted his shoulders in a negligent shrug. "It is far easier to feel nothing than... the sting of heartbreak."

"I thought that after Henry." Layering her palms to the edge of the table, she arched up on her heels. "But is it, truly, Rhys?" Alice shoved away from the mahogany piece and drifted close. The faintest hint of lilac filled his senses. "Just days ago, I myself thought the same... but now?" She tipped her head back, holding his gaze squarely. "I'm not altogether certain."

Rhys swallowed hard. Her lush mouth beckoned. Hooding his lashes, he dipped his head, lower—

A sharp voice sounded from the doorway, killing the moment. "Where have you been, Rhys Winston Grayson Brook—?" That sharp question came to a screeching halt.

Her cheeks ablaze, Alice leapt back.

And for the first time in the whole of his life, the impossible had been accomplished—his mother, the dowager marchioness of Guilford... had been silenced.

"It is fine," Rhys whispered for Alice's ears alone. The last thing his mother would do was reveal to the world that she'd found Alice and Rhys together, without a chaperone... not when it went against her marital hopes for Rhys.

Horror wreathing Alice's features, she dipped a hasty curtsy, and he ached to call her back. To tell her his mother's opinion mattered even less now than it had to him all those years ago when she'd found another young woman wanting.

In the end, he said nothing, and Alice escaped past the miserable harpie still frozen to the thin, Aubusson carpet.

The faint click of the door closing jerked his cold parent from her shock. "What in the blazes is the meaning of this?" She swept forward in a noisy rustle of her taffeta skirts. "You sneak off with that harlot—"

"Have a care," he warned in frosty tones. He'd be damned to hell before he allowed his mother to disparage Alice. With her spirit, wit, and honor, she was a far better person than any of the rotted souls he'd met in Polite Society.

The dowager marchioness pursed her lips. "Is this about your business dealings with her wastrel brother?"

The air hissed between Rhys' teeth. "My God, you truly are heartless." She believed Rhys' interest in Alice had something to do with a desire to grow his already plentiful coffers.

"Is it?" she demanded.

Rhys swiped his jacket from the sofa and shrugged into the garment. "Go to hell, Mama."

"What of Aria?" she implored. "Our familial connection. Surely, you'll not throw those expectations away on the Winterbourne girl. With her blood, she'll hurt you just as that other woman did."

Fury lanced through him. Stalking forward, he grabbed the door handle. "Rhys," she screeched, as he opened the oak panel. "Come back here. I am not finished. She will hurt you. Mark my—"

And with her furious diatribe trailing in his wake, Rhys took his leave.

CHAPTER 16

¶IT HAD BEEN ONE WEEK: one week since Alice and Rhys had entered into their arrangement.

Each morning, Alice and Rhys could be discovered walking the sprawling grounds of the Kent countryside. When they returned, they adjourned to the library where they read and shared their favorite literary works. And during the evening meals, Rhys maneuvered sitting beside Alice, and they spoke quietly, the rest of the room forgotten, about his business ventures and Alice's opinions on them.

Everyone attending the Marquess and Marchioness of Guilford's house party sighed over the rapid courtship between Alice and Rhys. And with their devotion to one another, they'd done a masterful job of convincing all that the pretense was real.

But somewhere along the way, the lines of reality and pretend had blurred for Alice. At some point, Rhys had reminded her how to smile, erased the heartache left by Henry's betrayal, and made her long, once more, for a dream she'd given up hope on—the love of a devoted, honorable, clever gentleman.

And there could be no doubting, despite his reputation as a scoundrel, Rhys was far nobler than all the lords in London. Unlike Henry, who'd cared more about his reputation as a barrister, Rhys was one who when he loved, did so deeply and without apology, and certainly didn't allow rank or Societal expectations to drive him.

But his heart had been broken beyond repair, and no one... certainly not Alice, could ever have anything with him.

It was why Alice desperately needed distance from him. Space with which to think, to order her thoughts, and to construct walls to keep herself safe from Rhys Brookfield's magnetic pull.

Or mayhap it is too late...

Standing beside the ceiling to floor windows in her room, she peered out through the crack in the curtains to where the guests gathered in the courtyard. She searched among the dark cloaks for one gentleman—and found him, with young Violet perched on his shoulders.

The little girl removed his hat and waved it about. The pair engaged in a back and forth tug of war with Rhys ultimately winning. He settled the black Empire hat atop Violet's head. The too-large article instantly sank over the eyes of the giggling child. Alice squeezed her eyes shut as her heart shifted perilously in her breast.

"Are you listening to me?" Lettie's concern-laden voice brought Alice's eyes reluctantly open. "I've been waiting for you—"

"I am not going," Alice said for the benefit of the young lady reflected back in the crystal panels.

Silence fell. "What do you mean you aren't coming?" Lettie demanded when she found her voice.

Alice toyed with a golden tassel affixed to the fabric. "Well, it means I won't be joining you."

Lettie took a hesitant step forward, when there had never been anything remotely cautious about her friend. "Have you and Rhys had a spat?"

Alice sought him out once more and found him.

She fisted her hands, as icy tendrils of jealousy swept through her.

Young Violet still cradled in his arms, Rhys now spoke with the dark-haired beauty his mother had hand-selected as his bride. Alice wanted to despise her. She wanted to find Aria Cunning loathsome and hateful as those stunning Diamonds of the First Water oftentimes were. Miss Cunning caught Violet's fingers and gave them a playful shake.

Alice sank her teeth into her lower lip. But she could not. The other woman, when they'd conversed, had proven only kind and clever and blast it, the manner of lady Alice would call friend.

Lettie hovered at Alice's side, looking out. "Is… this about Aria and Rhys?" she ventured. "Because I've seen the way he looks at you and I know my brother enough to say there is nothing between him and—"

"No," Alice rasped, spinning around, the curtain sliding back into place. She drew in a steadying breath, and tried again. "This has nothing to do with Miss Cunning and Rhys," she said in even tones. It had everything to do with Alice.

Lettie peered at her. "Then *what?*"

Tell her. She is your friend. She deserves the truth about this game of pretend you play with her brother.

Alice covered her face with her hands and breathed in. Then, letting her arms fall to her sides, she revealed the truth. "It is a lie."

Lettie puzzled her brow. "What?"

"Our courtship." Before her courage deserted her, Alice shared everything; from her and Rhys' first meeting in The Copse to Rhys' proposal. She took care to leave out the one stolen moment of passion in the library. When she'd finished, only silence met her recounting. Needing to fill the void, Alice wandered over to the edge of the window and pressed her forehead against the wall. "I'm sorry I kept all this from you," she said softly.

Lettie clasped her hands before her. "Mayhap your courtship with Rhys did begin as a ruse," she said with more seriousness than Alice had ever heard from her. "But somewhere along the way, something changed," her friend went on in an eerie echo of Alice's fears.

"You're wrong," she said, her voice emerging sharper than she intended.

"I might be," Lettie conceded. She rested a hand on Alice's shoulder. "But the fact that you are hiding from Rhys even now tells me that it's more likely I'm correct."

"I cannot…" Alice swallowed around the lump in her throat, unable to voice that fear aloud. *I love him.* Her legs weakened and she shot her hands out, catching the edge of the windowsill to keep upright. Her mind, heart, and soul immediately revolted at that whisper of a thought.

She could not love him. He was a rogue who'd had his heart broken once and had been abundantly clear with the fact that the last thing he desired was to walk the path of love, again. Just as she had vowed. But that had been before Rhys had barged into The Copse and flipped her world upside down.

"We've known one another not even a fortnight." Who was that entreaty for? Lettie or herself?

Lettie took Alice by the forearms. She brought her friend around to face her. "You were betrothed to Henry for more than a year. So mayhap, time truly means nothing in the scheme of one's heart."

Her pulse hammered loudly in Alice's ears.

She shook her head.

Lettie nodded.

No.

Lettie smiled. "Yes."

Restive, Alice rushed back to the window and found Rhys mingling below. Beating his gloves, he did a sweep of the guests. "But he doesn't want a bride." He'd had his heart broken and was content to live a bachelor's carefree existence. Wasn't he?

Lettie chuckled. "Men invariably don't know *what* they want. While we, women? We do." She wrinkled her nose. "Which is really what makes this," she swatted a hand in Alice's direction, "all so frustrating. I'm disappointed in you, Alice. I shouldn't have to convince you to trust your heart. You should do so yourself."

But she had, once before, and it had ended failingly bad.

She touched her forehead to the cool windowpane, finding Henry in the small crowd below. Or mayhap it had ended precisely as it had been intended. She hadn't loved Henry. She knew that now. Not truly. She'd loved the idea of what he represented and the bucolic future she'd dreamed of; the family she'd not had. With his staidness and single-minded devotion to his work, he could never have been that man.

Her gaze slid over to Lettie's older brother and their stares locked. A warmth unfurled in her belly. How was it possible for a man, more than a hundred feet below, to make her feel like she was the only woman in the world?

Rhys grinned. He lifted his palms in silent question.

She'd, however, made too many mistakes before; Henry, their betrothal, her public display. The caution that she'd allowed to drive her since The Scandal reared itself. Alice shook her head. "I cannot," she mouthed.

His smile dipped. "Of course, you can," his lips slowly articulated. He gathered the two pairs of ice skates resting at his feet. Holding them by their metal curls, he lifted them up. "A race?" he mouthed.

Alice hesitated, wanting to say no. Nay, needing to. With every encounter, she lost more and more of her heart to the roguish Rhys Brookfield.

Need that be so very tragic? What if she and Rhys, both with once broken hearts, could, in fact, heal one another? That whisper of a thought slid forward, dangerous in its appeal.

Rhys motioned once more for her to join him.

Alice smiled.

I am lost.

She nodded.

"Pretend courtship my arse," Lettie muttered. And taking Alice by the hand, she tugged her friend along.

OTHER THAN A SOLEMN "GOOD morning", Alice hadn't uttered a single word to him since she'd joined the gathering of guests a short while ago. Instead, as they made the trek to the lake, she remained more laconic than he'd ever known her to be.

Not even during their first meeting in The Copse.

He broke the silence. "I trust this means you're unable to skate."

Blinking like an owl startled from its perch, Alice stared questioningly up at him.

"First, there was your intention of skipping the lakeside revelry. Tsk. Tsk. That is certainly not like you."

"And you know me so well?" she asked curiously.

The unexpectedness of that question gave him pause.

For... he did. In a short time, they'd forged an unlikely friendship. He'd learned her many smiles and all their meanings. He knew the books she enjoyed and the ones she'd gladly use as kindling. Unnerved, he redirected his gaze to the party moving more quickly ahead of them. "You're afraid of racing me, then?" he put forward because, in this instance, it was safer to settle for the light teasing of before, than all the uncertainty that came with the unnamed emotions swirling in his chest.

Alice snorted, returning them to their usual camaraderie. "The arrogance of you, Rhys Brookfield. You're entirely too big."

"I beg your pardon?" he asked, indignantly. With his spare hand, he patted his flat stomach. He wasn't one of those paunchy lords who indulged in too much drink and dessert.

Clear, bell-like laughter spilled from Alice's lips, rolling around the countryside. "Tall," she clarified, stretching a palm above her head. "Muscu—" Color fired her cheeks.

Pure, masculine satisfaction gripped him. "What was that?"

She rolled her eyes. "Don't preen. It doesn't suit you."

They reached the clearing where the other guests had already taken seats on boulders and logs scattered about the frozen lake. Finding a quiet area on the fringe of the group, Rhys guided them over.

He held a hand out to assist Alice onto the fallen trunk but she was already settling herself onto the makeshift bench. Her emerald cloak fanned out behind her, revealing the hem of her sapphire blue gown... and for a too-brief instant, the hint of her trim lower legs. He swallowed hard. How had he failed to appreciate the inherent allure of those limbs until now? Or mayhap it was only this woman: who stirred his lust with a barely-there glimpse of her skin and flouted Societal conventions with an ease greater than his own?

You won't tell me, then?" he asked, affixing one of the metal skates to his boots.

"Tell you, what?"

"The reason you wished to remain indoors," Rhys elucidated. "Surely, it wasn't because you preferred to embroider with my dear mama, Lady Lovell, and Lady Hammell?"

Alice's lips pulled in the corners. "Decidedly not. I'd rather stick a needle in my eye than an embroidery frame."

He laughed. That sound was naturally stripped of the artifice and jaded cynicism that had held him in its snare since Anthony and Lillian. And how very good it felt to laugh again. Rhys looked up and the teasing reply died on his lips.

The sun's rays cast Alice in a soft glow; highlighting the shades of blonde to those luxuriant strands. He ached from his need to yank free his gloves and tangle his fingers in her hair once more.

"What is it?" she whispered.

Everything. It was the absolute upheaval of his world set into disarray by the spirited woman before him. "Nothing," he said gruffly. Did she hear the lie there? And why did that not terrify him as it should? "Your skate, madam," he murmured, reaching for the metal blade.

Without another word passing between them, Rhys strapped the skates to her boots and helped her stand.

The laughter of the other guests rang cheerfully through the countryside. Stepping onto the ice, he offered Alice his arm.

She glided forward with a long, fluid movements, doing a half-circle around him.

"You skate, Lady Alice," he called after her as she skated off.

Alice did a perfect pirouette, her skirts whipping about her ankles. She winged an eyebrow up. "Did you believe I lied?" she shot back, her gaze on him as she skated backwards.

"No." Clasping his hands behind him, Rhys lengthened his strides to reach her. His sharpened blades left a trail of dust in the ice. "I believed you did as a girl. I failed to consider you still, in fact, skated." After all, even his own sisters had abandoned the pursuits deemed too athletic to ever be proper by their mother.

"Should all joyful activities cease because a lady makes her entrance into Society?"

That was certainly the expectation among the *ton*. It was a belief Rhys' own straight-laced mother had ascribed to the whole of her lifetime. "Hardly," he acknowledged. "And yet, that is what so many do when stern mamas exert their influence."

Alice slowed her movements and glided to a near stop. "I never had a mother around to reign in my spirited ways," she said wistfully.

Her brother was Rhys' most recent business partner. However, those financial dealings they had with one another drove their entire relationship. Aside from the former rakish existence the Earl of Montfort had lived, the man's familial life had been his own, and of little interest to Rhys—until now. Rhys skated ahead, positioning himself in front of her. He crossed his legs back and forth, keeping pace with her forward movements. Questions swirled around his mind. In the time he'd come to know her, he'd learned so much about Alice Winterbourne and, yet, much of her life was still a mystery. "Do you have any memories of her?" It was the first time he'd ever asked any woman intimate questions about her family. They were details that had proven irrelevant—until Alice.

A gust of wind whipped about them, tossing her bonnet back. Not breaking stride, Alice adjusted the garish headwear he'd mocked at their first meeting, and now appreciated it as so endearingly her. Alice glided to a smooth stop at the edge of the lake where an old, gnarled oak's branches arched over the now frozen waters. Removing the hat, Alice turned it over in her hands, contemplating the garish article. "I never knew my mother," she said softly. "She died in childbirth." Alice paused. "She died birthing me," she quietly amended. "My father resented me the whole of my life for it."

An ache settled heavy in his chest for the loss she'd known. Desperate to imagine a sliver of happiness for the girl she'd been, he asked, "What of Montfort?" Before he'd become the rake who'd scandalized Polite Society, had he been one who'd looked after her and been a friend or playmate?

Her lips formed a half-grin. "Daniel couldn't have been bothered with me," she said without inflection. Rhys silently cursed his business partner to hell for having failed Alice. Having grown up without a mother, and both a father and brother invisible presences in her life, how strong she'd had to be. His admiration for Alice grew all the more. "Now, he is devoted," she said on a rush, defending a sibling who was undeserving of that loyalty. "Where other girls and young ladies were dealing with decorous mothers, I was riding across the countryside, trying spirits and cheroots, and living freely."

How very solitary the image she painted of her childhood. Rhys stared off to where Miles and his young family moved in careful circles over the ice. Philippa slowly pulled Faith by her hands, gliding along with her daughter. From where she stood along the shore, Lettie clapped loudly, cheering her nieces on.

How many years had he spent bemoaning his propriety-driven parents? They'd been endlessly proper, so devoted to the Guilford line, he'd resented their failure to see him as anything more than the spare to Miles' heir. However, Rhys had been blessed with loving siblings, and a mother and father who, even as they'd failed in many ways, had played a part in his becoming the man he had. He might have despised his mother for her interference with Lillian, but the truth remained—she'd saved him from himself.

Shame filled him for dwelling on the darker aspects of his family and not the gifts he'd enjoyed in them.

"This was hers," Alice murmured, pulling him back from his regret-filled musings. Settling onto the edge of a boulder, she lifted her bonnet—that same article he'd mocked upon their first meeting.

A vise cinched about his chest. How dismissive he'd been... with Alice and everyone. It made him wish he'd been a better person before her, and not because she'd opened his eyes to the truth of his character. "I am so sorry," he said hoarsely, claiming the spot beside her.

Alice chuckled. "It really is ugly."

He made a sound of protest.

"Oh, but it is. I know that. It's quite garish, with entirely too many adornments, and yet," she contemplated the frayed strings of that bonnet. A gentle wind rolled over the frozen lake and tugged at the ribbons. "I love it," she said softly. "When I was a girl, my father ordered every hint of her gone from our household. While everything was being carted away, I sneaked into her chambers and found this. It was one of the few articles that hadn't yet been removed. I plucked it from her bed and raced from the room."

Her telling was so vivid it conjured an image of Alice as she would have been then; a determined little girl, desperately clinging to a scrap of the mother she'd never known. Pain settled sharp in his chest.

"Every day, for so many years, I would just stare at this bonnet. It was a window into the life of a mother I'd never known. All these ribbons and flowers and..." Again laughing, Alice shook her head. "pins. I insisted the modiste who came to fit me create similar monstrosities."

"Not with the ribbons *and* flowers?"

"Oh, yes." Alice waggled her eyebrows. "*And* the pins." Her shoulders shook with the force of her amusement so pure and infectious that he joined in. "Along the hem, all the way up to my knees were these b-big billowing pink bows." She laughed, tears pouring down her cheeks as she held her palms out, demonstrating the size of those accents.

"S-Surely not?" he managed through his own mirth.

"And there were metal medallions around my waist th-that would jingle when I w-walked." Alice doubled over, clutching at her middle. Little snorts escaped her.

His laughter abating, Rhys caressed his eyes over her, and something shifted deep in his chest. Hers were not the practiced giggles or sultry laughs of previous lovers. Rather, there was an unfettered beauty to her mirth that held him enthralled.

Her amusement faded, and she dusted the moisture from her cheeks. "And then one day, I must have been eight or nine... I wanted to sneak away from my lessons and take one of my father's mounts for a ride."

"But you were wearing that dress," he ventured.

"Precisely," she confirmed with a nod.

"It would have been impossible to ride in such a monstrosity."

"For me?" She snorted. "Hardly. I would have just rucked it up."

His grin widened as he imagined the spirited imp she'd been as a girl. Her daughters would one day be the same; golden-curled, troublesome minxes who tossed flawless snowballs and sneaked off from their lessons. Only, in his mind's eye, that small child was embroiled in a snow battle between Alice and Rhys, and not some nameless stranger.

And I want that future...

The air left him on a whoosh; terror and denial all rolling together. The last thing he wanted or needed was marriage.

Wasn't it?

Alice continued through his riot of emotions. She lifted an index finger. "The *true* difficulty came in trying to sneak away. Every time I turned a corner, my nasty nursemaid would call out, 'I hear you, Lady Alice'," she said, her voice pitched high. Alice let her hand fall to her lap, and gazed out to where Violet and Faith now skated with their parents. A longing smile graced her lips. "I raced into the one place no one was permitted entry—my mother's chambers." The wind whipped a stray curl across her cheek and, reflexively, Rhys gathered that strand and tucked it behind her ear. He hung, enrapt by her words, wanting to know everything about her. He'd sort through the significance of that at a later time. For now, he wanted the remainder of her tale, and then she held out that gift. "I was out of breath, leaning against the door panel, and there was this... *silence*." She closed her eyes. "The kind that rings in your ears and hums. I can still hear it now." Alice opened her eyes. "And that is when I realized," she murmured.

He leaned closer. "What?"

"I could continue wearing those dresses, clinging to the past. All the while allowing my miserable nursemaid to find me." Alice held his gaze. "Or I could shed them and live for now."

Those handful of words were wrapped with layers of meanings.

How long had he been trapped by a past of hurt and betrayal? Only, he'd allowed himself to be fixed on Lillian and Anthony's treachery, and his mother's role in breaking up his betrothal.

Emotion wadded in Rhys' throat.

He covered one of Alice's hands with his. Alice glanced at their connected fingers, and then held his gaze.

And together, with the joyful guests skating in the distance, Alice and Rhys simply sat and there was a soothing peace in just being with her.

CHAPTER 17

⁋IT WAS MADNESS.

It was the height of foolishness in those romantic tales she'd once read—and had, of late, with Rhys' encouragement, begun reading again.

It was folly at every level.

Alice beat a frantic path back and forth over the Aubusson carpet.

Outside, the earlier calm of the weather had given way to great winds that howled forlornly over the countryside. Those gusts battered the windowpanes as if Mother Nature herself sought to beat down the door and shake sense into Alice's head. To remind her of the great folly she'd made before… over another man.

And yet—

Alice jerked to a stop, her night skirts tangling about her legs. She forced herself to confront head on the realization she'd fought.

"I love him," she whispered the truth aloud, lending it a reality that sent panic through her. "I love Rhys Brookfield." Notorious rogue and wicked charmer. Her heart thudded hard against her ribcage. And yet, he was so much more than the world saw; so much more than he let the world see of him.

He possessed a clever humor that unfailingly brought her to laughter, but was also a scholar who could debate legal texts and romantic literature with equal acumen. Unlike her former betrothed, who'd turned his nose up at pleasurable pursuits, Rhys reveled in them and had reminded Alice herself of the joy to be found around her.

He was both a devoted brother and a loving uncle who played child's games with his young nieces.

And God save her, in the short time Alice had been here with Rhys, she'd fallen hopelessly and helplessly in love with him.

Alice's legs gave out and she caught the back of the caned vanity chair to keep from falling. Her mind railed against the very thought that had been rolling terrifyingly around her thoughts that day. She'd loved and lost in the most spectacularly humiliating way with Henry, and had vowed to never be made the fool again.

Alice slid into the folds of the white painted seat and stared blankly ahead.

These feelings, however, stirring deep inside her breast defied pride and past mistakes. What had come before with Henry she could readily acknowledge now had not truly been love, but rather the dream of *being* in love.

And this, paralyzing, terror-inducing sentiment was anything but the grandiose portrait she'd painted in her mind two years ago.

Alice sucked a breath in slowly through her clenched teeth. "He doesn't want to marry," she directed that at her pale visage reflected back in the Moorish side vanity cabinet. "This has all been a pretense and nothing more." Except, even as that utterance slid from her lips, the inherent lie echoed back at her.

From her and Rhys' first meeting, there had been a charged awareness between them. She might be a virgin still at nine and ten, but there could be no mistaking the burn in his eyes each time she entered a room or the passion spilling from his frame as he'd embraced her. No, those sentiments were real—in every way. She'd tasted enough bliss in Rhys' arms to recognize a mutual desire in his eyes.

Alice chewed at the tip of her index finger, shredding the nail. But what did that truly mean? He lusted after her. The ease of his smile and laughter bespoke a man who very much enjoyed her company.

Was that enough for a man such as Rhys, however? Could he set aside past heartbreaks and trust himself to love again, more specifically—to love her?

Alice dropped her head onto the vanity. "You are assuming

he could love you," she muttered, lightly knocking her forehead against the wood. Rogues and rakes did *not* marry. Alice knew that well. Yes, her brother had... but that was one gentleman in a sea of other scoundrels.

A light rapping sounded at the front of the room.

Her eyes sought the Boulle mantel clock.

Twenty minutes after eleven o'clock.

It had been inevitable. With the guests since retired for the evening, Lettie would seek her out now. She groaned. It had been too much to hope her friend would have let the matter of Alice and Rhys' pretend courtship rest. Another knock filled the room, this one louder, more determined. "I am sleeping," she called out.

Silence fell, and then—

"I would be remiss if I did not point out that by your answer alone, you are still very much awake." The unexpected, muffled tones of Lady Guilford faintly penetrated the oak panel.

Alice's stomach lurched. "Oh, bloody hell," she whispered, her horrified gaze locked on the mirror and that panel reflected over her shoulder.

What could the marchioness want with *her* and at this hour, no less?

Lady Guilford again scratched at the panel.

Alice shoved to her feet, sending the legs of her chair scraping the hardwood floor. Lurching across the room, she grabbed the handle.

Alice drew in a deep breath and opened the door.

The marchioness stared back, a kindly smile wreathing her delicate features. "Alice," she greeted with a warm familiarity of one who'd forever called her friend and not just met at the house party hosted by Lady Guilford.

"My lady," she said belatedly, dropping a curtsy. Still attired in a deep purple satin gown, the other woman evinced regal grace and elegance. Alice gripped the closures at the front of her wrapper. "Won't you please come in?"

Lettie's sister-in-law waved her hand. "Please, just Philippa," she murmured, closing the heavy panel behind them. "I hope you're enjoying your time here."

"Oh, immensely. Very much so." While those words held truth now, that hadn't been the case before Rhys' arrival. Before then, she'd been downtrodden and pitiable. Rhys had opened her eyes to the person she'd allowed herself to become and she never again wanted to be that pathetic creature she was before he entered her life.

They stared at one another through a stilted silence.

"My mother-in-law has not been overly kind to you," the marchioness blurted.

Of all the statements, questions, or pleasantries to come, that had certainly been the least of which Alice expected from her hostess. "My lady?" she asked, carefully. After all, what in blazes did one say to that?

"Philippa," the other woman corrected. "Please, sit," she motioned to the nearby Rococo floral upholstered chair. "Mine was not so much a question as an observation," she continued after Alice had settled herself onto the edge of her seat with her hands primly folded. Lady Guilford sank unceremoniously onto the needlepoint stool.

Alice weighed her words before replying. "Her Ladyship has not said anything to make me feel unwelcome," she reassured. There. That was at the very least true as a formality. The cold glances and scowls directed Alice's way, however, had spoken volumes about the woman's opinion.

Lettie's sister-in-law shook her head. "There are other ways to make a person feel unwanted," she said, unerringly accurate in the path Alice's thoughts had wandered. "I came from the billiards room where my husband and his brother were playing." She collected her hands and gave them a slight squeeze. "I have never seen Rhys as happy as he has been this past fortnight with you."

This is why she'd come. Just like Lettie, Philippa, the Marchioness of Guilford, had believed the lie. "I'm sure you are mistaken," she said softly, wishing the other women were correct. All the while, knowing Rhys had been ready with a smile from when they'd first met. The memory of their first exchange in The Copse slipped in and a smile pulled at her lips. Well… not at first. "Rhys…" Her cheeks warmed. "*Lord* Rhys, he is always cheerful."

"Not like this," Philippa protested. "He cares about you. It is there in the way he watches your every movement and the way you two are around one another. As though the world has fallen away but for you two."

Alice's heart did a somersault. "Truly?"

The marchioness grinned. "*Truly.*" Her smile quickly faded. "My husband and I are both aware of my mother-in-law's… expectations for Rhys."

Miss Cunning.

"Miss Cunning," Philippa murmured.

She'd spoken aloud.

Alice's gut clenched.

"My mother-in-law believes she knows what is best for her children, and attempts to guide them toward that which she thinks is right…" She wrinkled her nose. "Including their spouses. But she loves her children and, as a mother myself, I appreciate that means she is not altogether bad."

Alice stared quizzically at the other woman. "Why are you telling me this?" she asked slowly.

"I expect the dowager marchioness will eventually interfere."

"You speak as one who knows," she observed.

"She came to me and called into question my worth as a woman and mother." A fierce glint lit the marchioness' eyes. "I'll not allow her to do that to anyone else, and certainly not a guest in my household." Philippa sank onto the stool. "She will not be content until Rhys weds Miss Cunning." Not unless. Rather, until. One word and yet it clawed at her insides. "But no one has the place to interfere in matters of the heart." Using the footstool to push herself upright, the marchioness stood. "Forgive me for intruding so late on your sleep. With the house party ending soon, I thought it essential I not wait any longer for us to speak."

"Oh, I was not sleeping." Alice jumped up. "I was—"

Philippa winked.

"You were jesting," she said with a smile, recalling the lie she'd called out.

"I was." She started for the doorway.

"My lady… Philippa," she called after her.

Lettie's sister-in-law glanced back.

"Thank you," Alice said.

"It was my pleasure. Oh, and Alice? My husband was planning to take his leave a short while ago of Rhys. He most definitely left him in the Billiards Room… alone." She winked. And with that, the other woman took her leave.

In the silence, with only herself once more for company, the marchioness' words and warning played around her mind. As did the encouragement she'd sent Alice with that wink.

He cares about you. It is there in the way he watches your every movement and the way you two are around one another. As though the world has fallen away but for you two...

Alice fisted the sides of her wrapper. Perhaps, Philippa was correct. Or perhaps, Alice merely wished her to be correct. Regardless, Alice had never been a coward.

"I love him," she repeated. This time, that utterance didn't usher in terror but rather a thrill that set her heart into a double-time rhythm. And she'd not forgive herself if she did not tell him.

The Billiards Room.

Grabbing the door handle, Alice sprinted from the room. With determination fueling her steps, she rushed through Lord Guilford's quiet household. The periodic groan of an aged floorboard pierced the silence. Gone was the fear that had dogged her this day. In its place was a giddiness... a thrilling anticipation at what might be with him.

Alice raced around the corner—and collided with a tall, solidly built gentleman.

Strong hands instantly caught Alice, steadying her before she tumbled on her buttocks. "Forgive m..." That breathless apology died a swift death. "Oh."

Her former betrothed adjusted his wire-rimmed spectacles. "Allice," he greeted, a slight slur to his speech.

There had been a time, not so very long ago, when the mere sight of this man had filled her with sadness. Now, she accepted that she'd merely mourned the future she wanted—love, a family, a doting husband. Henry had represented the vehicle with which to obtain those dreams. Now, she saw that if they had married, how unfair it would have been to the both of them.

"If you'll excuse me?" She made to step around him, but he matched her movements.

His gaze, always deferential and direct now moved up and down her person, lingering on her bare feet and then settling on her slightly gaping wrapper.

Gasping, Alice clutched the garment closed.

"You shouldn't be wandering the halls... as you are."

The initial shock of running into him abated. Now, Alice noted the details that had previously escaped her: the rumpled, slightly out of mode green jacket, the heavy scent of spirits wafting from his person, his bloodshot eyes.

"You're foxed," she blurted. Henry, who'd never even danced a waltz with her because of the immodesty of that set, now stood before her ape-drunk.

He took an uneven step forward and Alice easily moved from his path.

"You are off to seeeee himmm, aren't you?" Her former betrothed stumbled, knocking into the wall.

Alice stole a frantic glance about. The last thing she needed was being caught alone, in discussion with her former intended—her now drunken former betrothed. "I don't answer to you, Henry," she said tightly. How had she ever imagined a future with a man who'd be so controlling of her actions? Again, Alice made to leave but he blocked her retreat.

Henry leaned a shoulder against the wall. "Do youuuu love him-mmm?"

The last person deserving of that admission from her lips was the one before her now. No, when she uttered those three words they would be for Rhys.

"You are drunk," she said. "It is late and it would be scandalous if we were discovered toget—eek."

Henry took her arm in a surprisingly strong grip. "You *doooo*," he whispered. "Or you thiiiink you doooo, anyway. But you don't." He pitched forward, propelling Alice against the wall, crushing her with his body. His hand tightened about her forearm.

Alice tightened her mouth. "Unhand me."

His once-beloved features contorted into a paroxysm of anguish. "I love you."

She blanched. "For the love of all that is holy, you are *married*."

He rested his brow against hers. "It shooould have been you. It wasss a mistake."

Unease swirled inside her. This was Pup Pratt, harmless as a dove. And yet stinking of spirits and unrelenting with his touch. "You made your decision," she said calmly, in a bid to reason with him. Logic had always ruled his existence. "You have a wife."

"Was thiisss to make me jealous," he breathed against her ear.

"Because if it was, Alice, it worked outrageously wellll."

The irony was not lost on her that of all the people who'd believed Alice and Rhys' pretend courtship was, in fact, the one person the ruse had been for. And he had seen it for what it was. "You presume much," she bit out. Alice gave a hard shove, but he pressed his body to hers.

Panic roared to life.

"I missss you. So very much," he groaned and Alice recoiled.

"Henry, do not—"

His mouth slammed down on hers obliterating that demand, overwhelming her with the heavy scent of brandy. She angled her head sideways, attempting to escape him. He thrust his tongue inside her mouth.

Rage blotted out all her panic. Gripping him by his shirtfront she raised her knee, but he caught her movement, caressing her leg through her skirts.

"My goodness. You shameful wanton." That outraged cry broke through Henry's liquor-soaked brain. Panting, he jumped back...

And coward that he'd proven himself to be on numerous scores, Henry fled, tripping over himself with the speed by which he made his escape.

Alice's heart fell, sliding to her belly and then sinking all the way to her toes as she faced their audience. Alone.

"Shameful. Utterly shameful." The seething dowager marchioness glowered at Alice.

Ignoring the stinging diatribe the older woman proceeded to unleash, she trained her attention not on the Marquess of Guilford who flanked her right side but the other gentleman.

Silent.

Immobile.

Grey-faced.

"Rhys," Alice whispered.

He opened and closed his mouth several times, no words coming out.

Alice stared riveted, horror lancing through her, as a memory tripped in. She touched her fingers to lips still swollen from Henry's assault.

A loud buzzing filled her ears.

It was just a kiss. But it didn't matter. It was what that kiss represented.

Betrayal. The end of a dream. The death of a friendship...

Footsteps sounded from a nearby corridor, jolting Alice and the Brookfields from their dazed state.

"I suggest you take yourself off, Lady Alice, before you earn yourself any more attention this evening." Rhys' mother glanced pointedly at Alice's gaping wrapper.

Alice clenched the sides of the modest article, gripping the fabric tight for the weak lifeline it was. "It was not how it looked," she said, proud of that even deliverance, one she offered not for this harpie's benefit but for the stone-faced man beside her.

"Oh, and how did it look?" the dowager marchioness snapped. "As though you were shamefully pressed against the wall by your former betrothed." Her voice rose. "The same man you threw yourself at on the steps of St. George's Church?"

Rhys' body jerked.

Alice locked her gaze on him. "I can explain—"

"My son has heard that before, haven't you, Rhys?" his mother snapped.

"Mother," the marquess quietly admonished, whatever other words he uttered were lost in his hushed tones.

All the while, Alice's eyes remained fixed on Rhys.

Rhys, who may as well have been carved of granite.

Say something. She silently pleaded with him. *Say you know I'd never give myself in any way to Henry Pratt. That you know I love you...*

Only, why should he know that? She'd never told him. And he believed that everything that had come to pass was nothing more than pretend. Yet, if that were the case, why should he feel anything at discovering Alice with Henry?

Too late. She'd been too late.

Lord Lovell turned the corner and abruptly stopped. "I do say," he squinted, "is that you Rhys Brookfield?" the wizened viscount boomed, loud enough to bring the entire household awake. "And Miles and...?" His brown eyes widened on Alice. "Oh," he blurted, scratching at his cravat.

"Lord Archibald," Rhys' brother greeted with the aplomb only a powerful marquess could manage.

Viscount Lovell blinked slowly. "Highly unusual... this..." He gestured to Alice's wrapper.

Bile climbed up the back of her throat. Could the gentleman see her swollen lips, too, in this instance? She briefly closed her eyes as horror assaulted her senses.

"Indeed, it is," Rhys' mother seethed.

Another scandal... over the same man, and yet entirely wrong in how it now appeared to the world.

She peeked over at Rhys and her heart stumbled. The sharp, chiseled planes of his face were an immobile mask, bearing no hint of the teasing gentleman who'd reminded her what it was to feel and laugh... and love. *Look at me,* she silently implored. *Look at me and know I am not like that woman who hurt you...*

Instead, his stare remained on Lord Lovell.

"Peculiar night this one is," the viscount puzzled aloud. "A moment ago, I saw my Sybil's brother-in-law running down the hall. Nearly knocked me down, he did. I wouldn't take the youngest Pratt do be racing about." He chuckled, his gaunt frame shaking with mirth. "Now my son-in-law, Nolan? I trust he'd be one to do so."

Through his prattling, Alice stood frozen, feeling like an actor in a play who hadn't the benefit of her lines.

The night could not very well get any worse.

"Lord Lovell, where are you?" The leading Societal hostess rounded the corner.

Alice's face crumpled as she was, yet again, proven wrong.

The viscountess slapped a hand to her breast as her gaze went from Alice to Rhys. "Oh... my. My."

"It is not how it looks, Lady Lovell," Rhys' mother snapped. "It was this one," she whipped a hand in Alice's direction. Panic threatened to drag her down and she braced for the revelation that would thoroughly destroy her. Nor did she give a jot about what the *ton* said. Only Rhys mattered. "And M—"

"Miles, who was good enough to help the lady when she became lost." Rhys' quiet interruption managed the seemingly impossible—it silenced the greatest gossip in London.

Her heart soared at that defense and Rhys briefly looked to her.

And all the hope she'd foolishly allowed herself at that gesture was dashed by the glint of indifference in his gaze; that sentiment all the more painful than had his eyes brimmed with rage and hurt.

Lady Lovell tipped her head. "Oh?"

The marquess cleared his throat. "Might I suggest we adjourn for the evening?" he offered, pulling Alice back from the brink of madness.

"Thank you for your assistance… my lord," Alice managed and, bringing her shoulders back, started the long, painful trek to her rooms.

As soon as she reached the next corridor and found herself alone, Alice took flight.

A sheen of tears blurred her vision and she damned those useless drops as in her mind she relived Rhys' response. Suspicion and anger had darkened his eyes and then… an absolute nothingness. His mistrust had been as palpable as if he'd condemned her with the same harsh words his mother had.

He'd been too jaded by his former betrothed's betrayal to see that which had been before him and the truth of that left her bereft inside.

A short while later, attired in a proper gown, ensconced in one of Lord Guilford's carriages, Alice continued her flight home… and away from Rhys Brookfield.

CHAPTER 18

⁹IN THE THIRTEEN DAYS SINCE Rhys had arrived for his brother's house party, his life had come full circle.

"What in the blazes are you doing?"

The following morning, the sun not even yet risen, Lettie stormed the billiards room, stealing the futile moment of peace Rhys had been in search of.

"I thought it would be self-explanatory," he drawled. He let his cue stick fly, landing a perfect strike. "I am playing billiards."

The crack of the balls filled the room, usually calming, and now—

Nothing.

Alice had been in Pup Pratt's arms. She'd had that pompous bastard's lips on hers. He'd given her leave to sever their arrangement before the house party had concluded. Nothing could have provided a greater death knell to their whirlwind courtship than Alice being discovered… with her former love.

His grip tightened reflexively around the stick, draining the blood from his knuckles.

"Alice," his termagant of a sister clipped out. "I'm speaking of Alice and… you."

Alice and Rhys. They had done it. They had crafted a masterful display for his family and friends. "What of her?" he forced himself to say, infusing a bored nonchalance to that query. "It is my understanding the lady took her leave this morning." Even as he said it, agony sluiced away at his chest; the jagged ache of a thousand knives being thrust into his heart. They'd known one another thirteen days. Thirteen damned days. And yet, she'd shown him how to laugh again. She'd kicked down the walls he'd built about himself, keeping the whole world out, and let her inside. *Fool. You bloody fool.*

Lettie slammed her palm down on the felt. "That is what you'd say?" she cried. "You are in love with her."

Love her? Alice? It was preposterous. Madness. It was… true. God help him, somewhere along the way, truth and pretend had merged, and upended his entire world. He swallowed around the despair stuck in his throat. *I love her.*

Feeling Lettie's eyes on him, Rhys started a path around the table, considering his next shot.

Planting her hands on her hips, Lettie moved into his path. She wrinkled her nose. "Are you cup shot?"

"No."

His too-clever-than-was-good-for-anybody sister knitted her eyebrows into a single line.

"Very well, I'm a little foxed," he mumbled. The half-bottle of brandy he'd consumed since Alice had fled the hall last evening, however, had little effect on his misery; despair continued to invade corners of his being that had been previously empty, parts of himself that she'd brought to life.

And now she is gone.

Rhys' throat moved spasmodically as the energy drained from his legs. Sliding to the floor, he leaned against the billiards table, borrowing support from the mahogany leg. "She is gone," he forced himself to say those three words aloud.

Their game of pretend had come to an end, serving them both *well*: Rhys had been spared his mother's matchmaking attempts and, by the passionate embrace he'd stumbled upon last evening between Pratt and Alice, the pup had been gripped by jealousy. Red, searing, vicious poison that destroyed. The kind eating Rhys alive like a fast-moving cancer even now.

The floorboards groaned and he dimly registered Lettie settling onto the floor beside him. His always garrulous sister laid her head against his shoulder and, this time, she said nothing.

"I miss h-her." His voice broke.

"Then go to her," Lettie urged. She gave another wrinkle of her nose. "Not now necessarily. You stink like you've been rolling around the stables."

An agonized laugh escaped him. "Oh, poppet." He ruffled the top of her head, the same way he once had when she was a small girl. "It's complicated."

She swatted at his hand. "I'm not a child. You love Alice. Alice loves you."

"Alice loves Pratt." That admission cracked another part of his heart and the already useless organ crumbled under the truth there.

His sister worried at her lower lip. "Is this about her being discovered last evening... with him?"

"You know about that?"

"I overheard Mother speaking to Miles," she muttered, layering her cheek against her skirts. "I did not believe it."

"I saw it," he said gruffly. How was his voice so steady?

Lettie stared contemplatively at the doorway. "There has to be more there. There just has to. She never loved Henry. Not truly."

The portion of his foolish heart that lived only for hope, jumped. "Did she tell you that?"

The hesitation there told Rhys more clearly than words the answer before his sister spoke. "No. But I *know* her and I've seen you both together and it is... magic." She clasped her hands to her breast and, in this moment, she was transformed back into the troublesome, starry-eyed girl of long ago.

It was pretend. That answer hung on his lips. In the end, he couldn't shatter Lettie's naïve but poignantly beautiful dream of love.

A light rapping on the door spared Rhys from saying more.

"Enter," they both called out.

Philippa ducked her head inside. She did a search of the room, and then her gaze snagged on where Rhys and Lettie sat. "Forgive me for interrupting," she said quietly. "I was wondering if I might speak with you."

"Of course," Lettie said, hopping up.

"No..." Philippa's pretty blue eyes went to Rhys. "Your brother, that is."

Oh, bloody hell. Intervention from his sister-in-law now, too.

Lettie inclined her head. "I must warn you," she said, skipping over. "He stinks." His youngest sibling lowered her voice to a whisper loud enough to be heard around the room. "Badly."

Philippa grinned. "I will uh… take care to leave a sizeable distance between us when we speak."

Lettie winked and took her leave. She slammed the door hard in her wake.

Reluctantly, Rhys came to his feet. "Philippa," he greeted, dropping a deep bow.

The lady jerked to a stop several paces away. She touched gloved fingertips to her nose. "Uh… yes. Well, it appears your sister was not exaggerating."

"How may I be of assistance?" he drawled, fetching his cue stick.

"Miles shared with me the situation you and he both stumbled upon late last evening." She folded her hands primly at her waist.

"The situation?" he echoed, taking his next shot. "Is that what my mother has taken to referring to it as?"

Philippa went silent.

Rhys looked over his shoulder.

A frown marred her lips. "She cannot very well take to calling it a scandal when she still carries the hope you'll marry Miss Cunning."

No, that had always been the aspiration and expectation. He brought his arm back and propelled the stick forward. "My dear mama will take great care that…" A vise strangled his heart as the memory assaulted him. Pratt's hands on Alice as she'd been in nothing more than her nightshift. The other man's groans as he'd—"My mother will say nothing," he finished in deadened tones.

His sister-in-law frowned. "Is that what you believe?" she said crisply. "That I have some worry about what will be said about my house party?" Hurt outrage tinged her voice.

He scrubbed his spare hand over the stubble on his unshaven cheeks. "Forgive me."

Philippa waved him off. "That lady loves you, Rhys Brookfield. That is what I've come to say."

The stick slipped from his fingers and clattered to the floor. It rolled to a stop at his sister-in-law's slippers.

"You are wrong," he said hoarsely, wanting her to be correct. Wishing it were so.

"Sometimes, I am." Her eyes twinkled. "This, however, is not one of those times. Prior to the situation in the hallway, we had spoken in her chambers. I mentioned you were in the billiards room with my husband."

Hope flared in his chest, born of his want and desperation. "You spoke to her?"

She nodded.

He took a frantic step forward and then forced himself to stop. "What did you...?"

"What did I say to her?" She arched a brow. "I encouraged her to follow her heart."

Follow her heart.

And that is precisely what she'd done. She'd followed it all the way to Pratt's arms and an embrace that would be forever etched in Rhys' mind.

But what if Philippa is correct...?

The tantalizing prospect whispered forward.

"And you believe that talk you shared was leading her to me?" he ventured hopefully. How to explain then that kiss? That bloody embrace that fueled Rhys' bloodlust, filling him with a primitive need to tear Pup Pratt apart limb from scrawny limb?

"I would never presume to know what is in her heart," Philippa said regretfully. "I do believe, however, *you* know the answer to that better than I, or anyone, ever could."

With that, Philippa took her leave and Rhys was left alone with only that veiled statement for company.

CHAPTER 19

ℐT WAS COMING.

After all, it was inevitable.

Just as it had been a certainty following Alice's storming of St. George's.

The Scandal.

Or what happened when a lady found herself embroiled in not one, but two of the greatest public disgraces of the Season?

Would the *ton* create one name for the two events? Or would they simply ascribe a moniker to Alice herself?

Alice's previous fall from grace had been swift and complete, which was why five days after she'd fled Lord and Lady Guilford's country estate, she was so blasted confused.

There hadn't been so much as a word whispered among servants or written in the papers and Alice would know. She'd spent the past five mornings scouring those pages for a hint of a mention.

Uncaring about what was printed about her, the greater worry came from Daniel, who'd developed an older brother's worry twenty years too late.

It was only a matter of time until he learned of Alice's latest scandal... and with his business partner. And then, she would tell him and Daphne everything—well, not everything, but *something*.

For now, she opted for the coward's way—delaying.

Her nephew perched on her hip, Alice rushed into the foyer. "Haply," she greeted, with a forced smile. "Has the...?"

"Nothing yet, my lady," the ancient butler, Haply, murmured from his post by the front door.

Alex caught one of Alice's curls and yanked hard. "You're certain?" she pressed, gently disentangling the strand from his determined little fingers.

A twinkle lit the loyal servant's gaze. "My vision and hearing are not what they once were but I promise I will know when it arrives."

The thump of a cane striking marble announced the arrival of Alice's sister-in-law. "There you are."

She bit the inside of her cheek. Must Daphne be one who rose before the morning sun made its ascent? It rather complicated all this subterfuge business. "I was unable to sleep," she lied, her voice creeping up an octave.

Limping over, Daphne eyed her peculiarly. "Uh... I was not referring to you." She tipped her head.

Alice followed her stare to the plump bundle in her arms. "Of course," she said on a rush, making to hand her nephew over to his devoted mama.

He fidgeted, squirming away from Daphne. Twining his arms about Alice's neck, he clung tight.

"It appears my son has other ideas."

"That is just because your Aunt Alice sneaks you her dessert every night. Isn't that right? Isn't that right?" she cooed, bouncing him in her arms.

The babe squealed and clapped excitedly.

Alice cradled his plump body close and buried her head into his riotous curls. Only in these moments when she held her beloved nephew, did the misery abate. Even those reprieves, however, were fleeting and gave way to a fantasy she saw in her mind: Rhys' babe with luscious, golden curls and a dimpled smile, being carried about on his doting papa's shoulders.

A sheen of tears filled her eyes. Using her nephew's frame to shield herself, she dusted her eyes along his linen gown. Her sister-in-law leveled a clever gaze on Alice.

Please do not let her pry. Please let her be content with the illusion of Alice as a happy, doting aunt and not the woebegone creature who'd consistently read through the scandal sheets each morn.

"You are waiting for the newspapers," Daphne murmured, the

unexpectedness of that observation jolted Alice.

Her cheeks warming, she rocked Alex.

"Bab," Alex pouted, thumping his fist in the air. "Ba–ba–ba."

She caught a tiny blow to her head. "You are going to be a brilliant pugilist someday," she vowed in a sing–song voice. "Better than Gentleman Jackson. Better than anyone in all of England." His lower lip quivered. "In the whole of England," she corrected, spinning him in a quick circle until laughter spilled from his lips. Reluctantly, she placed him in Daphne's arms. As the other woman adjusted her cane, she shifted the boy into the crook of her opposite shoulder. Despite his earlier protestations, he snuggled against his mother's breast. Daphne brushed her lips over his brow.

The pair presented an idyllic image as glorious in its beauty as the Mother Mary with Jesus cradled in her arms. And Alice hated herself for envying her sister–in–law that joy. *I want that… I want it all… with Rhys…*

Her heart spasmed.

Do not think of him. Think of the latest scandal about to ensue which was vastly less painful than thoughts of how very happy she'd been with Rhys.

A footman strode into the hall with a silver tray in hand. "Your papers, my lady," he murmured, the way one might when presenting the crown to the king.

Alice raced over and plucked the first scandal sheet to arrive that morn. Unfolding it, she frantically skimmed the front page. Scandals such as hers invariably found themselves on the front of those useless rags, not buried several pages in at some obscure location.

Releasing a painful breath, she snapped it closed and glanced over.

Daphne pointed to the copy in Alice's hands. "You were never one to read scandal sheets."

No, she hadn't been. So how to explain her inordinate fascination with them now without revealing her latest scandal? Alice shifted on her feet.

Her sister–in–law didn't again speak until the footman and butler took their leave.

"But here you are," Daphne persisted, limping closer. "Each morning, waiting for the latest columns."

"You know that?" she squawked, wanting to call that revealing query back.

The ghost of a smile played at her sister-in-law's lips. "I know that."

Bloody, bloody hell. If Daphne had gathered the reason Alice rushed belowstairs each morning then surely Daniel also had.

Daphne cleared her throat. "Is your frantic search for the morning gossip columns perhaps at all connected to your early return from Lord and Lady Guilford's?"

Alice winced, letting her silence answer for her.

Her sister-in-law sighed. "I see."

"You don't," she whispered. "Not truly."

And what will you tell your brother? That she was dragged into a scandal by the pompous arse she'd been betrothed to? Oh, and there was the whole matter of her make-believe courtship with Rhys—her brother's most recent partner in business. "Does Daniel know?" she squeezed out the dreaded question.

"Does Daniel know what?"

Blast, damn, and double-damn.

The two women looked to the tall figure striding forward. Her brother stopped alongside his wife and dropped a kiss on her lips, before scooping his son up.

Feeling like an interloper on that beautiful moment, she glanced to the opposite corridor. Slinking off, Alice made her escape.

She made it no more than four steps.

"Stop," Daniel instructed and she froze, her slipper suspended.

Alice forced herself to complete the step.

"What is this all about?"

"*This?*" She searched her mind for a diversionary reply.

His brow lowered, shadowing his face with suspicion.

Daphne, as she had so often done in the years she'd been part of Alice's life, rescued her. "She was taking Alex to the breakfast room."

Her brother frowned. "By way of the foyer?"

Alice gritted her teeth. It had been vastly easier to go on with her own affairs when he'd been the detached sibling. Alas, it appeared there was no happy medium of loving brother... and one who allowed her a life of her own. "I was speaking to Haply about..." From just beyond her husband's shoulder, Daphne held a palm aloft, urging that thought to cessation. Alice cleared her throat.

The suspicion deepened in her brother's eyes and he took a step closer. "What were you speaking to Haply about at this hour?"

"I was… I was…" Alice frantically searched for a response and then annoyance slipped in. Daniel had lived the life of a black-hearted scoundrel more years than he hadn't. What right did he have to question any of her actions or decisions? She brought her shoulders back. "I was waiting for the newspaper."

His mouth opened and closed several times. "The newspaper?" he echoed. "That merits secrecy?" As soon as the words left him, Daniel's face shuttered. "What is it?" he asked gruffly.

Alex squirmed in his father's arms.

"Here, I will take him," Alice insisted, gathering her nephew.

Another footman rushed forward, with several papers upon his tray. He stopped, and looked between the assembled Winter-bournes. "Uh, these have arrived."

Daniel reached for the latest scandal sheets.

Darting over, Alice intercepted them, plucking them from the tray. "I'll take those."

"What in the blazes?" her brother muttered.

A hard knock at the doorway brought their attention to the door.

"Who's come to call now?" Daniel muttered. "The bloody King of England?"

Slightly winded, Haply ambled forward and drew the door open.

A charge of awareness coursed through Alice and she drank in the sight of the towering, broad-bear of a figure framed in the doorway. Afraid these past days missing him as she had, that she'd conjured him out of the air.

For he was here. Now.

Rhys, as devastatingly beautiful in the flesh as he'd been in her remembrances of him this week.

Doffing his hat, he took in the crowded foyer, before settling his gaze briefly on Alice.

Her arms tightened reflexively around her nephew and he squirmed, batting at her head in protest. She immediately lightened her grip.

Rhys' stare locked with hers. The piercing intensity of it sucked the breath from her lungs.

"Brookfield?" Daniel shattered that pull. "I believed our meeting was not until later this afternoon."

A bitter cold chased away the thrill of seeing him.

Of course. "You're here on business," she whispered, the revelation slipped out.

Everyone swiveled their heads in Alice's direction.

Her brother puzzled his brow. "Do you know... Brookfield?"

Striding through the entranceway, Rhys approached with long, sleek steps that set his black, wool cloak swirling about his ankles. Ignoring her brother entirely, Rhys stopped before Alice. "I am here on business," he confirmed, dashing the last sliver of hope responsible for her still frantically pounding heart.

"Oh," she managed through bitterness stinging her throat. She hugged her nephew close. "I will leave you and my brother to your... affairs."

"You misunderstand, Alice," Rhys called after her and she came to a jerky halt.

"Alice?" Daniel echoed, his expression darkening at Rhys' intimate use of her Christian name.

"I came to speak with you," he said somberly.

Alice's heart jumped and she dimly registered Daphne rushing over and scooping up Alex.

He is here for me...

UNTIL RHYS DREW HIS LAST breath and took his leave for the great hereafter, he would always remember Alice as she'd been when Montfort's door had been opened: a babe cradled close to her chest, as natural as if the boy himself had been born to her.

And he hungered for that life with her.

"What do you mean you've come to speak with my sister?" Lord Montfort growled. He took a threatening step forward, jerking Rhys back from those tempting musings.

The pretty, redheaded young woman at his side, laid a staying hand on his sleeve. She murmured something in hushed tones.

"I would like to speak to your sister, Montfort," Rhys said quietly.

"I'll ask you one more time before I throw you out on your damned arse," his business partner gritted out. "How do you know my sister?"

Given the vein bulging at the earl's temple, it wouldn't do for Rhys to point out that he, in fact, hadn't asked that same question. Rather, Montfort had wondered about the business Rhys had with his sister. The other man was rightfully suspicious. If a wicked scoundrel like Rhys had shown up for one of his sisters, he'd do far worse than throw the bugger out on his arse. As such, the earl was deserving of some explanation. He cleared his throat. "I—"

"You needn't explain yourself to my brother," Alice interjected in brusque tones. Wholly in command, asserting herself over her brother, there was nothing meek, mild, or demure about her. And how he loved her for her spirit.

"Yes, yes, he does." Seething, Montfort took another step closer.

The other woman stepped between the earl and Rhys, and thrust the squirming babe in her arms into Montfort's arms.

The tension immediately left the earl, as he folded the boy in a tender embrace.

"Forgive my husband," she said, confirming her identity. "I'm Daphne Winterbourne, the Countess of Montfort."

Rhys sketched a bow. "My lady." The lady was an ally. That much was clear.

The countess smiled. "Allow me to accompany you and Alice to the parlor." She paused to favor her husband with a stern look. "Will you bring Alex to the nursery."

A silent battle waged between husband and wife; some unspoken language that only they two understood. Over the tops of their heads, Rhys' gaze caught Alice's.

She offered him a tentative smile, and the hope that had sent him here breathed to life. For the first time since she'd gone, he grinned.

"Shall we?" Lady Montfort interjected, ending that silent connection. Without awaiting to see whether anyone followed, she started forward. The bottom of her cane marked an incessant beat upon the floor as she led the way, her pace made slow by the slight drag of her left leg. Casting a glance back at him, Alice fell into step alongside her sister-in-law.

"I'll have answers, Brookfield," Montfort vowed on a steely whisper that contained the threat of death.

He lifted his head in acknowledgement. "After I speak with the lady." The earl's gaze burning into his back, Rhys strode after the pair of ladies.

Perhaps if he were the respectable gent like Pup Pratt who'd snagged Alice's heart, Rhys would have done the honorable thing and spoken to her brother. He would have asked the other man for her hand in marriage and had a proper courtship, betrothal, and then a staid marriage.

But Rhys was not, nor would he ever be one of those sorts. He didn't know a bloody thing about being proper, and he knew even less about marriage and courtship. They were anathema to everything he'd vowed.

"Here we are," the countess murmured, bringing them to a stop outside a cheerfully lit parlor. She motioned them inside. "I'll remain on guard for my husband," she whispered, a mischievous twinkle glittered in her eyes.

Nor could there be any question that, even now, Montfort was, no doubt, racing through the stucco townhouse to hand the babe off so he might listen at the keyhole.

After Alice and Rhys had entered, the countess drew the door closed behind them.

He'd thought of nothing but her these past five days. Nay, she'd been all that had consumed him since he'd found her in The Copse. And yet, in this instant, all the carefully crafted words, questions, and thoughts he'd assembled in his mind melted.

Alice clasped her hands before her. "I trust you are... well?" she asked, breaking the impasse, proving herself, once again, more brave with her forthrightness than he'd ever been in the whole of his roguish existence.

"I am... well," his voice emerged garbled. Fingers shaking, he reached inside his cloak and fished around. "You left this." He pressed the small leather tome into her palm.

Alice stared at the cover, briefly tracing the title etched in gold. "Oh."

Did he imagine the disappointment in that single syllable? Was it merely crafted of his own yearning?

Folding his hands behind him, Rhys rocked on his heels. "I had this planned."

"Planned?" she repeated, slowly lifting her head from the book. Her golden lashes veiled her eyes, shielding her thoughts.

Terror rattled around his chest.

He managed an unsteady nod. "What I was going to say when I came here. I've thought of nothing else since I set out. I had it scripted in my mind."

The pink tip of her tongue darted out and traced the seam of her lips. "What were you going to say?"

"I don't know," he explained hoarsely, turning his palms up. "Everything in here," he touched his head and then moved his fingers to his chest. "And here. It is all jumbled. It has been that way since you entered my life... and then left."

Alice set her book down slowly on a rose-inlaid sidetable. "Try."

Try.

"My heart was broken," he said quietly. "Badly. After Lillian, I never wanted to love again but, more, I thought I was unable to love—until you, Alice."

She sucked in a shuddery breath. "You... *love* me?"

How could she not know?

"My life was empty—until you. You reminded me what it was to laugh and smile." An agonized laugh rumbled from his chest. "I never knew there was a woman like you. You are clever and spirited and you throw a snowball, Alice. And skate."

She cocked her head.

He scrubbed a hand over his face. "My God, I'm blundering this." Rhys began to pace, his cloak snapping angrily about his legs. "I always knew what to say. I would have once had pretty words for you, *perfect* ones, and they came easy to me." He took her hands in his, lightly squeezing them. The warmth of her palms was a balm to his trembling ones. They gave him strength, allowing him to continue. "Those roguish words once came easy because I didn't *feel*. You made me feel." His throat spasmed. He released her hands. "The night I saw you with Pratt... I was destroyed in ways that even Lillian's betrayal hadn't left me."

"Oh, Rhys," she whispered, brushing her fingers over his cheek.

He leaned into that caress, craving more of her tender touch.

She let her hands fall to her sides. "Is that why you didn't come sooner?"

The hurt there shredded him, but also stirred hope within him.

"No," he shook his head. "That is not why."

Alice bit at her lower lip.

"I know you love him and I've accepted that you always will, b–but…" His voice broke. "I love you so very desperately, I will take even the smallest piece of your heart, if you'll but trust it to me." He sank to a knee.

Alice slapped a hand to her mouth, catching the gasp that filtered from her lips. "What are you doing?" she breathed, backing up a step.

Rhys withdrew the thick ivory velum; marked, inked, and sealed. "I wanted to come sooner but I wanted to have this with me." He set it down. "It is special license from the Archbishop."

"You want me to marry you?"

"It is all I want," he said hoarsely. It was all he'd never known he wanted. "But my desires are secondary." Her happiness was everything and, even as it would break his soul to lose Alice, if that brought her joy, he'd set her free.

The clock ticked away atop the mantel, stretching the silence into a never-ending beat that drilled a slow, hollow wall of emptiness inside.

And when she spoke, hers was not the simple "yes" he longed for.

"You would marry me, Rhys, even believing I'm in love with Henry."

How he despised that name and all it represented. "I would," he said unequivocally.

Then, one word contained within that string of others, penetrated his misery, and he replayed that statement over in his head.

… *You would marry me, even believing I'm in love with Henry…*

"I do not love him, Rhys."

His heart slowed to a stop. "You do not?" It had been that thought that had eaten him alive since he'd come upon her and Pratt together.

"I do not." She took a hesitant step closer, when there had never been anything tentative about Alice Winterbourne.

"I saw you—"

"You saw *him* kissing *me*."

What was she saying? Rhys' mind raced and then slowed to a stop. "I saw—"

"He was drunk," she said bluntly. "And jealous… because of my feelings for you."

"And it was not a display to sever our pretend courtship?" he breathed that revelation out on a slow exhale.

She gave her head a tight shake. "Certainly not. Your sister-in-law paid me a visit. We spoke, and she encouraged me to follow my heart."

It was as Philippa had said. A lightness suffused his chest… and then as quick as it flickered to life, died as the implications settled around his mind. An animalistic growl started low and climbed to his throat. Primal rage consumed him. "Then Pratt's embrace?"

"He forced on me."

The air exploded from his lungs on a sharp hiss. He closed his eyes briefly, forcing his mind back to that night. Rhys had been so consumed by his own grief and heartache, he'd failed to see that which was before him. Hatred consumed him; for himself for failing to see and protect her as she'd deserved and loathing for Pratt who'd dared put his hands upon her.

I'll kill him.

"You won't."

Unaware he'd uttered that threat aloud, his eyes flew open. She'd defend a cur who'd never deserved her and who was long overdue for a good thrashing?

Alice continued. "You won't kill him because he's a pathetic man who'll suffer an empty life with a woman he does not love because of his lust for power. That's punishment enough. No, I never loved Henry," she said softly, drifting closer and then stopping when a mere handsbreadth separated them. "I loved the idea of love. I loved the idea of someone I could sit and read with; a man who didn't try to change me but accepted me as one who'd forever challenge Societal conventions. And I found him." She cupped his face. "In you." Alice lowered her brow to his. "I love you, Rhys Brookfield."

"You love me?" he asked hoarsely.

"Only you. It has only ever been you." She smiled a watery smile. "I just did not know it until you rescued me in The Copse, and then you saved me in every way."

His heart sped up. "Nay, we rescued one another." Gathering her hands in his, he raised them to his mouth, placing a lingering kiss on the inside of her wrist. "Is that a yes, Alice?"

Her grin widened. "That is a yes." She hurled herself into his arms and he caught her, holding her close.

Montfort's steady stream of black curses filtered through the oak panel. Alice and Rhys' laughter melded together as they let go of their pasts and embraced the future that awaited them—together.

THE END

If you enjoyed *To Tempt a Scoundrel*, Book 2 in
The Brethren series, check out Book 1, *The Spy Who Seduced Her*

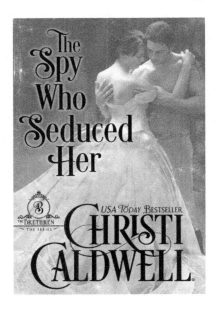

A WIDOW WITH A PAST... The last thing Victoria Barrett, the
Viscountess Waters, has any interest in is romance. When the only
man she's ever loved was killed she endured an arranged marriage
to a cruel man in order to survive. Now widowed, her only focus
is on clearing her son's name from the charge of murder. That is
until the love of her life returns from the grave.

A leader of a once great agency... Nathaniel Archer, the Earl
of Exeter head of the Crown's elite organization, The Brethren, is
back on British soil. Captured and tortured 20 years ago, he clung
to memories of his first love until he could escape. Discovering she
has married whilst he was captive, Nathaniel sets aside the distrac-
tions of love...until an unexpected case is thrust upon him—to
solve the murder of the Viscount Waters. There is just one compli-
cation: the prime suspect's mother is none other than Victoria, the
woman he once loved with his very soul.

Secrets will be uncovered and passions rekindled. Victoria and
Nathaniel must trust one another if they hope to start anew—in
love and life. But will duty destroy their last chance?

OTHER BOOKS BY
CHRISTI CALDWELL

TO ENCHANT A WICKED DUKE
Book 13 in the "Heart of a Duke" Series by Christi Caldwell

A Devil in Disguise

Years ago, when Nick Tallings, the recent Duke of Huntly, watched his family destroyed at the hands of a merciless nobleman, he vowed revenge. But his efforts had been futile, as his enemy, Lord Rutland is without weakness.

Until now…

With his rival finally happily married, Nick is able to set his ruthless scheme into motion. His plot hinges upon Lord Rutland's innocent, empty-headed sister-in-law, Justina Barrett. Nick will ruin her, marry her, and then leave her brokenhearted.

A Lady Dreaming of Love

From the moment Justina Barrett makes her Come Out, she is labeled a Diamond. Even with her ruthless father determined to sell her off to the highest bidder, Justina never gives up on her hope for a good, honorable gentleman who values her wit more than her looks.

A Not-So-Chance Meeting

Nick's ploy to ensnare Justina falls neatly into place in the streets of London. With each carefully orchestrated encounter, he slips further and further inside the lady's heart, never anticipating that Justina, with her quick wit and strength, will break down his own defenses. As Nick's plans begins to unravel, he's left to determine which is more important—Justina's love or his vow for vengeance. But can Justina ever forgive the duke who deceived her?

ONE WINTER WITH A BARON
Book 12 in the "Heart of a Duke" Series by Christi Caldwell

A clever spinster:
Content with her spinster lifestyle, Miss Sybil Cunning wants to prove that a future as an unmarried woman is the only life for her. As a bluestocking who values hard, empirical data, Sybil needs help with her research. Nolan Pratt, Baron Webb, one of society's most scandalous rakes, is the perfect gentleman to help her. After all, he inspires fear in proper mothers and desire within their daughters.

A notorious rake:
Society may be aware of Nolan Pratt, Baron's Webb's wicked ways, but what he has carefully hidden is his miserable handling of his family's finances. When Sybil presents him the opportunity to earn much-needed funds, he can't refuse.

A winter to remember:
However, what begins as a business arrangement becomes something more and with every meeting, Sybil slips inside his heart. Can this clever woman look beneath the veneer of a coldhearted rake to see the man Nolan truly is?

TO REDEEM A RAKE
Book 11 in the "Heart of a Duke" Series by Christi Caldwell

He's spent years scandalizing society.
Now, this rake must change his ways.

Society's most infamous scoundrel, Daniel Winterbourne, the Earl of Montfort, has been promised a small fortune if he can relinquish his wayward, carousing lifestyle. And behaving means he must also help find a respectable companion for his youngest sister—someone who will guide her and whom she can emulate. However, Daniel knows no such woman. But when he encounters a childhood friend, Daniel believes she may just be the answer to all of his problems.

Having been secretly humiliated by an unscrupulous blackguard years earlier, Miss Daphne Smith dreams of finding work at Ladies of Hope, an institution that provides an education for disabled women. With her sordid past and a disfigured leg, few opportunities arise for a woman such as she. Knowing Daniel's history, she wishes to avoid him, but working for his sister is exactly the stepping stone she needs.

Their attraction intensifies as Daniel and Daphne grow closer, preparing his sister for the London Season. But Daniel must resist his desire for a woman tarnished by scandal while Daphne is reminded of the boy she once knew. Can society's most notorious rake redeem his reputation and become the man Daphne deserves?

TO WOO A WIDOW

Book 10 in the "Heart of a Duke" Series by Christi Caldwell

They see a brokenhearted widow.
She's far from shattered.

Lady Philippa Winston is never marrying again. After her late husband's cruelty that she kept so well hidden, she has no desire to search for love.

Years ago, Miles Brookfield, the Marquess of Guilford, made a frivolous vow he never thought would come to fruition—he promised to marry his mother's goddaughter if he was unwed by the age of thirty. Now, to his dismay, he's faced with honoring that pledge. But when he encounters the beautiful and intriguing Lady Philippa, Miles knows his true path in life. It's up to him to break down every belief Philippa carries about gentlemen, proving that not only is love real, but that he is the man deserving of her sheltered heart.

Will Philippa let down her guard and allow Miles to woo a widow in desperate need of his love?

THE LURE OF A RAKE
Book 9 in the "Heart of a Duke" Series by Christi Caldwell

A Lady Dreaming of Love

Lady Genevieve Farendale has a scandalous past. Jilted at the altar years earlier and exiled by her family, she's now returned to London to prove she can be a proper lady. Even though she's not given up on the hope of marrying for love, she's wary of trusting again. Then she meets Cedric Falcot, the Marquess of St. Albans whose seductive ways set her heart aflutter. But with her sordid history, Genevieve knows a rake can also easily destroy her.

An Unlikely Pairing

What begins as a chance encounter between Cedric and Genevieve becomes something more. As they continue to meet, passions stir. But with Genevieve's hope for true love, she fears Cedric will be unable to give up his wayward lifestyle. After all, Cedric has spent years protecting his heart, and keeping everyone out. Slowly, she chips away at all the walls he's built, but when he falters, Genevieve can't offer him redemption. Now, it's up to Cedric to prove to Genevieve that the love of a man is far more powerful than the lure of a rake.

TO TRUST A ROGUE
Book 8 in the "Heart of a Duke" Series by Christi Caldwell

A rogue

Marcus, the Viscount Wessex has carefully crafted the image of rogue and charmer for Polite Society. Under that façade, however, dwells a man whose dreams were shattered almost eight years earlier by a young lady who captured his heart, pledged her love, and then left him, with nothing more than a curt note.

A widow

Eight years earlier, faced with no other choice, Mrs. Eleanor Collins, fled London and the only man she ever loved, Marcus, Viscount Wessex. She has now returned to serve as a companion for her elderly aunt with a daughter in tow. Even though they're next door neighbors, there is little reason for her to move in the same circles as Marcus, just in case, she vows to avoid him, for he reminds her of all she lost when she left.

Reunited

As their paths continue to cross, Marcus finds his desire for Eleanor just as strong, but he learned long ago she's not to be trusted. He will offer her a place in his bed, but not anything more. Only, Eleanor has no interest in this new, roguish man. The more time they spend together, the protective wall they've constructed to keep the other out, begin to break. With all the betrayals and secrets between them, Marcus has to open his heart again. And Eleanor must decide if it's ever safe to trust a rogue.

To Wed His Christmas Lady
Book 7 in the "Heart of a Duke" Series by Christi Caldwell

She's longing to be loved:

Lady Cara Falcot has only served one purpose to her loathsome father—to increase his power through a marriage to the future Duke of Billingsley. As such, she's built protective walls about her heart, and presents an icy facade to the world around her. Journeying home from her finishing school for the Christmas holidays, Cara's carriage is stranded during a winter storm. She's forced to tarry at a ramshackle inn, where she immediately antagonizes another patron—William.

He's avoiding his duty in favor of one last adventure:

William Hargrove, the Marquess of Grafton has wanted only one thing in life—to avoid the future match his parents would have him make to a cold, duke's daughter. He's returning home from a blissful eight years of traveling the world to see to his responsibilities. But when a winter storm interrupts his trip and lands him at a falling-down inn, he's forced to share company with a commanding Lady Cara who initially reminds him exactly of the woman he so desperately wants to avoid.

A Christmas snowstorm ushers in the spirit of the season:

At the holiday time, these two people who despise each other due to first perceptions are offered renewed beginnings and fresh starts. As this gruff stranger breaks down the walls she's built about herself, Cara has to determine whether she can truly open her heart to trusting that any man is capable of good and that she herself is capable of love. And William has to set aside all previous thoughts he's carried of the polished ladies like Cara, to be the man to show her that love.

THE HEART OF A SCOUNDREL
Book 6 in the "Heart of a Duke" Series by Christi Caldwell

Ruthless, wicked, and dark, the Marquess of Rutland rouses terror in the breast of ladies and nobleman alike. All Edmund wants in life is power. After he was publically humiliated by his one love Lady Margaret, he vowed vengeance, using Margaret's niece, as his pawn. Except, he's thwarted by another, more enticing target— Miss Phoebe Barrett.

Miss Phoebe Barrett knows precisely the shame she's been born to. Because her father is a shocking letch she's learned to form her own opinions on a person's worth. After a chance meeting with the Marquess of Rutland, she is captivated by the mysterious man. He, too, is a victim of society's scorn, but the more encounters she has with Edmund, the more she knows there is powerful depth and emotion to the jaded marquess.

The lady wreaks havoc on Edmund's plans for revenge and he finds he wants Phoebe, at all costs. As she's drawn into the darkness of his world, Phoebe risks being destroyed by Edmund's ruthlessness. And Phoebe who desires love at all costs, has to determine if she can ever truly trust the heart of a scoundrel.

TO LOVE A LORD
Book 5 in the "Heart of a Duke" Series by Christi Caldwell

All she wants is security:

The last place finishing school instructor Mrs. Jane Munroe belongs, is in polite Society. Vowing to never wed, she's been scuttled around from post to post. Now she finds herself in the Marquess of Waverly's household. She's never met a nobleman she liked, and when she meets the pompous, arrogant marquess, she remembers why. But soon, she discovers Gabriel is unlike any gentleman she's ever known.

All he wants is a companion for his sister:

What Gabriel finds himself with instead, is a fiery spirited, bespectacled woman who entices him at every corner and challenges his age-old vow to never trust his heart to a woman. But… there is something suspicious about his sister's companion. And he is determined to find out just what it is.

All they need is each other:

As Gabriel and Jane confront the truth of their feelings, the lies and secrets between them begin to unravel. And Jane is left to decide whether or not it is ever truly safe to love a lord.

LOVED BY A DUKE
Book 4 in the "Heart of a Duke" Series by Christi Caldwell

For ten years, Lady Daisy Meadows has been in love with Auric, the Duke of Crawford. Ever since his gallant rescue years earlier, Daisy knew she was destined to be his Duchess. Unfortunately, Auric sees her as his best friend's sister and nothing more. But perhaps, if she can manage to find the fabled heart of a duke pendant, she will win over the heart of her duke.

Auric, the Duke of Crawford enjoys Daisy's company. The last thing he is interested in however, is pursuing a romance with a woman he's known since she was in leading strings. This season, Daisy is turning up in the oddest places and he cannot help but notice that she is no longer a girl. But Auric wouldn't do something as foolhardy as to fall in love with Daisy. He couldn't. Not with the guilt he carries over his past sins... Not when he has no right to her heart...But perhaps, just perhaps, she can forgive the past and trust that he'd forever cherish her heart—but will she let him?

THE LOVE OF A ROGUE
Book 3 in the "Heart of a Duke" Series by Christi Caldwell

Lady Imogen Moore hasn't had an easy time of it since she made her Come Out. With her betrothed, a powerful duke breaking it off to wed her sister, she's become the *tons* favorite piece of gossip. Never again wanting to experience the pain of a broken heart, she's resolved to make a match with a polite, respectable gentleman. The last thing she wants is another reckless rogue.

Lord Alex Edgerton has a problem. His brother, tired of Alex's carousing has charged him with chaperoning their remaining, unwed sister about *ton* events. Shopping? No, thank you. Attending the theatre? He'd rather be at Forbidden Pleasures with a scantily clad beauty upon his lap. The task of *chaperone* becomes even more of a bother when his sister drags along her dearest friend, Lady Imogen to social functions. The last thing he wants in his life is a young, innocent English miss.

Except, as Alex and Imogen are thrown together, passions flare and Alex comes to find he not only wants Imogen in his bed, but also in his heart. Yet now he must convince Imogen to risk all, on the heart of a rogue.

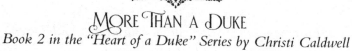

More Than a Duke
Book 2 in the "Heart of a Duke" Series by Christi Caldwell

Polite Society doesn't take Lady Anne Adamson seriously. However, Anne isn't just another pretty young miss. When she discovers her father betrayed her mother's love and her family descended into poverty, Anne comes up with a plan to marry a respectable, powerful, and honorable gentleman—a man nothing like her philandering father.

Armed with the heart of a duke pendant, fabled to land the wearer a duke's heart, she decides to enlist the aid of the notorious Harry, 6th Earl of Stanhope. A scoundrel with a scandalous past, he is the last gentleman she'd ever wed...however, his reputation marks him the perfect man to school her in the art of seduction so she might ensnare the illustrious Duke of Crawford.

Harry, the Earl of Stanhope is a jaded, cynical rogue who lives for his own pleasures. Having been thrown over by the only woman he ever loved so she could wed a duke, he's not at all surprised when Lady Anne approaches him with her scheme to capture another duke's affection. He's come to appreciate that all women are in fact greedy, title-grasping, self-indulgent creatures. And with Anne's history of grating on his every last nerve, she is the last woman he'd ever agree to school in the art of seduction. Only his friendship with the lady's sister compels him to help.

What begins as a pretend courtship, born of lessons on seduction, becomes something more leaving Anne to decide if she can give her heart to a reckless rogue, and Harry must decide if he's willing to again trust in a lady's love.

FOR LOVE OF THE DUKE
First Full-Length Book in the "Heart of a Duke" Series
by Christi Caldwell

After the tragic death of his wife, Jasper, the 8th Duke of Bainbridge buried himself away in the dark cold walls of his home, Castle Blackwood. When he's coaxed out of his self-imposed exile to attend the amusements of the Frost Fair, his life is irrevocably changed by his fateful meeting with Lady Katherine Adamson.

With her tight brown ringlets and silly white-ruffled gowns, Lady Katherine Adamson has found her dance card empty for two Seasons. After her father's passing, Katherine learned the unreliability of men, and is determined to depend on no one, except herself. Until she meets Jasper...

In a desperate bid to avoid a match arranged by her family, Katherine makes the Duke of Bainbridge a shocking proposition—one that he accepts.

Only, as Katherine begins to love Jasper, she finds the arrangement agreed upon is not enough. And Jasper is left to decide if protecting his heart is more important than fighting for Katherine's love.

IN NEED OF A DUKE
A Prequel Novella to "The Heart of a Duke" Series
by Christi Caldwell

In Need of a Duke: (Author's Note: This is a prequel novella to "The Heart of a Duke" series by Christi Caldwell. It was originally available in "The Heart of a Duke" Collection and is now being published as an individual novella.

~★~

It features a new prologue and epilogue.

Years earlier, a gypsy woman passed to Lady Aldora Adamson and her friends a heart pendant that promised them each the heart of a duke.

Now, a young lady, with her family facing ruin and scandal, Lady Aldora doesn't have time for mythical stories about cheap baubles. She needs to save her sisters and brother by marrying a titled gentleman with wealth and power to his name. She sets her bespectacled sights upon the Marquess of St. James.

Turned out by his father after a tragic scandal, Lord Michael Knightly has grown into a powerful, but self-made man. With the whispers and stares that still follow him, he would rather be anywhere but London…

Until he meets Lady Aldora, a young woman who mistakes him for his brother, the Marquess of St. James. The connection between Aldora and Michael is immediate and as they come to know one another, Aldora's feelings for Michael war with her sisterly responsibilities. With her family's dire situation, a man of Michael's scandalous past will never do.

Ultimately, Aldora must choose between her responsibilities as a sister and her love for Michael.

ONCE A WALLFLOWER, AT LAST HIS LOVE
Book 6 in the Scandalous Seasons Series

Responsible, practical Miss Hermione Rogers, has been crafting stories as the notorious Mr. Michael Michaelmas and selling them for a meager wage to support her siblings. The only real way to ensure her family's ruinous debts are paid, however, is to marry. Tall, thin, and plain, she has no expectation of success. In London for her first Season she seizes the chance to write the tale of a brooding duke. In her research, she finds Sebastian Fitzhugh, the 5th Duke of Mallen, who unfortunately is perfectly affable, charming, and so nicely… configured… he takes her breath away. He lacks all the character traits she needs for her story, but alas, any duke will have to do.

Sebastian Fitzhugh, the 5th Duke of Mallen has been deceived so many times during the high-stakes game of courtship, he's lost faith in Society women. Yet, after a chance encounter with Hermione, he finds himself intrigued. Not a woman he'd normally consider beautiful, the young lady's practical bent, her forthright nature and her tendency to turn up in the oddest places has his interests... roused. He'd like to trust her, he'd like to do a whole lot more with her too, but should he?

A Marquess For Christmas
Book 5 in the Scandalous Seasons Series

Lady Patrina Tidemore gave up on the ridiculous notion of true love after having her heart shattered and her trust destroyed by a black-hearted cad. Used as a pawn in a game of revenge against her brother, Patrina returns to London from a failed elopement with a tattered reputation and little hope for a respectable match. The only peace she finds is in her solitude on the cold winter days at Hyde Park. And even that is yanked from her by two little hellions who just happen to have a devastatingly handsome, but coldly aloof father, the Marquess of Beaufort. Something about the lord stirs the dreams she'd once carried for an honorable gentleman's love.

Weston Aldridge, the 4th Marquess of Beaufort was deceived and betrayed by his late wife. In her faithlessness, he's come to view women as self-serving, indulgent creatures. Except, after a series of chance encounters with Patrina, he comes to appreciate how uniquely different she is than all women he's ever known.

At the Christmastide season, a time of hope and new beginnings, Patrina and Weston, unexpectedly learn true love in one another. However, as Patrina's scandalous past threatens their future and the happiness of his children, they are both left to determine if love is enough.

Always a Rogue, Forever Her Love
Book 4 in the Scandalous Seasons Series

Miss Juliet Marshville is spitting mad. With one guardian missing, and the other singularly uninterested in her fate, she is at the mercy of her wastrel brother who loses her beloved childhood home to a man known as Sin. Determined to reclaim control of Rosecliff Cottage and her own fate, Juliet arranges a meeting with the notorious rogue and demands the return of her property.

Jonathan Tidemore, 5th Earl of Sinclair, known to the *ton* as Sin, is exceptionally lucky in life and at the gaming tables. He has just one problem. Well...four, really. His incorrigible sisters have driven off yet another governess. This time, however, his mother demands he find an appropriate replacement.

When Miss Juliet Marshville boldly demands the return of her precious cottage, he takes advantage of his sudden good fortune and puts an offer to her; turn his sisters into proper English ladies, and he'll return Rosecliff Cottage to Juliet's possession.

Jonathan comes to appreciate Juliet's spirit, courage, and clever wit, and decides to claim the fiery beauty as his mistress. Juliet, however, will be mistress for no man. Nor could she ever love a man who callously stole her home in a game of cards. As Jonathan begins to see Juliet as more than a spirited beauty to warm his bed, he realizes she could be a lady he could love the rest of his life, if only he can convince the proud Juliet that he's worthy of her hand and heart.

Always Proper, Suddenly Scandalous
Book 3 in the Scandalous Seasons Series

Geoffrey Winters, Viscount Redbrooke was not always the hard, unrelenting lord driven by propriety. After a tragic mistake, he resolved to honor his responsibility to the Redbrooke line and live a life, free of scandal. Knowing his duty is to wed a proper, respectable English miss, he selects Lady Beatrice Dennington, daughter of the Duke of Somerset, the perfect woman for him. Until he meets Miss Abigail Stone...

To distance herself from a personal scandal, Abigail Stone flees America to visit her uncle, the Duke of Somerset. Determined to never trust a man again, she is helplessly intrigued by the hard, too-proper Geoffrey. With his strict appreciation for decorum and order, he is nothing like the man' she's always dreamed of.

Abigail is everything Geoffrey does not need. She upends his carefully ordered world at every encounter. As they begin to care for one another, Abigail carefully guards the secret that resulted in her journey to England.

Only, if Geoffrey learns the truth about Abigail, he must decide which he holds most dear: his place in Society or Abigail's place in his heart.

NEVER COURTED, SUDDENLY WED
Book 2 in the Scandalous Seasons Series

Christopher Ansley, Earl of Waxham, has constructed a perfect image for the *ton*—the ladies love him and his company is desired by all. Only two people know the truth about Waxham's secret. Unfortunately, one of them is Miss Sophie Winters.

Sophie Winters has known Christopher since she was in leading strings. As children, they delighted in tormenting each other. Now at two and twenty, she still has a tendency to find herself in scrapes, and her marital prospects are slim.

When his father threatens to expose his shame to the *ton*, unless he weds Sophie for her dowry, Christopher concocts a plan to remain a bachelor. What he didn't plan on was falling in love with the lively, impetuous Sophie. As secrets are exposed, will Christopher's love be enough when she discovers his role in his father's scheme?

Forever Betrothed, Never the Bride
Book 1 in the Scandalous Seasons Series

Hopeless romantic Lady Emmaline Fitzhugh is tired of sitting with the wallflowers, waiting for her betrothed to come to his senses and marry her. When Emmaline reads one too many reports of his scandalous liaisons in the gossip rags, she takes matters into her own hands.

War-torn veteran Lord Drake devotes himself to forgetting his days on the Peninsula through an endless round of meaningless associations. He no longer wants to feel anything, but Lady Emmaline is making it hard to maintain a state of numbness. With her zest for life, she awakens his passion and desire for love.

The one woman Drake has spent the better part of his life avoiding is now the only woman he needs, but he is no longer a man worthy of his Emmaline. It is up to her to show him the healing power of love.

A Season of Hope
A Danby Novella

Five years ago when her love, Marcus Wheatley, failed to return from fighting Napoleon's forces, Lady Olivia Foster buried her heart. Unable to betray Marcus's memory, Olivia has gone out of her way to run off prospective suitors. At three and twenty she considers herself firmly on the shelf. Her father, however, disagrees and accepts an offer for Olivia's hand in marriage. Yet it's Christmas, when anything can happen…

Olivia receives a well-timed summons from her grandfather, the Duke of Danby, and eagerly embraces the reprieve from her betrothal.

Only, when Olivia arrives at Danby Castle she realizes the Christmas season represents hope, second chances, and even miracles.

ᴄWinning a Lady's Heart
A Danby Novella

Author's Note: This is a novella that was originally available in A Summons From The Castle (The Regency Christmas Summons Collection). It is being published as an individual novella.

~★~

For Lady Alexandra, being the source of a cold, calculated wager is bad enough…but when it is waged by Nathaniel Michael Winters, 5th Earl of Pembroke, the man she's in love with, it results in a broken heart, the scandal of the season, and a summons from her grandfather – the Duke of Danby.

To escape Society's gossip, she hurries to her meeting with the duke, determined to put memories of the earl far behind. Except the duke has other plans for Alexandra…plans which include the 5th Earl of Pembroke!

ᴄTempted by a Lady's ᴄSmile
Book 4 in the "Lords of Honor" Series

Richard Jonas has loved but one woman—a woman who belongs to his brother. Refusing to suffer any longer, he evades his family in order to barricade his heart from unrequited love. While attending a friend's summer party, Richard's approach to love is changed after sharing a passionate and life-altering kiss with a vibrant and mysterious woman. Believing he was incapable of loving again, Richard finds himself tempted by a young lady determined to marry his best friend.

Gemma Reed has not been treated kindly by the *ton*. Often disregarded for her appearance and interests unlike those of a proper lady, Gemma heads to house party to win the heart of Lord Westfield, the man she's loved for years. But her plan is set off course by the tempting and intriguing, Richard Jonas.

A chance meeting creates a new path for Richard and Gemma to forage—but can two people, scorned and shunned by those they've loved from afar, let down their guards to find true happiness?

"RESCUED BY A LADY'S LOVE"
Book 3 in the "Lords of Honor" Series

Destitute and determined to finally be free of any man's shackles, Lily Benedict sets out to salvage her honor. With no choice but to commit a crime that will save her from her past, she enters the home of the recluse, Derek Winters, the new Duke of Blackthorne. But entering the "Beast of Blackthorne's" lair proves more threatening than she ever imagined.

With half a face and a mangled leg, Derek—once rugged and charming—only exists within the confines of his home. Shunned by society, Derek is leery of the hauntingly beautiful Lily Benedict. As time passes, she slips past his defenses, reminding him how to live again. But when Lily's sordid past comes back, threatening her life, it's up to Derek to find the strength to become the hero he once was. Can they overcome the darkness of their sins to find a life of love and redemption?

CAPTIVATED BY A LADY'S CHARM
Book 2 in the "Lords of Honor" Series

In need of a wife...

Christian Villiers, the Marquess of St. Cyr, despises the role he's been cast into as fortune hunter but requires the funds to keep his marquisate solvent. Yet, the sins of his past cloud his future, preventing him from seeing beyond his fateful actions at the Battle of Toulouse. For he knows inevitably it will catch up with him, and everyone will remember his actions on the battlefield that cost so many so much—particularly his best friend.

In want of a husband…

Lady Prudence Tidemore's life is plagued by familial scandals, which makes her own marital prospects rather grim. Surely there is one gentleman of the ton who can look past her family and see just her and all she has to offer?

When Prudence runs into Christian on a London street, the charming, roguish gentleman immediately captures her attention. But then a chance meeting becomes a waltz, and now…

A Perfect Match…

All she must do is convince Christian to forget the cold requirements he has for his future marchioness. But the demons in his past prevent him from turning himself over to love. One thing is certain—Prudence wants the marquess and is determined to have him in her life, now and forever. It's just a matter of convincing Christian he wants the same.

SEDUCED BY A LADY'S HEART
Book 1 in the "Lords of Honor" Series

You met Lieutenant Lucien Jones in "Forever Betrothed, Never the Bride" when he was a broken soldier returned from fighting Boney's forces. This is his story of triumph and happily-ever-after!

~*~

Lieutenant Lucien Jones, son of a viscount, returned from war, to find his wife and child dead. Blaming his father for the commission that sent him off to fight Boney's forces, he was content to languish at London Hospital… until offered employment on the Marquess of Drake's staff. Through his position, Lucien found purpose in life and is content to keep his past buried.

Lady Eloise Yardley has loved Lucien since they were children. Having long ago given up on the dream of him, she married another. Years later, she is a young, lonely widow who does not fit in with the ton. When Lucien's family enlists her aid to reunite father and son, she leaps at the opportunity to not only aid her former friend, but to also escape London.

Lucien doesn't know what scheme Eloise has concocted, but

knowing her as he does, when she pays a visit to his employer, he knows she's up to something. The last thing he wants is the temptation that this new, older, mature Eloise presents; a tantalizing reminder of happier times and peace.

Yet Eloise is determined to win Lucien's love once and for all… if only Lucien can set aside the pain of his past and risk all on a lady's heart.

ONLY FOR THEIR LOVE
Book 3 in the "The Theodosia Sword" Series

Miss Carol Cresswall bore witness to her parents' loveless union and is determined to avoid that same miserable fate. Her mother has altogether different plans—plans that include a match between Carol and Lord Gregory Renshaw. Despite his wealth and power, Carol has no interest in marrying a pompous man who goes out of his way to ignore her. Now, with their families coming together for the Christmastide season it's her mother's last-ditch effort to get them together. And Carol plans to avoid Gregory at all costs.

Lord Gregory Renshaw has no intentions of falling prey to his mother's schemes to marry him off to a proper debutante she's picked out. Over the years, he has carefully sidestepped all endeavors to be matched with any of the grasping ladies.

But a sudden Christmastide Scandal has the potential show Carol and Gregory that they've spent years running from the one thing they've always needed.

ONLY FOR HER HONOR
Book 2 in the "The Theodosia Sword" Series

A wounded soldier:

When Captain Lucas Rayne returned from fighting Boney's forces, he was a shell of a man. A recluse who doesn't leave his family's estate, he's content to shut himself away. Until he meets Eve...

A woman alone in the world:

Eve Ormond spent most of her life following the drum alongside her late father. When his shameful actions bring death and pain to English soldiers, Eve is forced back to England, an outcast. With no family or marital prospects she needs employment and finds it in Captain Lucas Rayne's home. A man whose life was ruined by her father, Eve has no place inside his household. With few options available, however, Eve takes the post. What she never anticipates is how with their every meeting, this honorable, hurting soldier slips inside her heart.

The Secrets Between Them:

The more time Lucas spends with Eve, he remembers what it is to be alive and he lets the walls protecting his heart down. When the secrets between them come to light will their love be enough? Or are they two destined for heartbreak?

ONLY FOR HIS LADY
Book 1 in the "The Theodosia Sword" Series

A curse. A sword. And the thief who stole her heart.

The Rayne family is trapped in a rut of bad luck. And now, it's up to Lady Theodosia Rayne to steal back the Theodosia sword, a gladius that was pilfered by the rival, loathed Renshaw family. Hopefully, recovering the stolen sword will break the cycle and reverse her family's fate.

Damian Renshaw, the Duke of Devlin, is feared by all—all, that is, except Lady Theodosia, the brazen spitfire who enters his home and wrestles an ancient relic from his wall. Intrigued by the vivacious woman, Devlin has no intentions of relinquishing the sword to her.

As Theodosia and Damian battle for ownership, passion ignites. Now, they are torn between their age-old feud and the fire that burns between them. Can two forbidden lovers find a way to make amends before their families' war tears them apart?

MY LADY OF DECEPTION
Book 1 in the "Brethren of the Lords" Series

This dark, sweeping Regency novel was previously only offered as part of the limited edition box sets: "From the Ballroom and Beyond", "Romancing the Rogue", and "Dark Deceptions". Now, available for the first time on its own, exclusively through Amazon is "My Lady of Deception".

~★~

Everybody has a secret. Some are more dangerous than others.

For Georgina Wilcox, only child of the notorious traitor known as "The Fox", there are too many secrets to count. However, after her interference results in great tragedy, she resolves to never help another… until she meets Adam Markham.

Lord Adam Markham is captured by The Fox. Imprisoned, Adam loses everything he holds dear. As his days in captivity grow, he finds himself fascinated by the young maid, Georgina, who cares for him.

When the carefully crafted lies she's built between them begin to crumble, Georgina realizes she will do anything to prove her love and loyalty to Adam—even it means at the expense of her own life.

NON-FICTION WORKS BY
CHRISTI CALDWELL

Uninterrupted Joy: Memoir: My Journey through Infertility, Pregnancy, and Special Needs

The following journey was never intended for publication. It was written from a mother, to her unborn child. The words detailed her struggle through infertility and the joy of finally being pregnant. A stunning revelation at her son's birth opened a world of both fear and discovery. This is the story of one mother's love and hope and…her quest for uninterrupted joy.

BIOGRAPHY

Christi Caldwell is the bestselling author of historical romance novels set in the Regency era. Christi blames Judith McNaught's *Whitney, My Love,* for luring her into the world of historical romance. While sitting in her graduate school apartment at the University of Connecticut, Christi decided to set aside her notes and try her hand at writing romance. She believes the most perfect heroes and heroines have imperfections and rather enjoys tormenting them before crafting a well-deserved happily ever after!

When Christi isn't writing the stories of flawed heroes and heroines, she can be found in her Southern Connecticut home with her courageous son, and caring for twin princesses-in-training!

Visit www.christicaldwellauthor.com to learn more about what Christi is working on, or join her on Facebook at *Christi Caldwell Author,* and Twitter *@ChristiCaldwell*

For first glimpse at covers, excerpts, and free bonus material, be sure to sign up for my monthly newsletter! Each month one subscriber will win a $35 Amazon Gift Card!

Made in United States
North Haven, CT
22 December 2022

29978792R00117